continued . . .

ALSO BY LuANN McLANE

CONTEMPORARY ROMANCES

EROTIC ROMANCES

Walking on Sunshine

A Cricket Creek Novel

LuAnn McLane

A SIGNET ECLIPSE BOOK

SIGNET ECLIPSE
Published by the Penguin Group
Penguin Group (USA) LLC, 375 Hudson Street,
New York, New York 10014

USA | Canada | UK | Ireland | Australia | New Zealand | India | South Africa | China
penguin.com
A Penguin Random House Company

First published by Signet Eclipse, an imprint of New American Library,
a division of Penguin Group (USA) LLC

First Printing, May 2015

ISBN 978-0-451-47049-2

Printed in the United States of America
10 9 8 7 6 5 4 3 2 1

I want to dedicate this book to my childhood pen pal, Florence Scott. Through writing letters, we forged a friendship that reached across the ocean and has lasted more than forty years.

Acknowledgments

I would like to thank my lovely English friends in Naples, Florida. You were the inspiration for my side trip from Cricket Creek, Kentucky, to London, England. I appreciate all of the love, laughter, and support you've given me over the past few years.

Thanks again to the amazing editorial staff at New American Library. From the gorgeous covers to the details in copyediting, I couldn't ask for a better finished product. Also, thanks so much to Jessica Brock for promoting the Cricket Creek series. The reviews, blogs and tweets are the result of your hard work and enthusiasm. And a special thank-you goes out to my editor, Danielle Perez. From brainstorming ideas to tackling revisions, working with you has been a joy.

As always, I want to extend a thank-you to my agent, Jenny Bent. Your advice and knowledge are invaluable and I could not have made this journey without you.

1

Risk It for the Biscuit

"RUSTY, GET BACK HERE RIGHT THIS MINUTE!" MATTIE shouted at her brother's Irish setter, but he bolted from the kitchen with the slab of country ham dangling from his chops. "I mean it!" Mattie rushed after Rusty, knowing full well that he wasn't about to stop. Although the meat could no longer be served to her customers, Mattie felt the need to scold the naughty dog and deprive him of his prize. She also felt the need to scold her brother Mason for leaving Rusty with her again while he went fishing. Apparently Rusty, who used to be quite the docile dog while riding in Mason's bass boat, now felt the sudden urge to jump in the water without warning.

"I swear I'm never saving you a bone *ever* again!" Fuming, Mattie dodged tables and chairs while chasing Rusty around the dining room, glad that the restaurant wasn't open for breakfast just yet. For an old dog, Rusty still managed some impressive speed and agility, but this was the second ham heist this week, so Mattie was determined to catch him. Country ham and biscuits was a popular item on the breakfast menu! When Rusty headed for the big booth in the back of the dining room, Mattie threw caution to the wind and did a half dive, half slide across the hardwood floor, hoping to snag him around his haunches and bring him to the justice he so richly deserved...

And came up with nothing but air.

With a groan, Mattie pounded her fists on the floor. She pictured Rusty doing a wheezy doggy laugh while munching on the salty slab of ham. "I'm gonna tell on you!" Mattie threatened with a bit more fist pounding. After another moment she started pushing up to her feet, but she looked ahead and spotted shoes. Yeah, shoes, not boots. Kinda fancy shoes at that....

"Excuse me. Are you ... are you ... quite all right?" asked an unusual male voice that made her pause, putting her in a Pilates plank position.

Two things immediately went through Mattie's head. Number one was that the question held a measure of concern at her plight rather than the amusement that was usually dealt her way; and number two was that his accent was a distinctively clipped British one rather than a slow, Southern drawl. Mattie quickly scooted to her knees apparently just as he squatted, because suddenly they were eye to oh ... very blue eyes. She swallowed, staring. The man was simply gorgeous.

"Um ..." He tilted his shaggy blond head to the side. "Is something amiss?"

"No, I ... uh ..." What did he just ask? Her brain suddenly left the building. "Oh, a ... ham," she managed, and then realized it sounded as if she were clearing her throat. "H-ham. I was running after the ham."

"You were chasing after a ham?" He shoved his fingers through his blond hair, making it stand on end.

Mattie had the urge to reach over and smooth it back into its beautiful style. There was something vaguely familiar about him that she couldn't quite place.

"So the ham ran away, did it?"

"Yes ... well, no. It was a dog."

"A dog named Ham? Now it makes sense."

"What? No . . ." Mattie shook her head hard, making her ponytail swing back and forth.

"Are you quite certain you're all right?"

"Yes, why do you keep asking that?"

"Well, mainly because you *were* facedown while pounding your fists on the floor when I walked in. Cause for some concern, I'd say."

Mattie looked down at her fists. "Oh, right, I guess I was."

"Early in the day to be so unsettled, don't you think?" he asked gently. "Is there anything I can do? Search for the runaway ham perhaps?"

"I . . ." It was *hard to think* when he looked so cute, sounded so, well, so damn sexy. Mattie suddenly felt silly having been caught in her fit of frustration on the floor like some kind of crazy person. Should she admit that she was trying to tackle a dog? Would that be better or worse than chasing a ham? "I . . . I was having a . . . moment."

"Ah." He gave her a crooked grin that made a fluttery thing happen in her stomach. Must be hunger pains. "Haven't had your coffee yet? I can sympathize. You'd best serve me up a cup or I'll be joining you in your fist-pounding moment." He stood up and then reached down to help her to her feet.

Mattie took his offered hand, finding his warm, firm grasp to be so pleasant that she felt reluctant to let go. Realizing that she was clinging to his hand, she masked her lingering hold with an introduction. "I'm Mattie Mayfield, by the way. Welcome to Breakfast, Books, and Bait . . . or BBB for short." She then gave his hand a firm squeeze as her daddy had taught her.

"Well, thank you for the rather odd but warm welcome, Mattie Mayfield. I am duly charmed and also rather fascinated by the wide range of seemingly unrelated items you have to offer here at BBB." He looked over to the bags of fishing bait shelved on the far wall. "Are the worms all dead, then?"

Mattie nodded. "Well, no, I mean not *dead*. Artificial, you know, plastic, mostly used for bass fishing."

"Ah, and the fish fall for that, do they?" he asked with another boyishly cute grin.

"Oddly, yes."

He chuckled. "It must be quite the letdown to be lured in by a silly piece of plastic instead of a tasty worm. I'd spit it out straightaway."

Mattie had to laugh. "Yes, but there's that tiny complication called the hook."

"Oh . . . true enough." He winced. "Ouch. Adding insult to injury and then end up in a frying pan."

"No, no . . . *no*." Mattie scrunched up her nose. "You really don't want to consume anything caught in the Ohio River." She waved a hand in the direction of the bait. "This is all mostly for catch and release, for sport and tournaments my brothers host."

"We?"

Mattie jabbed her thumb toward the window that overlooked the dock. "My family owns Mayfield Marina," she answered with a measure of pride. For some reason she felt it important that he think she was more accomplished than simply slinging hash and baking biscuits, not that there was anything wrong with an honest day's work. "So, what can I get for you?" she asked a bit crisply.

He looked past the bait to the rear of the shop where Mattie kept her selection of books. "I think I'll pass on the bait, but breakfast sounds lovely. And perhaps a book later."

"Have a seat and I'll bring you a menu."

"All right, then."

Mattie thought he'd opt for a booth, but he followed her to the counter lined with old-fashioned round swivel stools in deep red. Mattie had been serving up breakfast for several years, and her melt-in-your-mouth biscuits were raved about, but she suddenly found herself feeling a bit nervous. "Coffee?"

"Please."

"So, are you just passing through Cricket Creek and happened to stop down here by the marina?" Mattie asked while pouring strong coffee into a sturdy china mug. When hit with a fit of nerves, Mattie, who was usually a bit on the quiet side, tended to chatter.

He reached for a little plastic tub of cream from the dish she put in front of him. "No, actually I just bought the A-frame cabin right next door."

"You did?" From his blue polo shirt to his fancy shoes, he didn't seem the type to settle down in Cricket Creek, but then again the little town had had quite a few unexpected people moving here over the past few years. "Wow." Wait. There really was something familiar about him. Where had she seen him before?

"I'm sorry. I neglected to introduce myself. I'm Garret Ruleman."

"Oh!" Mattie nearly dropped the menu she'd been about to hand to him. She had seen him all right, on the cover of tabloids at the checkout lane at the grocery story. "You are?"

"Last time I looked at my license," he said while pouring cream into his coffee.

Feeling a bit silly by her question, Mattie decided to add a little sass. "Maybe you should check just to be sure."

"All right, then, I'll have a look." He reached around for his wallet, then flipped it open. "Yes, I'm still Garret Ruleman. Damn the luck," he added with an arch of an eyebrow and a slight grin.

"So you moved to Cricket Creek to live near your father?" Rick Ruleman, famous rock star, owned My Way Records, which was located just a few miles away from the marina. It was well known that Garret and his father shared a rocky relationship, and Mattie suddenly wished she'd kept her doggone mouth shut.

"No, actually I'm back in town to rekindle my relationship with Addison Monroe." He calmly took a sip of his coffee and peered at her over the rim of the mug.

Mattie couldn't hold back her gasp. Garret and Addison's broken engagement had been splashed all over the tabloids and was the reason Addison ended up opening up a bridal shop, of all things, in Cricket Creek. Garret looked familiar because she'd seen his face in print so many times and not usually in a flattering situation. "Addison is, um, married to Reid Greenfield, now," Mattie informed him in a hesitant stage whisper.

"You don't say . . . well, bollocks, that throws a monkey wrench into my plans." When his mouth twitched Mattie knew he'd been messing with her. He took another sip of coffee and then added more cream. "This stuff is going to make my hair stand on end."

"It's already standing on end, but maybe that will offset the fact that your nose is going to grow from fibbing," Mattie grumbled.

He reached up and touched his nose. "Wouldn't want that to happen. Actually Addison and I have mended our fences and I've met Reid. He's a great chap and Addison should thank her lucky stars that she dodged the bullet and dumped the likes of me."

His grin suggested that he was joking, but there was something in Garret's eyes that made Mattie want to give his shoulder a reassuring squeeze.

"So I had you going, did I?"

"That little deception wasn't one bit funny."

"I didn't really think you'd fall for it. I was just goofing on you."

"Goofing?"

"English slang for teasing."

"Well, you'd think that I'd wise up, but I manage to fall for nearly everything." *I could fall for you* zinged through her brain, but she chalked it up to a lack of coffee in her system. "I think I have *tease me* tattooed on my forehead."

Narrowing his eyes, Garret peered at her forehead as if trying to see the tattoo. "Hmm, you do. Get that thing removed straightaway."

"Good advice," Mattie said, and then topped off his coffee.

"Actually I'm a studio musician and a talent scout for My Way Records." Garret took a sip of the steaming brew. "But yes, it's good to live near my father," he added, but Mattie thought his smile appeared forced and he started studying the menu as if there would be a pop quiz afterward.

"Do you have any questions about the menu?"

"I do, in fact." Garret looked up at her. "What in the world is redeye gravy?"

"Gravy made with coffee and the drippings from fried country ham." She sighed. "But unfortunately I can't offer redeye gravy or country ham on biscuits."

"Ah . . . right, since the ham ran away with the dish and the spoon?"

Mattie nodded. "Something like that."

"Pity, I was curious."

"Well, I do make sausage gravy that will have you sigh with delight."

"As it so happens, I adore sighing with delight," Garret informed her with a slow grin that caused the butterflies in Mattie's stomach to take flight once again. "I'm sold." It looked as if he was about to say more when his phone started playing "Hard Day's Night." Standing up, he pulled his cell from his pocket and frowned at the screen. "Excuse me," he said, and then answered the call. "Hello, love," he said, making Mattie wonder if he was speaking to his girlfriend. "Ah yes, darling, I can be there by noon."

Mattie felt an expected pang of disappointment that took her by surprise. Feeling silly, she quickly turned away and started fussing with rolling silverware in napkins. The breakfast crowd would be arriving soon and she'd best be thinking about getting ready rather than mooning over her sexy new neighbor. Besides, *let's get real,* Mattie thought to herself. Now that she knew who he was, she remembered that Garret Ruleman's bad boy reputation preceded him like his shadow. Along with Addison Monroe, daughter of famous finance guru Melinda Monroe, Garret had been linked to various famous actresses and models. If she remembered correctly, his mother was also some kind of celebrity. Garret might have been goofing on her, as he said, but Mattie was quite certain that she was as far from being his type as a girl could possibly get. With a sigh Mattie sternly reminded herself that she was already an expert in the not-his-type field, having been ass over teacups in love with Colby Campbell since, well, ever since she could remember.

Unfortunately there were several problems with loving Colby, starting with him being Mason's best friend, which made Mattie off-limits because of some sort of hard-and-fast guy code rule. In addition, the four-year age difference between them had thrown Mattie into the annoying kid sister category while growing up. But at twenty-six she figured that gap should surely be closed! And face it, Mattie thought, she was no longer a *kid* but a grown woman, not that Colby seemed to notice. And if Mattie wanted to be honest (and she didn't), that was also where the not-his-type part came into play. Colby always had some sort of prissy, big-haired blonde, some leggy, girlie thing hanging on his arm, and Mattie was anything but a girlie-girl. Mattie usually wore her long blond hair pulled up into a ponytail or in a braid down her back and she was neither prissy nor leggy. Still, in spite of having the deck stacked against her, every time he walked in the door, Mattie's heart beat like a big bass drum.

Unrequited love truly sucked.

Complicating Mattie's love life—or rather the lack thereof—was that her brother Danny, two years her junior, also adhered to the ridiculous don't-date-my-sister rule, leaving Mattie friend-zoned by most of the eligible bachelors close to her age in town. Perhaps if her brothers would get married they would be busy raising families and back off watching her love life like a doggone hawk. In fact, their parents had become so frustrated by their lack of grandchildren that they up and moved to

Florida, vowing not to return to Cricket Creek until they had at least one grandbaby.

Mattie stood up on her tiptoes and fumbled around in the cabinet for a coffee filter. Her brothers got blessed with the tall genes, while she stood barely over five foot two. She was also left-handed and the only blonde in the bunch, but she shared the same hazel eyes as her father. Her mother claimed that Mattie's eyes were like mood rings, changing color depending upon her disposition.

Mattie measured the coffee grounds while trying to listen to Garret's conversation. Eavesdropping was one of her favorite ways to pass the time while serving breakfast. From the old-timers' breakfast club's corny jokes to the really tall fish tales to the gossip from the ladies who came in to browse through the selection of romance novels, Mattie was thoroughly entertained every single morning. While Mattie wasn't one to repeat gossip, she sure did get a kick out of listening to it.

After the coffee started hissing and dripping into the carafe, Mattie decided she needed to refill the saltshakers that were running low. She rose on tiptoe once again, but this time her fingers refused to coax the salt container to slide her way.

"Hey, love, do you need some help?" Garret asked in that sweet-ass accent of his.

Love? Wait. Did he just call her love? Before Mattie could process the whole love thing, he was standing behind her reaching up for the elusive canister of salt. She could feel the heat from his body standing so close to hers, and *wow*, did he smell heavenly ... something spicy and, well, *delicious*! She had the urge to lean back against him and when he stepped to the side to hand her the salt, she wanted to grab him by the shirt and bury her nose next to his chest just to soak up the smell.

Instead Mattie had a saucy *I didn't need your help* on the tip of her tongue, but then her fingers brushed against his and she felt a zing all the way to her doggone toes. Still, she lifted her chin, searching her befuddled brain for a retort of some sort, but he tilted his head and said, "You have the most amazing eyes. What color are they?"

"C-color?"

"Yes, I thought brown at first, but now they look green with a hint of blue. Quite lovely, actually."

Mattie was used to teasing rather than compliments and she stood there feeling rather perplexed. She licked her bottom lip, something she did when confused, and damn if his gaze didn't seem to drop to her mouth. Mattie swallowed and although warning bells chimed in her head about bad boy Garret Ruleman, she tipped her head up and leaned closer . . . suddenly prepared to risk it for the biscuit.

But just as her eyes started to flutter shut in anticipation of their mouths meeting, Mattie spotted none other than Colby Campbell walk through the front door. Startled, she took a quick step away from Garret and then frowned at him as if he'd done something wrong rather than offer his help. What in the hell had just gotten into her, anyway? Kissing a total stranger wasn't like her at all! She shot Garret a frown so he got the message.

"Everything okay, Mattie?" Colby asked in that big brother tone that never failed to set her teeth on edge.

"Yeah, um, Garret was just helping me reach a canister of salt. Weren't you, Garret?" she asked, but kept her focus on Colby. When Garret remained silent she gave him a little nudge with her elbow and then looked up at him.

"Well, actually . . ."

The mischief in Garret's blue eyes made Mattie's heart start to hammer. She looked at him and held her breath.

2

Scattered, Smothered, and Covered

"I WAS JUST ABOUT READY TO ORDER BISCUITS AND GRAVY when I spotted Mattie in need of some assistance," Garret explained, and could sense the tension leave Mattie's body. Was this giant bloke dressed in boots and camo really cute little Mattie's boyfriend?

"Because I'm so dang short," Mattie chimed in. "Couldn't reach the salt," she added as if she needed to give Colby an explanation so he wouldn't be jealous. But Garret noticed that Colby didn't seem all that concerned.

"I was just being neighborly," Garret said, and that seemed to get Colby's attention.

"Neighborly?" He grinned. "You sure don't sound like you're from around here."

"True enough. L.A. and London with a bit of Chicago tossed in. But I bought the cabin down by the river."

"Oh, hey, welcome to Cricket Creek." He stuck out his hand. "I'm Colby Campbell."

"Garret Ruleman," Garret said, and shook Colby's hand. He saw recognition on Colby's face but didn't want to deal with it, so he said quickly, "Good to meet you. Now that I'm no longer needed, I'll just have a seat over at a booth." Garret's statement went mostly unnoticed by an obviously smitten Mattie.

"Okay," Mattie said absently, and didn't bother to flick a glance in Garret's direction. Since Garret was rather used to women fawning all over him, he found Mattie's rapid dismissal refreshing in a weird way. Odd, but he could have sworn she was about to let him kiss her just moments ago. Perhaps he'd been mistaken, because she only seemed to have eyes for Colby. Pity, because he found her utterly charming. After picking up his coffee mug, Garret walked over to a booth by the wall and proceeded to watch the rather interesting scene unfold.

"I'm in dire need of coffee," Colby announced.

"Comin' right up." Mattie put a mug in front of Colby, who swung one long jean-clad leg over the stool and sat down. "Just to let you know there's no country ham this mornin'."

"Again?" Colby grumbled. "And here I was wantin' some of your redeye gravy."

"Sorry 'bout your luck." Mattie sighed and then fisted her hands on her hips. "Rusty ran off with the ham. I chased after his sorry hide but came up empty-handed." She wiggled her fingers in the air to demonstrate. "I'm gonna give Mason a piece of my mind about the situation. I love ol' Rusty to the moon and back, but I can't have him stealing my breakfast supplies."

"I don't blame you one bit," Colby said with a nod.

Ah, so Mattie was chasing after a dog, Garret thought, and had to grin. He would have loved to see her in action. He'd also love to have his breakfast served, but Mattie was totally focused on Colby. But then as if reading Garret's mind she glanced in his direction.

"I'll be back in a minute," she said to Colby, and then walked Garret's way with the coffeepot in her hand.

"Did you decide what you want?" Mattie asked with

what appeared to be a grateful smile. She obviously regretted the brief heated moment they'd shared. Of course perhaps the heat was all on his end. If he really had been crazy enough to try to steal a kiss, he would most likely have gotten a roundhouse to the jaw. Risky business, he thought, but perhaps one worth taking.

"I'll have the biscuits and sausage gravy that is sure to make me sigh with *pleasure*."

Her eyes rounded and she glanced over at Colby, who seemed oblivious of her adoration. Couldn't the big clod see how cute Mattie was in her cutoff jeans and scuffed cowboy boots? She tilted her head to the side, making her long ponytail slip over her shoulder. "I believe I said de-*light*."

"Right . . . my mistake."

"Eggs?"

"Over easy."

"Grits?"

"Never had them, but they sound, well, gritty."

"My grits are smooth and creamy. Give them a try. You won't be sorry."

"Causing another groan of sheer pleasure?" Garret asked, and was rewarded with a scowl that had a cute blush behind it.

"Another sigh of delight."

Garret shrugged. "Semantics . . ."

"Butter or cheese?"

"What do you suggest?"

"I prefer cheesy grits, but that's just me."

"Sold."

"Hash browns?" she continued with a crisp business-like tone that made Garret grin.

"Um . . ." Garret wondered how he was going to consume all that food, but he'd just bet that Colby over at the counter would scarf down a manly breakfast, so he nodded. "Of course."

"Scattered, smothered, and covered?"

"Who, what, and where?"

Mattie laughed and Garret decided he liked the soft, slightly throaty sound. She slowly repeated the choices.

"Are you trying to kill me? Because it sure sounds like a grisly murder."

"Scattered on the grill, covered with onions, and smothered with cheese."

"Well, then, yes, you are definitely trying to kill me."

"Then you will surely die with a big smile on your face."

Garret had to chuckle. "All right, then, scatter, smother, and cover me."

"Waffles, toast, or pancakes?"

"No!" Garret raised his hands skyward. "I must draw the line somewhere . . . . dear God, the biscuits are more than enough carbs."

Mattie laughed again. "Juice?"

"Just water, please, but keep the coffee coming."

"Will do." Mattie nodded and turned on her heel. He noticed that she kept glancing at Colby, who had his nose buried in a newspaper. When she walked over to refill his coffee mug, he ordered a huge breakfast feast, including a stack of pancakes. It kind of irked Garret that the dude didn't seem to have an ounce of fat on his damn body. A few minutes later a whole crew of guys dressed and built like Colby entered the restaurant. There was a lot of back slapping and joke telling. Garret had to admit that he was envious of their camaraderie. But what he didn't like was the constant teasing of Mattie. When Colby tugged her ponytail as she walked by, Garret longed to stomp over there and smack the big clod upside his head.

While waiting for his breakfast, Garret played with his cell phone but listened to their conversation that was apparently English but might just as well have been in a foreign language, since Garret failed to understand most of what they were talking about. What in the world was flipping and pitching lily pads? And apparently mudding was some sort of pastime that they were going to engage in over the weekend. Did they sling it at each other while flipping lily pads? The conversation led into some of them trying to get their girlfriends to go noodling in a nearby lake. Garret thought they must mean something like skinny-dipping. Knowing that he needed to learn the local lingo, he listened closely.

"Sherry won't even consider going noodling," said some big dude they called Squirrel. "What do you think, Danny?"

"Too scared, I guess," said Danny. "Mattie would be too."

"Nah, I just bet Mattie would do it," Colby said, drawing Mattie's attention away from the griddle.

"Of course I would," Mattie boasted, and then turned to flip several pancakes. "When are y'all goin'?" she asked over her shoulder.

Garret took a sip of his coffee, not liking the idea at all, and then wondered why he considered it his business.

Danny laughed, drawing a frown from Mattie. "You'd never stick your hand in a catfish hole, Mattie. Get real."

"I'm not afraid of a catfish," she scoffed before handing him a huge stack of pancakes.

"You'd be too scared of a water moccasin," Danny said.

"I would not," Mattie argued.

Garret had the feeling they weren't talking about a shoe.

"Right, you're scared to death of snakes," Danny insisted. "You even screamed at that fake one I put behind the counter last week."

"That was a riot," Colby said, and gave Danny and Squirrel a high five. They all laughed.

Mattie narrowed her eyes and pointed her spatula at Danny. "I thought you said that Mason put the fake snake there."

"It was Colby." Danny jammed his thumb in his friend's direction.

"No way." Colby held up his hands in protest. "Wasn't me."

"Well, I wasn't scared, just startled," Mattie insisted. "Even Rusty thought it was real and started barking his fool head off. And I will go noodling with you to prove it," she added. "And show y'all up by winnin' the weigh-in." With a lift of her chin she turned back to the griddle, cooking at the speed of light. A minute later she brought Garret's huge breakfast over to him and put it on the table. "More coffee?"

"When you get the chance," Garret said, and suddenly wanted to get up and help her wait on those big clods who seemed to love to get her goat. "What is noodling, again?"

"You wade through the water until you find a catfish hole. Then you stick your hand in there."

"What? Don't they bite?" Garret could only shake his head that this was actually some sort of sport that one would willingly engage in.

"When they clamp their mouth shut you grab them by the gills and haul them out of the water. It's not too dangerous. You usually only get little scratches or cuts."

"Sounds horrid."

Mattie glanced over at the front counter and then lowered her voice. "It's not the catfish that are dangerous but the snakes or snapping turtles or beavers who take over the catfish holes as their home."

Garret felt a flash of alarm. "You're not really going to do this nonsense, are you?"

Mattie shrugged. "Maybe." She gave Colby a glance and Garret wondered if she would do this insane activity to impress him. Apparently so.

"Good God, I'll pay you *not* to do it. Name your price," Garret offered, but she only laughed as if he was joking, though he wasn't.

"You're funny, you know that? I'll bring more coffee over in a minute."

"Thank you." Garret wanted to tell her that he was dead serious, but she turned on her heel and hurried back to the griddle, where she cracked eggs one-handed and then started rapidly flipping food, making her ponytail swing back and forth. Garret had a hard time not staring at her cute bum in those little cutoff jeans. After she served up the big breakfast feast, the blokes dove into their food with gusto and to Garret's relief the teasing finally ceased.

Mattie seemed to take it all in stride as she handed menus to a sweet older couple whom she addressed as Clyde and Miss Patty.

"You two still have that newlywed glow about you," Mattie said as she poured coffee into their mugs.

"I'm not at all surprised that it shows." Clyde reached over and picked up Miss Patty's hand. When he bestowed her knuckles with light kisses, she blushed. "I couldn't be happier."

"Oh, you're such a sweet talker," Miss Patty said with a wave of her hand, but the blush deepened.

Newlyweds? There was something so endearing about them that Garret had to smile. He felt an odd stab of longing and in that same moment Mattie turned and came walking his way.

"They're cute, aren't they?"

"Adorable."

While Mattie poured steaming coffee into his mug she asked, "How is everything?"

Garret responded with a long sigh and she laughed. "You're right. I'll die happy."

"Let me know if you need anything else," she said, sounding a little bit breathless.

"Don't you have any help?" Garret asked, thinking that she could use someone to either cook or wait tables for her.

Mattie shrugged. "Sometimes I have Bubba Brown in here helpin' me cook and clear tables, but he's a bit under the weather, so I'm all by myself today." It seemed like a daunting task to have to do everything on her own, but she seemed to be able to handle it. "And my brother Danny over at the counter will help me clean up if he doesn't have boats to work on today. I'd rather be busy than standing around twiddling my thumbs." She shot him a grin. "Keeps me outta trouble."

"I hope it keeps you from sticking your hand in a catfish hole," he grumbled, but she just laughed again.

"Maybe you should come along."

"Not on your life," Garret said, trying to imagine doing such a foolish thing.

"Don't say I didn't offer," Mattie said in a tone that suggested that she knew he wouldn't accept, making him suddenly want to.

But when she started to turn away, Garret felt the need to stop her. He surprised himself by saying, "Seriously, Mattie, don't do something that could potentially cause you harm just to prove yourself." He supposed that he could relate, since he'd felt the need to prove himself most of his life. Her smile faded and Garret thought she was going to tell him to mind his own business, and she would be right. He should. "I won't," she promised softly, and then went back to work.

Garret looked down at the enormous amount of food on his plate and started eating the biscuits and gravy. Mattie was a damn good cook, which made him marvel at how she could get everything done to perfection without any assistance. He toyed around with his phone, checking messages and playing on Facebook while trying to make a dent in his breakfast. While he used to love to sleep in, these days Garret was an early riser and there still didn't seem to be enough hours in the day to get everything done. But he liked his schedule being full and wondered how he had ever thought that life was good when he didn't have a damn thing to do. And Mattie was right. Staying busy kept Garret out of trouble, something he used to get into on a regular basis. Three-day benders and raising hell no longer appealed to him.

Garret looked down at a text message from his father, reminding him about the meeting with country superstar Shane McCray that was to take place tomorrow. Recently retired from touring, Shane was going to help open Sully's South, a venue to showcase singers/songwriters in the vein of the famous Bluebird Café in Nashville. Sully's South was the brainchild of Maria Sully, songwriter extraordinaire who took a position in the publishing end of My Way Records after returning to Cricket Creek to reunite with her ex-husband, Pete, who owned Sully's Tavern and Concert Hall. Cricket Creek, Kentucky, was quickly becoming a mecca for musicians.

Along with his performing on guitar as a studio musician, Garret's other role with his father's recording studio was as a talent scout and he absolutely loved finding fresh new voices. Funny that he'd once longed to be famous like his father and now his job was making other musicians into stars.

When Mattie started clearing dishes from tables, Garret realized he'd outstayed the other customers who were starting to leave. By some miracle he'd managed to consume most of his breakfast—even the smothered and covered mountain of hash browns.

"Can I get you anything else?" Mattie asked, and grinned when she saw his nearly empty plate.

"Yes, a crane to heft me out of here."

Mattie laughed. "Well, there are plenty of activities to do around here this time of year to burn up some calories."

"Like noodling? Um, I don't think so. And I don't even want to know what mudding is."

"Well, there are some tamer things to do like swimming, fishing, and hiking. We rent boats and WaveRunners down at the dock if you're interested. My brother Danny can hook you up. Mason is a fishing guide if you want to try your hand at bass fishing. They really do fall for the artificial bait."

"You swim in the river?"

"Only close to the dock back here in the cove. The current is pretty swift and can be dangerous when you get out into the main channel of the Ohio River. Up near the dam the river is wide like a lake and we head up there whenever we can to go tubing or water-skiing."

"Tubing? Sounds a bit odd."

"Not really. It's when you sit in a big inner tube that's hooked with a ski rope to the back of a boat. You have to hang on for dear life while the driver tries to shake you off by bringing you back over the huge waves from the wake of the boat. Mason takes particular delight in shaking me from the Tube."

"Again, I think I'll shy away from noodling and tubing and . . . mudding."

"Hey, it's a small town. We have to make our own fun."

"How about a good ol' swimming pool? Do you have one of those around by any chance?"

"Sorry." Mattie laughed. "No concrete pool back here, but we do have a nice-sized lake on the property with campsites nearby." She shook her head as she handed him his bill. "There are electric hookups, no room service, I'm afraid."

"Pity." Garret made a show of sighing. He'd actually done some hiking in some pretty remote places all around the world, but he found it rather amusing for her to think he was a total city boy.

"We provide cabins up by the lake too. My own cabin is located on the opposite side and I have my own little dock. Trust me, it's safe to swim in if you like. And you can just sit in a tube."

"Now, that I could do."

"Come on up for a swim any time you like. I only chase strangers away with my shotgun, so you're safe."

Garret imagined her with a big shotgun and was rendered speechless.

"I'm just kidding."

Thank God. "I knew that."

"Sure you did." Mattie laughed again. "Well, it was nice to meet you, Garret. I hope you'll come back for breakfast on a regular basis."

"No doubt about that. You're an amazing cook, Mattie Mayfield."

"Why, thank you."

Her smile seemed shy at his compliment, making him wonder if all those blokes took her for granted.

"And it's nice to know you're my neighbor. How far away is your cabin on the lake?" he asked.

"Just a rather short walk through the path in the woods or a couple of miles down the main road that winds through the marina if you go by car. Unless it rains I usually walk."

"Sounds peaceful." Garret nodded and he was about to ask if she might show him around later when some customers walked through the door, taking her attention away from him. He left a generous tip and walked outside into the warm sunshine. As he made his way toward his cabin, he realized that he was smiling and that cute little Mattie had put the smile on his face.

Garret paused to take a few pictures of the stone and cedar structure to send to his mother, who lived in London. He missed her dearly and planned to visit her again as soon as he could fit in a bit of a holiday. Although he'd lived in way more luxurious homes in his lifetime, there was just something about this rustic A-frame that drew him in and made him feel at peace. The river view wasn't majestic like an ocean view, but Garret liked the calm sound of the river lapping against the shore.

Because the cabin had been used as a vacation rental, it had been fully furnished, another nice perk, since Garret was so busy traveling back and forth to Nashville. It helped that his stepmother, Maggie, was a real estate agent who did all the legwork for him. Garret shook his head when he thought about his hard-rocker father marrying such a down-to-earth sweetheart like Maggie. Garret adored Maggie, who in some ways reminded him of his London-born mother, who was much more grounded than people realized. He certainly would never have guessed that his dad would ever settle down at all, much less in a small town like Cricket Creek. And running a record label geared toward bluegrass and country music was another surprise. But then again, he'd always thought his dad had been living the life of his dreams when that couldn't have been further from the truth.

Garret understood. His own badass thumbing-his-nose-at-the-world persona that he'd created over the years was a complete farce. If Addison Monroe hadn't seen through him and called him out on it before giving back his engagement ring, he might still be chasing a dream he never really wanted in the first place. Like his father, music pumped through his blood with every heartbeat. But fame? He no longer cared and thank God he hadn't stooped to become a reality show star laughing-stock. When Addison had called him out on wanting to marry her so that they could star in their own television show, she hadn't been far from the truth. Creating amazing music in the studio and searching for new talent were much more rewarding.

Garret snapped a few pictures of the cabin and then took a few more of Mayfield Marina. When he heard shouting he turned around and laughed when he saw Mattie chasing the dog better known as the ham bandit.

"Rusty, get your sorry hide back here!" she yelled.

Chuckling, Garret took a video with his phone, wondering what tasty treat Rusty had snatched from the kitchen this time. When the ham bandit got away Mattie stood there with her hands on her hips and stomped one foot before taking angry strides back into the restaurant.

Still grinning, Garret opened the front door and decided to brew a bit more coffee to enjoy while sitting on the back deck that overlooked the marina and cove. While he'd someday take the time to put his personality into the décor, for right now the sturdy functional furniture was perfect.

Later that evening Garret thought he'd take a jog after the heat of the day dissipated. And just *maybe* he'd end up on the trail in the woods leading to Mattie's home by the lake. Garret had to grin. There wasn't a *maybe* in that thought. Although he knew he wasn't Mattie's type, since she seemed to be so into Colby, there was just something about her that made him want to get to know her better. He'd never had a girl who was only a friend, and the thought suddenly appealed to him. While the coffee brewed, Garret went into his office and picked up his laptop so he could make notes for the meeting with Shane and Maria.

Garret inhaled the pungent scent and smiled while thinking that not too long ago he didn't even know how to make his own coffee—or rather wouldn't have been *bothered* to make it and would have felt the need to have a barista create a frothy something or other with a long list of ingredients. Garret poured the strong coffee into the mug and smiled. Simplicity felt so much better. While he knew that he still had a way to go on his journey of self-discovery, he liked this new sense of purpose. And though he and Addison weren't meant to be together, he'd missed her friendship after their breakup. In the end Addison had seen through his false bravado. She'd told him that there was more to him than what he'd given himself credit for and she had challenged him to have the courage to dig deep and find it. The fact that Addison had truly cared about him had seeped into his bones and made him stronger, unbreakable. He thought again that he was so over being the bad boy son of a famous rock star and international fashion model. Instead of being famous for being famous, he wanted to create a career based on his own talent and accomplishments.

Taking his coffee and laptop out onto the back deck, he settled into the cushioned lounge chair and started brainstorming. He'd once turned his nose up at country music, thinking the down-home genre of music to be beneath him. But after meeting and working with the brilliant Maria Sully, he'd, well, changed his tune. Shane McCray was a Country Music Hall of Fame legend. His classic country songs transcended time and spoke to Garret on a basic level that he'd ignored in the past.

Timeless, Garret typed and then smiled when sparks of inspiration starting flooding his brain. He laughed, thinking that his brain was so happy to be used for something worthwhile that the ideas came faster than he could type. When he finally took another sip of coffee, it had gone cold, but he didn't care and drank it anyway. The meeting with Maria and Shane was going to be fantastic.

3
Skinny-Dipping

SHANE STRIPPED OFF HIS SWEATY RUNNING CLOTHES and let them drop into a soggy heap behind a potted plant on the pool deck. He added his shoes to the pile, peeled off his socks, and then dove into the deep end. The water felt deliciously soothing, sliding against his overheated body. He'd pushed too hard during his run, but now that he was retired he wanted to remain in decent shape. After breaking the surface, Shane flipped to his back and simply drifted. As he gazed up at the light blue sky dotted with fluffy clouds, he realized that he hadn't felt this calm in way too long.

Shane would never be ungrateful enough to complain about his success as a country music star, but the downside to fame was never having enough hours in the day to enjoy the fruits of his labor. His career had also cost him his marriage to his high school sweetheart, a woman he still at times missed. Thinking about Patsy brought a sigh past his lips. His ex-wife had moved on and was remarried with three children and he thought maybe two grandkids by now. They'd remained friendly, but the pain of the divorce caused Shane to never seriously consider marriage again. Shane wondered if Patsy knew how many of his early songs were written about loving her. Missing her. When they'd fallen in love their senior year in high school, neither of them could have predicted that just a few years later Shane would shoot to the top of the country music world so swiftly and stay there. Patsy simply couldn't deal with his absence, and God knows Shane often wondered if his career had been worth it. He didn't give a damn about the money or fame. He had remained a simple man with simple needs. In truth it was the fans that had kept him going. Shane knew all too well how much music meant to people.

It wasn't as if he still pined for Patsy every day, but since his retirement he had time to reflect upon his life and wonder what the future might bring. Always surrounded by people and yet he still suffered from bouts of loneliness.

Shane kicked his feet, sending water splashing. The direction of his thoughts disturbed his peaceful floating, so he pushed them aside and let music drift into his head.

Shane watched an eagle soar high up in the sky and smiled. One of the perks of moving from Nashville to his secluded home in Cricket Creek was the privacy. Nestled as it was deep in the woods on a hillside overlooking a winding section of the river, Shane no longer had to worry about paparazzi snapping pictures or tourist buses driving past his house. Nope, the only eyes possibly on him were animals scampering through the woods.

Shane flipped over and swam a few leisurely laps. Other than helping his songwriter friend Maria Sully with Sully's South, her showcase venue for discovering new music talent, the only thing Shane had to worry about was where he'd go fishing next. Having free time still felt odd, but he supposed he'd get used to it. He didn't want to be one of those stars who had a huge last tour hurrah only to come back a year later.

After a few more minutes Shane's stomach rumbled in empty protest and he hoped he'd find something in the fridge to eat for breakfast, which was the only meal he was capable of making. Flipping an egg was about as far as his cooking skills could take him. Unfortunately going to the grocery store was still an adventure where he walked around in a confused daze.

While there were a few excellent restaurants in Cricket Creek, Shane wanted to keep his existence on the down low. Nashville wasn't all that far from Cricket Creek and he sure didn't want to ruin his newfound privacy by luring the paparazzi to this small town. Nope, that would really suck, he thought, and decided he needed to watch some cooking shows now that he had the time. He'd read in the local paper that the chef at Wine and Diner conducted cooking classes, so perhaps he could sharpen his culinary skills and discover a new hobby. Learning to cook might be fun and serve a purpose as well.

After one last lap Shane glided to the side of the pool and hefted his body up over the edge. He stood up, letting the water sluice down his body. The warmth of the sunshine felt good and he closed his eyes and tilted his face upward. With a long groan he raised his arms above his head and stretched out the kinks.

"Oh dear God, you're naaaaa-ked!"

"What?" Startled, Shane opened his eyes and encountered a red-haired woman he'd never seen before. He lowered his hands to shield himself. Where in the hell had she come from? At least she didn't have a camera. She covered her eyes with her hands and took a big step backward.

"I . . . I . . ."

"Watch out for the lounge chair behind you," Shane warned when she nearly fell into it. The back of her calves hit the metal edge and she did a little hoppy side step, looking as if she were ready to start a line dance. Coming to an unsteady halt, she nodded but kept her eyes covered. Her flaming cheeks were nearly the same color as her hair. With her eyes still hidden she said, "I'm so, *so* sorry!" Her purse slid from the shoulder of her white blouse and hit the pavement with a thud. She dropped a folder she was carrying, causing papers to scatter.

"It's okay." Shane glanced around for his clothes but couldn't remember where he'd shed them, thinking that he could remember the lyrics to hundreds of songs but forgot where the hell he'd left his clothes just a little while ago. "But if you don't mind if I ask, who are you?" He looked around again, thinking perhaps he should jump back into the water.

"Laura Lee Carter. I ... I'm here about the house-keeping position. I went to the front door, but there was no answer and I s-saw your truck and ... and I thought I'd check back here, um, here. I ... I was supposed to interview with you at ten."

"Oh, I thought that was tomorrow," Shane admitted, thinking that having a personal assistant was something he was really going to miss.

"I'll come back another time," she offered, and hastily turned around but hit the chair again.

"No, hey, listen this is totally my fault. I just need to get dressed," he said. "As soon as I figure out where I left my clothes." Seriously what the hell? Did his damn shorts just get up and walk away? Was a raccoon wearing his running shoes? "They've got to be around here some-where."

She nodded but looked as if she wanted the ground to open up and swallow her up. He also noted that Laura Lee wore a plain blue pencil skirt hitting just above the knees and sensible blue pumps. She probably thought the outfit was all business, but Shane found the understated look somehow sexy and to his horror his body reacted. "Um ..." He spotted a towel draped on the chair behind her. Thank God for small favors. "Laura Lee, there's a towel on the lounge chair. Would you please toss it to me?"

"Oh ... oh, sure." She nodded vigorously, allowing a lock of her hair to escape the neat bun she had perched near the top of her head. The breeze blew the deep red curl across her face just before she whipped around to retrieve the towel. She turned back to him with her one hand still over her eyes and gave the towel a hard toss, sending it sailing over his head and into the pool. It amused Shane that she didn't simply close her eyes but felt the need to add her hand as protection against the possibility of viewing him naked again. Perhaps he wasn't in that great shape after all.

Laura Lee lowered her hand and looked at him. "You're still naaaa-ked!" she sputtered, forgetting for a second to shield her eyes. "And oh my God, are you Shane McCray?"

"In the, um, flesh," he said, hoping to make her laugh. He'd left out his real name in the ad, not wanting to give away where he lived or attract the wrong people. "You tossed the towel in the pool."

"Oh! I did?" Laura Lee surprised him by hurrying past him, dropping to her knees, and looking into the water. "I see it!"

He suddenly remembered that his clothes were behind a big potted plant near the deep end of the pool. "Laura Lee," he began, but before he could stop her she reached for the edge of the rapidly sinking towel and tumbled headfirst into the water with a big splash.

Shane's first impulse was to laugh, but when she flailed her arms around he thought that perhaps she couldn't swim. The water would only be slightly over her head, but he knew that when people thought they were drowning they panicked. "Here!" Shane leaned forward, offering his hand, but more of her hair had escaped, obscuring her vision.

And then she went under.

"Dammit!" Without wasting another second Shane jumped in and dove beneath the water. He reached for her, but as he suspected she was a tall woman and was able to stand up.

"Here," Laura Lee said with a little cough. Pushing the hair from her face, she shoved the wet towel in his direction. "Sorry. Again."

Shane took the heavy wet towel from her and wasn't quite sure if he should laugh or give Laura Lee a polite thank-you. For someone who was used to dealing with some pretty crazy situations, this one sure did take the cake. He wrapped the towel around his waist and tied the edges into a knot and tried not to chuckle at her expense.

"Well . . . I guess as interviews go, this pretty much puts me out of the running, so if you don't mind I'll just be on my way," she said with a slight quiver in her tone. When she started to wade through the water, Shane reached over and tapped her shoulder.

"Laura Lee?"

She slowly turned around.

"Are you kidding me? You dove into the pool to retrieve my towel. I'd say that goes beyond the call of duty and tells me that you'd be an excellent employee."

Laura Lee's mouth twitched and he didn't know if she was going to laugh or burst into tears. "In all honesty I fell, but let's go with the diving-in, excellent-employee theory," she said.

Shane finally laughed so hard that he slapped the water, splashing her. "Oh, sorry."

"I'm already soaked, so no harm done," Laura Lee said, making him laugh even harder.

"When can you start?"

"Seriously?" She blinked at him and even with smudged mascara and a sopping-wet bun sliding to the side, Laura Lee Carter was one pretty woman. Not that he would hire her for that reason. "Do you want to see my résumé?" She looked over her shoulder. "Oh, gone with the wind, I'm afraid."

For some reason Shane found her comment hysterically funny and laughed again. When she appeared a bit distraught he cleared his throat and tried for a serious tone. "So, tell me what it said on your résumé."

"Well . . ." When she lifted her chin and tried for a businesslike expression, he had to bite his tongue to keep from laughing. He was draped in a towel and she was fully clothed complete with her sensible shoes, standing in his pool. "I've had my own housekeeping business for the past year. I know that's not all that long, but I have several references to vouch for my excellence. I've lived in Cricket Creek all my life. If you wish to do a background check you will see that I've not had as much as a parking ticket. To find wrongdoing you'd have to go all the way back to high school when I got detention."

"And what did you do?"

"I broke the dress code by wearing my skirt too short."

"What a rebel," Shane said, and she finally laughed.

"I know, right?" She gave him a slight grin. "Actually my legs were growing way too fast for the length of my clothes, but I rather like the rebel idea."

"So, what got you into the housekeeping business?" Shane asked.

"It's always been my dream. Much like you and country music, I imagine. I'm just living the life, you know?"

He laughed. "No, seriously."

"Do you want the truth or the sugarcoated version?" Laura Lee asked, and then shook her head, making droplets fly. "I don't know why in the world that just came out of my mouth."

"Because I asked?"

"No, I mean—"

"Hey, I like straight shooters," Shane interrupted. "Don't sugarcoat it."

Laura Lee gave Shane a long look and then said, "I was married to a jackass who didn't allow me to work because it would detract from me waiting on him and keeping his house spotless. I got really good at cooking and cleaning."

"Allow you?" The notion infuriated Shane.

She shrugged. "I was at the tail end of the baby boomers. I thought I was doing the right thing by pleasing him just like I watched my mother do for my daddy. I believed it was my wifely duty."

"Was? Good for you."

"You got that right." She gave him a short laugh.

"Tell me more," Shane said, and for some reason he couldn't explain he had to know her story. "If you don't mind."

"You really want to know?"

"I do, but only if you want to tell me."

She hesitated but then said, "Well, Jack ... *short for jackass* ... traveled a lot for his job and had been cheating on me for years while he ignored me. He depleted our retirement account and savings in the process. Because of that, I did get the house in the divorce settlement, but I couldn't afford to maintain it, so I sold it." She paused and then said, "I used the money to buy a van, slapped my logo on the side, and started cleaning houses. Not glamorous but good honest work." She paused again and then added, "My story kinda sounds like one of your sad songs."

Shane tossed his head back and laughed. He was about to feel sorry for her, but she was a feisty redhead who had stiffened her backbone and landed on her feet. She laughed too, but there was a bit of a haunted quality in her green eyes that hit him in the gut. "You're a steel magnolia."

"Damn straight."

"So, did it say all that in your résumé?"

"No, and I can't believe I just told you all that personal stuff."

"I asked, remember?"

"You did. But hey, this is a small town and we all know a lot about each other, so it doesn't really bother me to tell. Good thing Jack moved away, because he wasn't welcome at too many places around Cricket Creek."

"Well-deserved shunning, I'd say. I'm starting to like this town more and more."

"I've lived here all my life and a lot of people have my back." Laura Lee laughed. "So, do I still have the job?"

"Is there any doubt?"

"Is that a yes?"

A sudden thought hit Shane and he gazed at her for a few seconds.

"You're rethinking your hasty offer? If you want to interview more people, I fully understand."

"Not at all." Shane shook his head. "I was just thinking that I'm embarrassed that I need a personal assistant to remind me of things like this interview, for instance. And I can't cook worth a lick. How do you feel about working for me full-time as my personal assistant, cook, and housekeeper? I know it sounds like a lot, but I'm retired . . . well, sort of anyway . . . and those three positions can be rolled into one. Plus, I still have an agent and manager and a staff that manages my other investments. Although I won't be recording or touring any longer, I'll do an occasional endorsement and charity functions. You would have to keep track of those things for me through them. Just hand me a sheet of paper telling me what I have to do that day."

"Oh my goodness." Her eyes widened. "But I have other clients to clean for."

"What kind of compensation would you need to give those up?"

"I don't know. I . . . um, what would my hours be?"

"A nine-to-five kind of thing mostly, but it could be flexible when you need it and of course you'd get vacation time. I eat breakfast after my morning run and I'm gone a lot too, so I won't be breathing down your neck. Lunch can be left in the fridge and dinner but only if I'll be here. If I don't have errands for you to run, you're welcome to use the pool and exercise room as part of your job perks. I might also need you to go to Sully's South or My Way Recording Studio with me once in a while."

She put a hand to her chest. "This is so unexpected. I don't know what to say."

"Would sixty thousand work?" Shane asked. He suspected his offer was much more than she was making.

Her pretty green eyes widened again. "I take that back. I do know what to say. Yes. I will take the job."

Shane laughed again, thinking that he was going to like having Laura Lee Carter around in his daily life. He was a good judge of character, and his gut told him that she would do an excellent job and could be trusted. "So, can you start tomorrow?"

"Yes."

"Good." Shane extended his hand and as expected she gave him a good grip. "I'll give you some details so you know what to do."

She nodded again but appeared slightly uneasy. "Um, when I said I was a good cook, I meant the basics, you know, home-style. I don't know how to do really fancy stuff."

"Laura Lee, just to let you know I've always thought the whole celebrity thing to be a bunch of hogwash. I'm just a good ol' boy who can sing. Trust me, I'm really easy to work for. And I don't go for the fancy stuff. Simple home-cooked meals will be perfect."

She let out a sigh of relief, making Shane smile. "Well, then I guess I'll see you tomorrow at nine. Make a list of your favorite meals and I'll go grocery shopping today. I'll leave a card for you with my e-mail address."

"Will do. I would walk you out but if you don't mind I'm not quite dressed for it."

Laura Lee laughed. "I can see myself out to my van."

Shane watched her slosh through the pool and walk up the steps. When she had to pause to find a shoe, he found it hard not to laugh but somehow managed not to. He tried not to notice how her wet clothes clung to her tall, shapely body when she emerged from the shallow end of the pool but felt another pull of attraction. She seemed like a sweet, down-to-earth woman who had been put through the wringer. He sternly reminded himself that she was his employee and he needed to keep his hands to himself. Still, he was looking forward to her company.

She picked up her scattered papers, chasing one down in a sudden gust of wind. "Do you want these?"

"I know all I need to know," Shane replied.

"Okay, then . . ." She slid her purse over her shoulder and gave him a crisp little nod that was at odds with her soggy status. "I'll be off."

"I'll send the list. See you tomorrow morning, Laura Lee." He had to grin when she sloshed away, leaving a wet trail in her wake.

4

Everybody's Got Somebody but Me

MATTIE SAT CROSS-LEGGED ON THE FLOOR AT THE BACK of the diner while browsing through the bottom shelf of the historical romance section of her books. "Hmm ..." She pulled one out and looked at a long-haired, bare-chested pirate on the front. "I wonder if I've read this one," she mused, and started reading the back cover. Mattie had a weakness for pirates and often imagined herself as the feisty heroine who after putting up a fight ended up having lusty sex with the swashbuckling hero. Tired to the bone after doing inventory, she wanted a book to read later that evening.

Rusty came over, flopped down, and rested his head on her thigh. "Ha. If you think that's gonna get you out of trouble you're dead wrong," Mattie said, but then petted Rusty's head until she heard him sigh. When she stopped he raised his head and gave her that sad look that got to her every time. "You know I can't stay mad at you," she said, and started scratching him behind the ears. While the old dog snored she started reading the first few pages of the story.

"Hey, Mattie, you here?" Rusty lifted his head at the

sound of Mason's voice and trotted to the front of the restaurant.

"In the back, Mason. Whatcha need?"

"You got any sexy shad? It's the only bait the bass seem to go for."

"I'm all out," Mattie shouted. "And would you let Rusty out?"

"Okay. Go on out, boy."

A moment later Mattie looked up to see Mason standing over her with his arms crossed over his chest. "Don't give me that look."

"You gotta be kidding me. I need shad-colored baits, Mattie."

Mattie sighed. "Like you said, it's the go-to bait right now, so I'm sold out. Don't be so cranky. I've got some ordered." She patted the floor next to her. "Pop a squat."

Mason bent his long jean-clad legs and sat down next to Mattie. "Sorry for being such an ass. You know how I get when the fish don't bite. It's not fun to take somebody out fishing for the day and come up empty-handed." He leaned in and gave her shoulder a shove. "I need to get you out on the water sometime soon."

"I'd like that. Maybe do a little bit of night fishing."

"You got it. We'll get Danny to come along. You can pay me back with some homemade fried chicken in Mama's cast-iron skillet. You talked to her or Dad lately?"

"Not in a day or two. They're practicing for a couples tournament coming up."

Mason nodded and then grinned down at the book she was reading. "I remember picking up one of Mama's books she was reading and my eyes just about popped out of my head when I read a page or so."

"Hey, it's the only action I'm getting right now, so don't knock it."

"No! Just stop!" He put his hands over his ears and shook his head. "On that note I think I'm heading over to the Bass Pro Shop and get some lures. Let me know when you can go fishing."

"I will. And I'll catch more than you and Danny put together."

Mason stood up. "Ha, we'll see about that. Hey, you up for a bonfire soon?"

"Sure, let's do it."

"I'll make some calls."

"Sweet."

"Catch ya later, little sis."

Mattie grinned as she watched her brother walk away. When he opened the doors Rusty came back and flopped back down next to her. She did on rare occasion outfish them but not too often. It sure would be a treat to get out on the water if only she could find the time. With a sigh Mattie went back to reading her book.

"Mattie? Yoo-hoo, are you here, girlie?"

"Back by the books, Laura Lee." Mattie grinned when she looked up and saw her mother's best friend. Laura Lee Carter was one of her favorite people in the whole world. "Get over here and pick out a book." She patted the space on the opposite side of where Rusty snored.

Laura Lee angled her head to check out the cover of the book. "Ah, pirates. Good choice."

"Well, you're the one who turned me on to romance novels when I was in high school. If my mama had known what I was reading, she would have thrown a hissy fit," Mattie said with a giggle.

Laura Lee put a fingertip to her lips. "Shhh, don't tell on me."

"Never," Mattie whispered, and Laura Lee laughed. She was such a wonderful person and had been put through so much. But through it all she'd managed to keep a smile on her face and her chin up.

Laura Lee picked up a book with a handsome High-lander on the cover. "Give me a man in a kilt," she said, and wiggled her eyebrows.

"Aren't you going to read the back?"

"I don't need to," Laura Lee replied, and hugged the

book to her chest. She reached over and patted Mattie's thigh. "So, how are you doing?"

"Fine." Mattie was a little startled by the question. "Why do you ask?"

"Oh, I don't know." Laura Lee tilted her head to the side. "I haven't seen that pretty smile of yours as often as I'd like. Anything bothering you, sweetie?"

"Well . . ." Mattie ran her fingers over the glossy cover for a moment and finally said, "I'd like to have a man in my life other than book boyfriends, I guess." She knew she could tell Laura Lee anything and she wouldn't breathe a word of it. "And I suppose I get kinda lonely for girl talk," she added with a little shrug. Mattie wasn't high on feeling sorry for herself, but when Laura Lee gave her a quick hug Mattie felt tightness in her chest.

"You know you can call me any time of the day or night with anything you need to talk about, Mattie."

"I sure do know that, Laura Lee." Mattie gave a smile, but it wobbled just a bit at the corners. She wasn't much of a crier either, but she had to swallow sudden hot emotion in her throat. "It's just that so many of my girlfriends are getting married and starting families. I mean, I'm in no hurry for that, but they don't get out as much and when they come over for bonfires down by the river, it seems that everybody's got somebody but me."

Laura Lee shook her head slowly. "Quite honestly I'm flabbergasted that nobody has snatched you up already."

"Ha . . ."

"Oh, would you just stop?" She gave Mattie's leg a shove, making Rusty groan in protest of the sudden movement. He yawned wide enough to crack his jaw and laid his head back down. "You're a catch and then some."

"I know . . . right?" Mattie said with a little grin. "Hey, I'm good at fishing and play a mean shortstop in softball." She gestured toward the kitchen. "And I make melt-in-your-mouth biscuits."

"And you're gorgeous."

"Of course there's that too." Mattie nodded and then laughed, but in truth she often wondered if guys did find her to be pretty. "Do you think we'll find our real-life hero? Our happily ever after?"

"Of course you will." Laura Lee's smile faltered just a bit, but Mattie noticed.

"Um, I said *we*."

"I do believe that ship has sailed for me." She leaned against the bookshelf and chuckled. "Or sank might be a better way of putting it."

"What? Why would you say such a fool thing?"

"Well . . ." Laura Lee rubbed her thumb over the edge of her book, making a flapping noise. "I'm fifty-five years old for one thing."

"So? Why does that matter?" Mattie sat up straighter. "I mean, what does age have to do with anything at all? Look at Kate and Ben at Whisper's Edge. They're, like, in their sixties and I've seen them holding hands, walking down Main Street. Ha! And what about Clyde and Miss Patty? They were having breakfast here earlier. I swear they were *glowing* and they're as old as the hills." She tapped her cheek for a second. "Oh, and Pete and Maria Sully? They're older than you and they rekindled a love that refused to die." Mattie shook her head. "When Maria came back from Nashville, everybody in town was rooting for those two to get back together, you included."

"Yeah, but—"

"Yeah, but what?" She pointed a finger at Laura Lee and continued. "And how about Myra at Wine and Diner? Myra and Owen are up there in age too. That man worships the ground she walks on."

"How do you know this?"

Mattie chuckled. "Because Myra says so all the time. Owen just nods and laughs in agreement. I can give you about another dozen examples if you want me to, not that you don't already know these people."

"You know what?" Laura Lee gave Mattie's leg another shove. "You walk around like a tough little cookie and you're nothing but a big old mushy romantic. Well, make that cute, young little romantic. You're no bigger than a minute."

"I know." Mattie didn't even try to dispute it because Laura Lee knew her inside out. "That's why I love reading these books. It's like there's always hope against all odds, ya know? I like the opposites-attract scenario when the hero and heroine are the two least likely people to fall for each other."

"And they banter back and forth until you're dying for them to just kiss and get it over with already."

"Exactly! What's your favorite?" Mattie asked, but before Laura Lee could answer they heard someone come through the front door.

"Hello? Mattie? Are you here?"

"Back here by the books," Mattie called out.

"Well, by the sound of him he's certainly not from around these parts." Laura Lee gave Mattie a curious look. "Who is it?"

"Garret Ruleman, Rick Ruleman's son," Mattie whispered just before he walked up to them.

"Ah, there you are." When they both started to scramble to their feet he shook his shaggy head. Rusty groaned in complaint and flopped down onto the floor. "No, stay seated and carry on. I just came back to browse through the books. I forgot to earlier." He leaned down and extended his hand to Laura Lee. "Hello there, I'm Garret Ruleman."

"Laura Lee Carter," she said, and Mattie noticed that she seemed to be charmed.

"Nice to meet you." Garret pointed down at Rusty. "The ham bandit, I'm guessing?"

"Yes. Add three biscuits to the growing list."

"Can't say that I blame him. Your biscuits were even better than your promise, Mattie. I'm going to have to add another mile to my evening run, but well worth the effort, I might add."

"Thanks." Mattie couldn't help smiling. She noted

that he had changed into a blue oxford shirt tucked into khaki pants. Business casual, but her brothers would consider Garret's clothes as dressing up. The subtle scent of his spicy aftershave slid her way, making her want to move closer. She almost did.

Garret looked down at the book in her hand. "What are you reading?"

Mattie held the book up. She fully expected a raised eyebrow or snide comment and braced herself.

"Ah, a romance novel. My mother adores them." He grinned and put one hand to the side of his mouth. "I have a confession," he said in a hushed tone.

Laura Lee and Mattie looked at him expectantly.

"I used to read Mum's books when she wasn't around." He pointed to the cover. "Lots of good information about women in there."

Laura Lee laughed. "More men should think like you."

"I'd say you're right." Garret shot her a crooked grin. "Mind if I have a look around?"

"Not at all," Mattie replied. "Mysteries and suspense are located at the back with some Westerns mixed in. Horror is to the right."

"Any self-help?" he asked. "I need a stack of those babies."

"Mixed in with the rack of other nonfiction," Mattie answered, and then realized he was joking. "All the books are one dollar and you just drop the buck in the fishbowl by the register. The money goes to a local charity for literacy, so feel free to be generous. Oh, and if you have any books you want to donate we will be grateful. And although you don't have to return anything, it helps the cause if you do."

"I'll remember that." Garret inhaled deeply. "Ah, I just love the smell of books, don't you?"

"I sure do," Mattie admitted, thinking that her brothers probably wouldn't admit to something like that. Of course none of them were big readers unless you counted

Fish and Stream or *Sports Illustrated*. "So you're a book lover."

"Some might be surprised by that fact, but I always have a stack of books on hand. My mother is responsible for my love of reading."

"Me too. I refused to go to bed until she read at least two or three books to me."

"You were better than me. I would always be obsessed with one particular book that I would beg for Mum to read over and over." He shook his head. "Annoying little chap."

"No, I think that's cute." Mattie imagined him as a little boy begging with that sweet accent and had to smile.

"Well, I had so many books memorized that Mum's friends thought I could read at the tender age of three, so she got some satisfaction out of it, I suppose."

"That's funny." Reading had always been Mattie's escape and she'd often dreamed of actually visiting some of the settings in her favorite historical romances. "Take your time browsing. I'm done for the day, but I'll be here for a while."

"All right, then, I'm going to go have a look. Good to meet you, Laura Lee. Mattie, always a pleasure."

Laura Lee gave Mattie a wow-he's-cute little nod, but she rolled her eyes.

When Garret disappeared around the corner, Laura Lee whispered, "What a charmer. I could listen to him talk all day long. Couldn't you?"

"I guess," Mattie conceded with a small nod. Although she did feel a pull of attraction, it kind of oddly felt as if she were cheating on Colby, so she pushed it aside. She could hear Garret pulling books from the shelves and moving about. With all the stories in the tabloids about his wild ways, Mattie wouldn't have pegged him as a big reader. She kind of wanted to stand up and peek over the middle shelf to see what he was looking through.

"Hey . . ." Laura Lee put her hand on Mattie's arm. "I have some news."

Mattie took one look at Laura Lee's eyes and knew this was going to be juicy. "Don't keep me hanging."

"Shane McCray just hired me as his housekeeper, cook, and personal assistant," she said in a low but excited tone.

"Shane McCray?" Mattie drew in a sharp breath. "For real?"

"I know it's pretty hard to believe. I'm still thinking it's all a dream and I'll wake up soon and be super pissed."

Mattie reached over and pinched her.

"Ouch!" she said with a laugh.

"You're awake."

"Mattie, I have to admit that I'm nervous. I know I can handle the cleaning part, but get real, what do I know about handling the affairs of a country music superstar? And what if he doesn't like my cooking?" She bit her bottom lip, clearly concerned. "I'm sure in the past he's had professional chefs slicing and dicing all sorts of fancy dishes. My meat loaf and mashed potatoes will seem so . . ." She looked up at the ceiling.

"So delicious? And are you kidding? You are the most organized person I know, hands down. Everything in your doggone house is labeled and in its place."

"Not everything."

"Oh, come on. Even your garage is nice and neat." It was her turn to give Laura Lee a shove. "And your cooking? Are you serious? You're an amazing cook. You taught me every bit as much as Mama. My biscuits would still be hard as bricks if you hadn't told me not to play with the dough too much. You're perfect for all three jobs."

"I hope you're right. I guess the whole celebrity thing is just throwing me for a loop."

"As my daddy would say, we all put our pants on one leg at a time."

"I know . . . but still."

Mattie thought about how Garret made her sort of nervous for that very reason. "Hey, but what about your other clients?"

"I know. I hate that part." Laura Lee blew out a sigh. "I have to give them notice. And, Mattie, I won't be able to help you clean the cabins up by the lake for the fishing tournaments. I'm so sorry."

"No worries." Mattie waved a dismissive hand at her. In truth she really didn't need the help but knew that Laura Lee could use the work after her jerk of an ex-husband had left her high and dry. "I'll make do."

"Thank you, sweetie. Well, I'd better get going. I just wanted to pop in and tell you my exciting news."

"I'm so glad you did! We'll have to go to Sully's soon to celebrate. I haven't been out in a while."

"Sure thing," Laura Lee said, and then pushed up to her feet. "I'll drop a buck in the jar on my way out."

Mattie nodded and stood up as well. When Garret noticed Laura Lee leaving he said, "Lovely to meet you, Laura Lee."

"It was nice to meet you too, Garret. Welcome to Cricket Creek. I hope you'll enjoy living here."

"I'm sure I will," he replied, but Mattie had to wonder how he would fit in. When he turned a book over and read the back jacket she suddenly felt compelled to walk over to him.

"Find anything interesting?"

He held up a Stephen King novel. "I don't think I've read this one."

"*It*?" Mattie shivered. "Oh, that would give me nightmares. I'm already afraid of clowns."

Garret laughed. "Me too."

"Really?" She liked that he admitted to his fear rather than denying it.

Garret nodded. "Oh yeah. Creepy buggers if you ask me." He circled his face with his index finger. "All that makeup gives me the willies. When I was a kid I couldn't even handle Ronald McDonald. Just give me my cheeseburger, dude."

"Dude?"

Garret laughed. "I lived in L.A., then Chicago for a

bit and spent a lot of my life in London. My vocabulary is an odd combination of all three. I would imagine that I'll soon be saying things like y'all with a Southern drawl."

"I can't imagine that."

"What are y'all doin' tonight?" he asked, making Mattie laugh.

"That sounded like a very bad impression of John Wayne."

"Sorry, I'll have to work on it. That's how I have to talk to get Siri to give me directions on my phone or she can't understand me. I've ended up in the wrong place more than once," he said, making Mattie laugh. "And now I have to learn what seems like a whole new language."

"Southern-speak? Give me an example and maybe I can set you straight."

He tapped his book for a second. "Okay, just what in the world does fixin' mean? I keep hearing the term and it confuses me."

"It means gettin' ready. Like, I'm fixin' to go to the store."

"Ah . . . makes rather odd sense now." Garret grinned at her. "How about best? It's used in a strange manner that baffles me."

"Best not?"

Garret nodded.

"It means don't."

"Oh, like you *best not* stick your hand in a catfish hole?"

"Did you just set me up for that?"

Garret laughed. "No, not that I wouldn't. I really think I need one of those translating books."

Mattie laughed. "A Southern-speak app on your phone would help."

"All the extra syllables get in the way for me too. It's like stretching a sentence like a rubber band. But I'm learning."

"I'll come up with a cheat sheet for ya."

"I need one." A moment passed and he looked down at his book. "I love to read horror into the night until every little noise in the house scares me."

"Why would you do that to yourself? Are you crazy?"

He tilted his head to the side. "I think most people would say yes to that question."

"I believe it." Mattie eyed the book and shook her head. "I'll stick to my romance novels, thank you very much."

"And this is coming from the girl who is going to stick her hand in a catfish hole." Garret thrust the novel toward her. "Give it a try."

"No way!" Mattie took a step backward as if the clown might bite her.

"How about this? If you read Stephen King's *It*, I'll read that romance novel you're holding so tightly."

"No, you won't," she scoffed.

"I will too."

"In public?"

"You're pushing it just a bit," Garret said with a grin.

"Ha, thought so."

"All right, then." Garret reached over and took the book from her. "Deal."

"What?"

Garret handed *It* to Mattie. "You heard me. A month from now we can get together over coffee with a book report in hand."

"Okay . . . okay." Mattie had to laugh. Garret was quite different than any guy she'd met before. "And you promised to read it in public. Here, so I can see you." She pointed at a table. "While you're eating breakfast."

"It's really hard to embarrass me. At one time that might have been the case, but I'm over caring what people think," he added, but Mattie wasn't really buying his declaration completely. He was cute and a bit cocky, but there was a vulnerable set to his mouth that didn't fool her.

"I hear ya." She lifted one shoulder. "I don't embarrass easily either. Trust me, my brothers and his friends try super hard to embarrass me but even if I am, I never let on." She suddenly wondered why she felt the need to tell him all this, and in truth they did embarrass her on occasion.

"Ah, never let them see you sweat."

"Exactly." Mattie nodded and she realized that he got it. The two of them might be more alike than what she first thought. "It's all in good fun. They don't mean any harm." She didn't want him to think ill of Mason and Danny, because they were good guys. "Do you have siblings?"

"Two younger half sisters named Sophia and Grace."

"They sound adorable."

"They were," he said with a fond smile and something else in his eyes that she couldn't quite read. "I had to participate in many a tea party, let me tell you."

Mattie laughed. "I'm picturing you in a tiara and feather boa."

"And you would be spot-on," Garret admitted, and Mattie thought he might make a super-cute dad and then wondered where in the world that thought came from. He leaned closer to her ear. "Don't tell anyone but I had bows in my hair on more than one occasion."

"What a fun big brother you must have been," Mattie said.

"I suppose I was at that," Garret said, but had a look of surprise on his face as if just now realizing it. "Because I was such a rascal I think everyone thought I was going to be jealous when they were born, but they were such cute little bundles that I loved them both straightaway." He got a rather wistful look on his face. "Very sweet little girls, those two. Still are to this day," he added, and then tilted his head to the side. "Well, no longer little. They're both tall like my mum," he said, and Mattie thought it was interesting that he didn't mention his stepfather but she thought it rude to ask.

"Are you still close to your sisters?" she asked, because he seemed to be.

"I don't get to see them as often as I'd like," he said with a rather sad smile. "But yes, we get along."

"And you? Were you well behaved when you were little?"

"As I mentioned I was a little rascal from the get-go. It was a wonder that my mum wanted more children after me."

"Oh, I doubt that," Mattie said.

"That I was a rascal?"

"No, that your mother wouldn't want to have more children because of you, silly."

"Why, thank you." Garret reached over and briefly touched her cheek. Mattie was used to tugs on her ponytail and shoves to her shoulder, making the small gesture so very tender. Something warm settled in her stomach, making her long to lean her cheek into his palm. "You're such a sweet girl as well, Mattie Mayfield."

"Oh, there might be some who would argue," Mattie said with a laugh. She pulled back and felt a little bit flustered.

Garret smiled and for some reason Mattie felt as if he could see through her toughness to the girl who wanted to have her hand held and share a kiss in the moonlight. He looked at her for a moment as if trying to decide what to say. "Well, I'd better push off." Garret held up the book and glanced at the shirtless pirate. "I'll start reading tonight, I think."

Mattie looked at the cover of her book. "I guess I will too," she said, but the creepy white-faced clown with the red nose and evil eyes seemed to be glaring directly at her. "Oh boy . . ."

"I hope you don't get too scared."

"No, you don't. You hope this scares the pants off me," she said, and then felt a blush heat her cheeks.

"Don't worry, I won't touch that line even though I want to."

"Thank you." Mattie slapped her hand over her face and laughed.

"Oh, stop." Garret pried her fingers away from her face. "See you soon, Mattie." He paused and then said, "Perhaps you can show me around Cricket Creek when you get the chance." It was funny but for someone used to the limelight he suddenly seemed a bit shy about asking. He seemed so bold but then somehow unsure, making Mattie want to give him some sort of reassurance.

"I'd be happy to show you around town."

"Fantastic. Well, I'm really going this time, although I hate to leave good company."

"Thank you."

"I'll probably see you at breakfast tomorrow." He patted his stomach. "Well, if I'm ever hungry again."

"Get used to Southern cookin'. We don't skimp." Mattie grinned, but as he walked away she shouted, "Garret, there are some business cards on the counter by the register. The second number is my cell phone. If you need anything or have questions about town, let me know."

He pivoted to look back at her. "Thanks, I'll do that." He gave her another nod and a wave.

When Mattie saw him pause and then stuff several bills into the book jar, she had to smile. She liked his company too, and as soon as he left she was already wondering when she'd see him again, hoping it was before breakfast. As a friend, of course. She still had her sights solidly set on Colby Campbell.

5

Holding Out for a Hero

 $\mathcal{G}$ ARRET'S EARLY-EVENING RUN TOOK HIM INTO THE PATH in the woods up toward the lake. He told himself it was so cool in the shade of the trees, but he knew it was an effort to head toward Mattie's cabin. He also told himself that simple curiosity caused his feet to have a mind of their own, but in truth he knew better. He liked her. Liking her felt . . . odd. In the past chatting up a woman was for selfish reasons. Either he wanted to get laid or there was something in it for him. Liking Mattie felt innocent and pure, leaving him feeling shitty about the way he'd conducted himself in the past and yet somehow a bit cleansed with this new attitude.

Garret took the bend in the path and headed uphill. Random twigs snapped beneath his shoes, sounding loud in the silence. At first he was pissed that he'd forgotten his earbuds, but the quiet filled him with a peacefulness that seemed to give him extra endurance. He felt as if he could run forever in these woods.

Long fingers of sunshine reached through the tree branches, touching everything like a warm caress. Garret breathed deep the scent of pine and damp soil. Although he loved the energy of the city, Garret also deeply appreciated nature. Those who knew him would be surprised, and then the thought gave him pause.

Who actually knew him?

The answer was simple and rather sad: *no one*. Not even his mum, really. How could anyone know him? Because he sure as hell didn't know himself. Since his breakup with Addison Monroe, Garret had been on a mission to improve the sorry-ass thing he called his life. His goal, if you could call it that, had always been to piss his father off in a misguided cry for attention. He got that now. But for many years rocker Rick Ruleman had only been concerned with himself. So Garret's antics went pretty much unnoticed except for the eager public who ate it up with a spoon so much so that he was offered a reality show about his engagement to Addison Monroe, daughter of the famous finance guru Melinda Monroe.

The breakup was his wake-up call. Garret had been a total wanker, trampling on hearts and not giving a damn. But when he realized that he had been turning into everything he hated about his father, he came to a screeching halt and took a long, hard look at himself. And he pretty much sucked.

Thinking about his over-the-top past, he shook his head and muttered, "Classic." There should be a damn reality show about him traveling around the country, no, make that the world, apologizing to every girl he'd been a jerk to. "Might be the longest-running reality show ever," he muttered, pushing harder. He had to laugh, though, when he pictured how many times they would open the door, see it was him, and give him a much deserved slap across his face.

When Garret came to a clearing he spotted the lake glistening in the waning sunlight. Basic brown cabins hugged the shoreline on the opposite side of the lake, each with its own small dock. A lovely stone and cedar cabin sat in the clearing apart from the rest. Wondering if the larger dwelling could be Mattie's home, he jogged closer. Sure enough, he spotted her sitting on the back deck, leaning back in a lounge chair. Upon closer inspection he noticed that she clutched a book in her hand. Grinning, Garret cupped his hands around his mouth and was about to shout out to her but then hesitated. There was a spark of attraction between them and he needed to tread softly. The last thing he wanted was to break another heart, especially someone who seemed as sweet as Mattie Mayfield. But he liked her.

As he was just about to jog away, a sudden notion hit him. Perhaps they could be friends, nothing more. "What a novel idea," he muttered with a sense of wonder, but one that appealed to him.

With that in mind, intruding upon her space seemed rude, so he turned and ran back toward his cabin, thinking with a chuckle that he had a romance novel to read.

After a quick shower Garret popped the top on a beer and took a good long guzzle. He threw together a huge cheddar cheese, tomato, and Branston pickle sandwich, added a handful of barbecue Pringles, and headed out to the back deck with his romance novel in hand. Because it was nearly dark he lit the outside light and settled into a lounge chair, propping his bare feet up onto the matching ottoman.

The story started with Dominick, the swashbuckling pirate hero, attacking the ship with lovely Isobel on board. As it turned out Isobel's father was Dominick's archenemy, so he promptly kidnapped her in his plot for revenge. Ah, but Dominick was enchanted by lovely Isobel, so what was a pirate to do? He locked her in his cabin while he brooded over his situation.

So engrossed in the story, Garret didn't hear the music coming from the dock until he looked up from the first chapter. The story, although not his cup of tea, had captured his attention and in truth he wanted to know how it would all play out in the end.

After dog-earing the page Garret stood up and stretched, thinking he might like another beer, when he heard shouts and laughter mingling with upbeat music. Curious, Garret walked over to the side of the deck and saw a bonfire shooting flames upward from a big stack of wood. Lounge chairs surrounded the circle of fieldstone, keeping the fire in check. Several coolers dotted the lawn and Garret guessed they were filled with beer. Garret spotted Mattie standing near the fire pit looking cute in cutoff jeans and a white button-down shirt tied around her waist showing just a hint of skin. He must have been so immersed in the story that he hadn't heard the commotion until now.

Loneliness washed over Garret and he wondered if Mattie had thought to invite him. He'd already put her phone number from her business card in his contacts. Maybe he could send her a random text message and hope that she'd ask him to join them. What would they do if he simply showed up? He'd crashed parties and done way crazier things in his life, but he found himself hesitating. He wouldn't fit in, but that wasn't anything new. The problem was that because he was a celebrity the girls tended to flock around him and the blokes tended to size him up and give him the evil eye. After a good dose of alcohol the girls would get flirty and the blokes even more pissed with someone ending up taking a swing. Garret found it amusing that because he was tall and lanky they always thought they could take him, but he kept in shape and was stronger than he looked.

"Not a fun scenario," Garret said under his breath. And when he spotted Mattie walking away from the crowd with Colby he felt a flash of a foreign emotion that could only be, wait . . . jealousy? Garret turned away and shook his head. Surely he must be mistaken. He barely knew the girl.

Another cold beer sounded pretty damn good, but just when he was about to head into the cabin Mattie's voice carried his way. He turned back around and after looking closer he spotted her standing on the dock nearest to his cabin. She was talking to Colby and her voice carried his way.

"I don't want to swim, Colby. I'm not in my suit. And it'll be cold coming out of the water."

"Come on, Mattie. The bonfire will warm you up."

"I don't really like swimming in the dark."

"That's what makes it fun. I'll stay close. I promise."

Garret saw Mattie glance toward the water and hesitate. Was she really going to do something that she didn't want to do just to impress the jackass? Garret's jaw clenched. Swimming in the cove might not be the safest thing to do this time of night.

"I don't know . . . ," Mattie said.

Colby took a step closer to Mattie. His unsteady gait suggested that he'd already had too much to drink. "Well, then, maybe I'll just have to throw you in."

"Colby . . . ," Mattie said in a wary tone. "Come on. Don't."

Garret had heard enough. "I wouldn't do that," he shouted, drawing both Mattie's and Colby's attention. They looked up at him.

"Do what?" Colby asked.

"Toss Mattie in the water. Don't do it, dude."

"I think you should mind your own business . . . *dude*."

"Garret, it's okay, really," Mattie said.

"Maybe Mattie wants me to throw her in," Colby challenged, and it was now very clear that he'd had one too many. "Dontcha, Mattie?"

"No, I — " she began, but shrieked when Colby scooped her up.

"Yes, you do."

"Stop it!" Garret saw red. Not caring if he broke his fool neck, he hopped over the side of the deck and hit the grass a few yards in front of the dock. When a sharp pain shot up his ankle, he knew he'd landed wrong, but he rushed over to the dock toward Colby, ignoring the pain. "Put her down. Now."

"Since when do I take orders from you, Garret?"

"Since right this damn minute."

"Colby, just put me down," Mattie pleaded. "Seriously."

"You heard her."

"I'm just playin', Mattie," Colby chided, but when he started to put her down he stumbled sideways, nearly losing his balance. He let go of Mattie and a moment later she went airborne with a shriek and landed with a splash.

"Mattie!" Pushing by a confused Colby, Garret jumped into the water and snaked his arm around Mattie. Coughing, she clung to him. "It's okay, I've got you. Just hang on." When she nodded against his neck Garret felt a wave of protectiveness wash over him and made his way back to the dock. "Can you get up the steps? You can hang on to me if you need to."

"I can do it," she answered with just enough of a tremble in her voice to make Garret want to smash his fist in Colby's face. Maybe he would just for the hell of it.

After they were standing on solid ground, Garret wrapped his arm around Mattie's waist, making sure she was steady on her feet. "Are you okay?"

Mattie gave him a quick nod. "Yeah," she said gruffly. "I was just startled."

"Mattie, damn, I'm so sorry," Colby said with a slight slur to his speech. "I wasn't really gonna toss you in. I was just playin'." He shot Garret a look that tried to place the blame on him. "You shoulda just kept out of it and this wouldn't have happened."

"It didn't look that way to me," Garret said stiffly. "Mattie doesn't deserve to get manhandled."

"Mattie knows I wouldn't cause her any harm," Colby said.

"You just did," Garret said.

"I didn't mean to. You know that, right, Mattie?" When Colby stepped closer Garret tightened his hold around her waist and planted his feet firmly on the dock.

"I know," Mattie said, and she pulled away from Garret. "It's fine, Garret. I know you meant well, but—"

"He shoulda kept out of it," Colby insisted, and took a step forward with his fists clenched at his sides.

"Colby! Just back off, okay?" Mattie pleaded.

"You better listen." Garret wasn't going to take a swing at the big clod, but he stood his ground. If Colby wanted a fight, he was going to get one and end up in the river just for spite.

"Hey, what's going on here?" They all looked over to see Danny walking onto the wooden dock. "Everything okay?" Danny asked, and looked at Garret as if he suspected he was the troublemaker.

Garret raised his hands upward. "Hey, I was just coming to the aid of your sister." He pointed at Colby. "This dude was going to toss her in the water."

"Seriously, Colby? What the hell, man?"

"I wasn't!" Colby insisted, but swayed a little.

"Sure looked that way to me," Garret said to Danny. "And she did end up in the water because of him. Dangerous if you ask me."

"No one is askin' you," Colby said. "Danny, I dropped Mattie in on accident. You b-believe me, r-right?"

"You okay, Mattie?" Danny asked, and gave Colby a pissed-off look that said he'd better shut up.

"Yeah," Mattie answered softly, but then shivered.

"Sorry, Garret. He's been hittin' some apple pie," Danny said with a shake of his head.

"I think he's been hitting more than apple pie," Garret said.

"Apple pie is moonshine. He's not usually like this," Mattie explained, and Garret felt a flash of anger that she was defending him.

"Sorry," Danny apologized again to Garret. "I'll get him outta here." He turned to Mattie. "You sure you're okay, sis? Do you want me to go and get Mason to come over while I get Colby out of here?"

"No, Danny, I don't want to ruin Mason's fun. I'll be fine," she said, but shivered again. "I just need to warm up."

"Let's go, Colby," Danny ordered firmly, and put his arm around his friend's waist. They started walking away with Colby apologizing profusely.

Garret turned to Mattie, who hugged her arms across her chest. "I'm sorry if I butted in, but that was a jackass thing he was going to do."

"He really wasn't going to toss me in," she insisted with just a hint of accusation in her tone.

"Oh, sod that."

"What does that mean?"

Garret shoved his fingers through his hair. "It means that's ridiculous and you know it."

"No, really. Colby was just teasing."

Garret felt a stab of disappointment. "Okay, I get it. Next time I'll mind my own business." He jabbed his thumb over his shoulder. "I'll just go back to my romance novel," he added, and turned away. A couple of steps later he swore, "Bollocks."

Mattie rushed forward. "Garret, you're limping! Are you hurt?"

"I'm fine," he said in a gentler tone. The concern in her eyes dissolved any anger he was feeling toward her.

"You must have twisted your ankle."

"I did, but trust me, I'll live."

"You need to ice it," she said. "I'll come with you." She placed a cold hand on his arm.

"Mattie, you're shivering. Find a towel and go stand by the fire." He angled his head in the direction of the fire pit. "Go join your friends. I'm really sorry I butted in," he said even though he wasn't one bit sorry. He would do the same damn thing again if he thought she was in any kind of danger.

"Oh my God, wait. Did you . . . did you jump from the *deck*?" She made it sound as if he'd taken a flying leap off a jagged cliff.

Garret nodded. He looked up and realized it was higher than he'd thought. "Yeah, so what?"

"Are you crazy?"

"I think we've established that fact already." He started walking, trying to hide the needles of pain shooting from his ankle up his leg. And he thought he might have a splinter in his foot too. *Bloody hell.*

Mattie followed him, shivering and sputtering. "What if you'd broken a leg . . . or your fool neck?"

Garret paused and gave her a look. "And what if you'd drowned in the damn river?"

"I wasn't going to drown, for Pete's sake! I grew up on this river!"

"What about snakes?"

"They swim away more afraid of us than we are of them."

"Yeah, that's what people say, but I never did buy in to that rubbish and I wasn't going to take that damn chance!" He really wanted to add a bit of a stomp to his gait but couldn't. "Why on earth are you following me?"

"I want to make sure you put ice on that ankle and that it's not broken."

"It's not broken. I've had enough broken bones to know. Go back to your party, Mattie. I'll be fine."

"You're as stubborn as a mule."

"I've been called way worse." He continued to hobble over to the steps leading to the back deck. Damn, it really was pretty far up there and he had to grin. "I bet Dominick the swashbuckling pirate would have jumped to your rescue." Garret meant it as a joke, but he heard her soft intake of breath, wondering what that meant. He would just bet if that clod Colby had come to her rescue Mattie would have been swooning and falling into his arms.

And then a thought hit him that he should probably discard, but when had that ever stopped him? "All right, then, follow me inside."

"Finally you're talking with some sense."

"I know—amazing, right? Almost never happens. Mark this day in history. I think I need to Tweet this."

"You don't have to be a jackass, you know."

Garret gave her a sideways glance. "And here I thought I was a mule."

They'd reached the bottom of the steps. "Aren't they about the same thing?"

"No." Garret paused with his hand on the railing. "Actually a jack is a male donkey or ass, thus the term jackass. When a jackass is bred to a female horse, the result is a mule. So there you have it." When she just blinked at him he chuckled. "I told you I read a lot. I am chock-full of useless knowledge unless you're playing trivia and then you'll want me on your team."

"They play trivia at Sully's Tavern on Thursdays. I'll keep that in mind."

Garret stepped aside for Mattie to climb the stairs first. He was being a gentleman, but the wet denim clung to her cute little bum and he couldn't stop himself from a bit of admiration. When they reached the deck he walked or rather limped over and slid the door open. "After you."

"This is nice," Mattie said with a look around, but when the air-conditioning hit her she immediately hugged her arms across her chest. He was a bit cold too. "I peeked in the windows when it was for sale, but I've never been inside."

"I know. I fell in love with the rustic beauty when my dad's wife, Maggie, showed it to me," Garret said. "Of course I'll eventually furnish it the way I want to, but this works for now." When he saw her shiver he said, "I'll round up some sweatpants and a shirt. You'll swim in them but at least be warm."

"No! I want you to get off that ankle."

"You won't stop me, you know, me being the jackass-slash-mule and all that. You know I think you need to shorten that term of endearment." He tapped his cheek. "Ah, how about Jamule?"

Mattie laughed. "All right, Jamule, I'll toss some ice in a plastic bag while you round up some dry clothing."

"You'll find the bags in the drawer closest to the dishwasher." With a nod Garret headed into the master bedroom and located a pair of gray sweatpants along with a T-shirt with the red London flag embossed on the front. He peeled off his wet clothes and found another pair of sweatpants and went into the bathroom to dry off. He looked at the shower with a bit of longing, wanting to wash off the river, but he didn't want Mattie to catch cold, so he tugged on the pants and pulled the drawstring. He looked at his reflection in the mirror and had to grin. Jumping off the back deck to the rescue?

He wasn't quite sure how Mattie was going to react to the proposition he'd just thought up, but these days he was all about giving what he wanted his best shot rather than not putting forth much effort. When he walked back into the living room, Mattie handed him a bag of crushed ice wrapped in a dish towel and pointed to the large leather sectional.

"Please get off that foot."

"Yes, ma'am." He handed her the clothes. "You can change in the bathroom off the master bedroom."

"Okay, thanks." Did she just give his chest a once-over?

"Oh, and the laundry room is next to the kitchen if you want to toss your wet clothes in the dryer."

"That's a good idea." Mattie nodded. "Now put the ice on your ankle to stop the swelling. Elevate it with a pillow and you need to take an ibuprofen to stop the inflammation. Do you have some?"

"In the medicine cabinet."

"Good. Hopefully you've just sprained or twisted it, but if the pain persists we need to get to the emergency room for X-rays."

"Why do you sound like a nurse?"

"Because my mom is a nurse. She wanted me to follow in her footsteps."

"Why didn't you?"

"Because . . ." She pushed a lock of wet hair from her face.

"Go on."

"Because I can't stomach the sight of . . . *blood*." She shivered and this time Garret knew it wasn't just from being cold. "And I detest *getting* a shot, so how could I ever *give one* to somebody? Having a nurse faint all the time might be a job hazard, don't you think?" She chuckled, but there was something in her eyes that looked so sad. "I really have admiration for what they do."

"And this disappointed your mum?"

She fiddled with the fringe on her shorts. "Yeah, because I had the grades and got into nursing school, but it just wasn't for me. I know she thinks that cooking breakfast and cleaning cabins isn't *living up to my potential*," Mattie said in a mock tone that must be an imitation of her mother's. She sighed. "Look, I know that she meant well. But I enjoy cooking, so what's wrong with that?" she asked in an emotional tone, but before Garret could answer she pivoted and headed into his bedroom to change. He sensed that she didn't want him to see her so vulnerable and had to shake his head. Mattie Mayfield wasn't as tough as she made herself out to be. Not by a long shot.

Damn, she was cute.

Garret eased down onto the cool leather couch and then used one of the decorative pillows to prop up his throbbing injury. Bending forward, he placed the bag of ice over his swollen ankle, wincing when the cold heaviness added to the discomfort. Looking toward his bedroom, he thought that wanting to please parents was another thing he and Mattie had in common. The difference in their circumstances was that Mattie's mother wanted her daughter to follow in her footsteps when Garret's father balked at Garret wanting to break into the music industry. At the time Garret had thought his father didn't want him to steal any of his rock legend thunder because in truth Garret was every bit as good a musician as the famous Rick Ruleman and he sure as hell wanted to prove it. It wasn't until recently that he learned that his father didn't want Garret to go down the wrong path and live a lonely life on the road. His father had also owned up to his mistakes, and his admission and apology went a long way toward mending their relationship, but it was still a work in progress. Of course Garret's own selfish antics hadn't helped, but that was all in the past and he was hell-bent on living for the future.

Garret leaned his head back against the cushion and blew out a sigh. When his relationship with his father had improved, they'd made the effort to start fresh. When Addison Monroe pointed out that Garret needed to make a name, a life for himself on his own merit rather than on the coattails of his dad, he'd scoffed at the notion. Why not cash in on his father's fame? He'd suffered enough because of it and had thought it his right to take advantage. But now he understood. And he felt so much better for it.

A moment later Mattie walked into the living room with her wet hair pulled up into a damp ponytail. She looked super feminine wearing Garret's way-too-big pants and shirt. She'd rolled up the waist, but the legs bunched up around her ankles. When she walked closer he noted that her toenails were painted a light shade of pink. When she saw him eyeing her feet she looked down as well.

"What are you looking at?"

"Your feet. They're cute."

"You're silly," she said, and it made Garret a bit sad that she didn't know how to take a compliment. He remembered her surprise when he'd admired her lovely eyes.

"Well, I guess that's a step up from a Jamule, although the term is kind of growing on me. I think it belongs in the Urban Dictionary."

"With your picture by it?" She laughed. "Yeah, I

know. I kinda like it too." She handed him the ibuprofen along with a bottle of water.

"Thanks." He took the pill, hoping it would ease the pain. "Hey, would you like something to drink? Beer? Wine?"

"Bourbon?"

"Sorry. Don't have any bourbon, I'm afraid."

"You're living in Kentucky now. You have to stock up on bourbon."

"I don't know much about it. Will you teach me?" he asked, thinking this was a pretty good way to slide into the direction he wanted this conversation to go.

"Sure. I know my way around good bourbon."

"And fishing?"

"You want to learn to fish too?" Mattie reached down and lifted the bag of ice from his ankle and gave it a look before gently putting it back in place.

"I do. Along with anything else that will help me fit in around here. Well, with the exception of noodling, I think."

"Really?" Mattie tilted her head while nibbling on the inside of her lip. "I had you pegged for someone who wants to stand out."

"A lot of people have me pegged as being something I'm not. And of course most of that is my own damn doing. But for once in my life I'd like to blend in. Or I guess just be accepted, really. I want to learn all about how to live in Cricket Creek. You know, tubing and all that."

"Wait a minute." Mattie grinned. "Let me get this straight. You want lessons in being a . . . well, a redneck?"

"Yes, I suppose I do. Are you willing?"

Mattie nibbled on the inside of her cheek and then held up her index finger. "On one condition."

"Only one?"

She nodded.

"Name it."

6

Here Comes the Sun

"THAT YOU TEACH ME HOW TO BE A . . . YOU KNOW . . .
lady," Mattie said, and felt a little surge of excitement at the prospect.

Garret frowned at her. "I don't think that you're *not* a lady, Mattie. Why don't you go grab us something to drink and we'll talk about it? I'd go myself, but—"

"Don't you dare move," Mattie ordered, and headed into the kitchen that was off to the side of the great room. She snagged two beers from the fridge and walked over and handed one to him before sitting down at the other end of the L-shaped sofa. She'd seen bare chests for as long as she could remember. But for some reason seeing *his* bare chest made her want to go over there and run her fingers over his skin. He had a golden tan with just a sprinkling of tawny chest hair. While his build wasn't as thick as Colby's, she found his wide shoulders and toned torso appealing.

"Mattie?"

"Um . . ." Oh, crap, she'd been staring. "Sorry. I was thinkin' of some questions," she lied.

"So I guess you're a bit of a tomboy. Am I right?"

"Okay, so sure, I was brought up right with manners and all that good stuff, but with having two brothers and working at the marina ever since I can remember, I've always been one of the boys. I never had much time to do things like hang out at the mall with girlfriends. I feel like I could be more refined, you know? My mama tried to get me to be more girlie, but in truth other than cooking, I preferred being outdoors. And to be honest she's kinda outdoorsy too."

"Nothing really wrong with that, I'd say."

"Yeah, I liked playing ball more than playing with dolls." She took a drink of her beer and then shrugged. "So there you have it."

"Well, I'm a guy, so I'm not sure how I can help you all that much."

"Well, I mean, your mama is a famous fashion model, so I think you know your way around how a girl should dress, right? London is full of fashion and you spent a lot of time there, right?"

"True."

She ran her fingertip over the edge of the can and waited for him to answer. "I mean, I know I don't have long legs and—"

"Your legs are just fine. Shapely, in fact."

Mattie looked down at her legs, not quite believing him.

"Somehow I think there's more to this than learning how to dress. Am I right?" he asked quietly.

"Yeah. . . ." Mattie swallowed hard and nodded. "I'm so over being treated like one of the guys. I mean, just like you said, it's my fault too but I want that to change." She patted her chest and felt hot moisture well up in her throat. "Don't get me wrong. I love fishing and softball and camping, but . . ." She closed her eyes and inhaled a shaky breath.

"But let me guess, you want flowers and candlelit dinners and dancing in the moonlight."

"Yeah." Mattie gave him a quick little nod. "I'm no

different than anybody else. I—I want a boyfriend. Someone to be there for me." *To fall madly in love with me,* she thought, but couldn't bring herself to say it.

"And you want to capture the attention of that big clod Colby?"

"He's not a big clod."

Garret gave her a long look of disagreement.

"Okay . . . I get where you're coming from." She tipped her head to the side. "He's not usually like he was earlier. Colby is a good guy, truly. He just had too much shine tonight."

If Garret had a different opinion he politely kept it to himself. "And you've had a crush on him forever."

"Um . . . yeah." She felt heat creep into her cheeks. "But he's always had some leggy, prissy thing on his arm."

"Maybe he's not the right guy for you if that's what he's after," Garret said slowly. "We just met, but I can tell you that there's more substance to you than just a pretty face. And I would find prissy quite annoying."

"Thank you," Mattie said, and gave him a smile. She had the sneaking suspicion that there were many more layers to Garret than most people realized as well. "I think we both might be a little misunderstood."

"Ah, part of our mystique."

Mattie laughed. "If you say so."

"Hey, I don't jump off of a sky-high deck for just anyone," he said with a laugh.

"Well, don't ever do that again." Mattie searched for the words to make Garret understand that Colby was everything she wanted in a guy . . . in a boyfriend. She watched the play of muscle when he lifted his arm to take a swig of his beer. *Until now,* went through her head, but she dismissed it. She was falling under his charming and rather rakish spell.

"I have to say that I'm surprised that one of these guys hasn't already gone after you, Mattie."

"Laura Lee was saying the same thing earlier." She

took a swig of her drink and tried to explain. "My brothers, Mason and Danny, were always so overprotective of me, so that never helped my situation. I became the kid sister to all the eligible boys near my age." She shrugged. "I fell into that unwanted role and now I need your help to break out."

"So I'm going to teach you how to stand out and you're going to teach me how to fit in. Interesting."

"That's a good plan, right?" Mattie laughed. "I'll show you the finer points of being a redneck."

"Think I can pull it off?"

"With that accent? And that Keith Urban hair? I'm not sure. It even sounds polite when you curse."

Garret laughed. "I have to ask. Is redneck a term you embrace?"

"Not always." Mattie shrugged. "The term redneck originated when farmers would get their necks burnt from toiling in the sun. It can be used as a derogatory term by some, but we let it roll off our backs. To us it means hardworking, down-home folk with good values. Television pokes fun with stupid reality shows and comedy, but I'm proud of where I come from." She leaned forward and patted her chest. "Who I am."

Garret took a sip of his beer. "Go on, then."

"What makes you think I had more to say?"

"I could see it in those expressive eyes of yours." Garret adjusted the bag of ice when it slid sideways. "Let's establish right now that we're friends. What you tell me goes nowhere. And no matter what you might think or have read about me, my word is good."

"I believe you." And in truth Mattie really had no concrete reason to trust Garret Ruleman, but she looked at the sincerity on his face and somehow just *did*. "Okay . . ." She licked her bottom lip and then after another deep breath mustered up the courage to say, "For once in my life I want to walk into a room and turn heads."

"Darling, you could stop traffic. You just don't know it."

"Oh, come on, do you think I could actually do that?"

"Are you kidding me?" Garret looked up at the ceiling and then back at her.

Mattie put one hand over her eyes. "Pretend I never asked you that. Please. God, I am such a dork."

"A dork? Who even says that?"

"Me?" she asked with a wince. "Proving my own point."

"Seriously do I need to limp over there and pry your hand from your pretty face again?" Garret lowered his head a notch and gave her a stern stare.

"Maybe," she said between her fingers, but when he started to push up from the cushions, she shook her head. "No! Don't you dare put weight on your ankle!" She lowered her hand to point over at him.

"Don't point that thing at me unless it's loaded."

She arched an eyebrow. "It is."

"All right, then I'd better behave."

"That's more like it, Jamule."

"I rather like that endearment." When Garret eased back against the cushions, Mattie breathed a sigh of relief. "Maybe I should get it tattooed across my chest. What do you think?"

"No!" Mattie hated the thought of him marring that gorgeous body. "I mean, I don't think that would be the image you're going for around here," she said in a softer tone.

"I was joking."

"Oh. Well, I was just giving you sound advice." She looked over at him and said firmly, "You know what?"

He raised his eyebrows. "What?"

"Try this on for size." Mattie lifted her chin and then lost her nerve.

"I'm waiting."

"I like you. What do you think about that?"

"Well . . ." Garret looked at her for a moment as if no one had ever said that to him.

"Cat got your tongue?"

"I never did understand that phrase. Do cats really get one's tongue?"

Mattie laughed. "I hope not, but if they did it would prevent speaking."

"True enough."

"I do like you." Mattie thought about all the crazy stories she'd read about him and wondered how many of them were fabricated or not even remotely true. "Has anybody ever said that to you before?"

"Of course, but in truth I haven't been all that likable, I'm afraid."

"Well, you are, so there."

"Has anyone ever told you you're pretty?" he countered.

"No," Mattie said because she thought she could tell this man, this so-called celebrity, anything. "I mean, my parents and granny, but they don't count."

"First of all, they do count. But no boy has ever said that to you?"

"Nope."

"Well, then, they are all . . ." He lifted one hand as if searching for the right word.

"Dumb asses?"

"Yes, as opposed to the very cool Jamule."

Mattie leaned against the butter-soft leather and looked over at Garret. "So, are we gonna do this?"

"Make each other over?"

Mattie nodded. "You make me into a hot chick and I turn you into an English redneck hybrid that will drive the local girls wild?"

"Yes, a new breed of . . . something never seen before around these parts. I like it." He gave her a nod. "All right, then. I'm in if you're in."

Mattie pushed up from the sofa and went over to shake his hand. "Deal." She gave him a firm handshake the way her daddy taught her.

"So, when do the joint classes begin?"

"I think the sooner the better, don't you agree?"

"Absolutely." Garret nodded. "I think the first thing

we need to do is shop. I need boots and you need heels. It's always best to look the part."

"Agreed."

"You have a passport, right?"

"A . . . passport?" Mattie felt her eyes widen. "Um, yes, I went on a cruise to the Bahamas with my parents last year and I had to get a passport. Why?"

"You never know. We might want to pay my mum a visit sometime." Garret grinned. "As you said she's a famous fashion model, so we might just want to get her input."

"You mean . . . go to *London*, and I don't mean London, Kentucky? You're joking, right?"

"There's a London, Kentucky?"

"Yes, and a Paris too." While her parents had taken family vacations, they'd visited places like Daytona Beach and Disney World. Other than the cruise to the Bahamas, she'd never been out of the country. She'd dreamed of visiting Europe but never thought it could really happen. In fact, she found the thought exciting but also intimidating.

"I did mean London, England. Don't look so stunned, love. It was only an offhand suggestion for a possible future excursion. We could Skype or something instead."

"I guess that hopping on a plane and heading to London is normal for you." She pointed to her chest. "For me? Not so much. Wait, not at all."

"Some might say that there's nothing normal about me." Garret chuckled but then shrugged. "I haven't made the effort to visit my mum enough lately," he said with a bit of a sad tone. "I need to change that."

"I know what you mean. I miss my parents too."

"I put my poor mum through hell with worry."

"Don't be so hard on yourself. My brothers were a bit on the wild side too. Trust me, country boys work hard but play harder."

"It just took me a bit longer than most to grow up."

He pointed to the sofa. "All right, then. Have a seat and let's put a schedule and game plan together. A week or so from now or whenever you're ready, we can make our debut somewhere in town."

"You mean when you're ready."

"That too."

"I'm a note taker. I need a pen and paper." Mattie rubbed her hands together. "Let's get this party started."

"I have a desk in my bedroom with a printer. Grab some of that paper and there should be a pen there too."

Mattie headed back into his bedroom and flipped on the light. She spotted his desk in the corner and hurried over to get the paper and pen, but before leaving his room she took a little nosy quick glance around. The bed was made but done up a little bit crooked as if dressing a bed wasn't something Garret was used to doing. For some reason the thought made her smile. Just the barest hint of his aftershave lingered in the air. The blue shirt he'd worn earlier was tossed onto the bedspread and she had the odd urge to pick up the shirt and hold it to her nose. "Okay, that would be weird," she whispered, but almost did it anyway.

Mattie shook her head and backed away. While there was no denying that she found Garret charming and attractive . . . and, okay, downright sexy, he'd just made it abundantly clear that he wanted to be friends.

He's far too worldly for the likes of me, Mattie thought as she walked over to turn off the light. And besides, Colby Campbell was the man she'd dreamed of and wanted for as long as she could remember. Garret Ruleman was her ticket to getting Colby, nothing more except for friendship, and she'd best remember that fact or she just might chase the man away.

With a smile on her face she walked into the living room and picked up a *Rolling Stone* magazine from the coffee table. Placing the paper over the glossy cover, she clicked the pen and then looked over at Garret. "Ready?"

"Yeah, baby," he replied with a grin.

While Mattie knew he'd just used the endearment in a joking Austin Powers accent, she still liked being called baby. Shaking that off, Mattie wrote her name and date at the top of the page and then added categories. With a lift of her chin she mustered up a businesslike tone of voice and said, "Well, then, let the lessons begin."

"Okay, so, what do you usually wear when you go out?"

"Go out?"

"Yes, like on the town. Happy hour or a concert or whatever."

"Oh . . ." The question made Mattie realize that she didn't go out all that much anymore, but she didn't want him to know that sad little fact. The last concert she'd been to was Reid Greenfield and South Street Riot when they'd opened for Shane McCray last summer. "Um, you know, blue jeans and some sort of top." Mostly T-shirts, but she was too embarrassed to divulge that boring little detail. "No wonder I'm still single. I need to step up my game."

"And that's what we shall do." Garret scooted up against the pillows. "Now, don't get me wrong, you wear jeans quite well, but a cute skirt would turn some heads. Show off your shapely legs."

Mattie wrote *cute skirts* under the wardrobe category. The thought that he found her short legs shapely made her feel a bit warm. She plucked at the shirt, hoping that he didn't notice her flushed face. Some girls never seemed to break a sweat. She wasn't one of them.

"And while cowboy boots are your personal style, you need to get some sandals and show off your pretty feet."

"My feet? Really?"

"Men find feet quite sexy." He glanced over at her feet. "And you have these perfect little toes."

Mattie laughed. "I've never given much thought to my toes, although I do keep my toenails painted. Feet, huh?"

"Absolutely."

Encouraged, she looked at him with her pen poised. "So, other than the obvious, what other body parts are important to pay attention to?"

"Hmm . . ." Garret sucked in his bottom lip for a second and then said, "Ah, I know, *shoulders*. The gentle slope of exposed shoulders is so very feminine." He smiled and added, "And the graceful nape of your neck. Think Audrey Hepburn."

Mattie made a note of it. "I love *Breakfast at Tiffany's*. Oh, but I could never be so graceful and elegant like her."

"Of course you could. You've got delicate bone structure." He angled his head. "You would photograph really well. I would love to take some photos of you."

"Really?"

"Yes, really. I've learned something about photography over the years. Mattie, your ponytail swinging back and forth is really endearing, but try one of those French twists. Simple . . . elegant. And you've got great hair. Is the blond natural? Or is that rude to ask?"

"Natural," Mattie replied, even though most people didn't believe her when she gave that truthful answer. "I was always a towhead and I spend so much time in the sunshine that my hair lightens on its own."

"Well, to be naturally that light is rare and gorgeous, so please don't change a thing."

Mattie reached up and touched the end of her damp ponytail, thinking that she didn't give her hair much thought other than how to keep it out of her way when she cooked. Under the category *hair* she wrote *Try a French twist*, then underlined *do not change the color*.

"What kind of jewelry do you wear?"

"Oh." Mattie looked up with surprise. "I don't. Since I'm either cooking or working around the marina, I can't wear jewelry. With my mama being a nurse and sometimes helping out around the dock, she didn't ever have many rings and stuff, so I never gave much thought to it, I guess."

"I mean, when you go out."

"Oh . . . well, I thought about getting my ears pierced, but the idea of poking a hole in my ear scared the bejesus out of me when I was younger, so I never bothered. It's the needle thing again."

"Well, since you wear your hair pulled back much of the time, earrings, even simple studs, would add a nice feminine touch."

Mattie envisioned getting holes poked through her earlobes and winced. "I don't know."

"I'll go with you and make silly faces so you laugh. I'll even hold your hand if you want me to."

"I sound like such a wimp. Afraid of silly things like clowns and getting my ears pierced. I just don't like needles. A tattoo would be completely out of the question."

Garret shook his head. "Vulnerability is so sweet, Mattie. You don't have to be tough all the time."

"I have a feeling you're gonna mention the noodling thing again."

"Thought about it."

Mattie had the strong urge to go over there and give Garret a hug. "You're nothing like all the stories written about you, are you?"

"So you read the tabloids, do you?"

"You have to do something while waiting in the checkout line at the grocery store. I always wondered if there was a grain of truth to any of it."

"Sometimes." Garret glanced away as if troubled, making Mattie wish she hadn't asked such a question. He just seemed so different than what she'd expected. "I liked the attention. I especially liked getting my father good and mad."

"It must have been hard that he was gone all the time. I suppose you were acting out. Normal behavior for such an abnormal life."

"Well, that's a brilliant way of putting it."

He smiled, but he seemed rather sad and she felt another urge to give Garret a hug. Mattie felt herself being drawn to him in ways that she didn't quite understand.

He shoved his fingers through his hair. "Oh, don't

look at me with such sympathy. I caused most of my misery, trust me."

"Addison must have seen something good in you, Garret. I know she broke off the engagement, but she must have fallen for you in the first place, right?"

He seemed to mull that over for a moment. "Addison was coming out of a breakup when we met. I made her laugh and forget about it." He paused and then said, "We were wrong for each other, but knowing I'd hurt the feelings of such a wonderful girl made me realize what a wanker I was and needed to change. Addison Monroe was my wake-up call."

"Wanker?"

"English slang for douche bag."

"Well, we all do things we regret. Maybe you're being too hard on yourself."

"Or not hard enough. I was a selfish and callous cad, not caring about anything but myself. Someone should have punched me in the face. Oh, wait. I think that happened a few times." He shook his head. "I was a closet nerd pretending to be a badass. A rather odd combination, don't you think?"

Mattie understood. "I'm a hopeless romantic and I'm tired of being treated like one of the guys. I totally get you, Garret."

"Well, that would be a first, Mattie Mayfield. No one has gotten me yet." He looked at her for a moment and then said, "We're quite a pair, aren't we?"

"That we are. Two peas in an odd pod."

He chuckled. "Normal is so overrated, don't you think?"

"I agree."

They talked about everything from music to baseball with several hours slipping by with ease. Mattie popped popcorn and kept changing his melting ice. They listened to his collection of Beatles albums while she kept adding things to her becoming-a-lady list.

After a while Mattie felt her eyes grow heavy, but she was enjoying his company and each time she started to

go he told her another story that had her in stitches. She
decided that she'd stay for just a few more minutes and
then hightail it home. She started her days with the ass
crack of dawn and needed to get home and catch some
sleep before her dreaded alarm rang. Maybe she'd just
close her eyes for a minute just to rest....

Mattie yawned and blinked a bit, not ready to open her
eyes and fully wake up. She stretched and then wondered why it was getting light, but her alarm didn't go off,
so she had a few more minutes to sleep. Serving breakfast meant she had to be an early riser, and there were
mornings when she longed to snuggle back into her pillow. This was one of them. Mattie turned to get a better
position in bed and heard a sort of squeaking sound. She
opened her eyes a slit. Wait . . .

She was on a sofa....

Mattie opened her eyes wide. Dear God, she was still
at Garret's cabin! She'd fallen asleep! Her slowly thud-
ding heart started to hammer. What the hell time was it?
When she looked over at the floor-to-ceiling window and
saw rays of sunshine reaching up into the muted darkness, Mattie barely stifled her gasp.

She leaned up slightly and spotted Garret sound
asleep on the other end of the sofa. His bare shoulders
peeked out from a cover, making Mattie realize that she
also had a soft throw draped over her body. She racked
her brain to remember when covers had been brought
out and came up blank. Garret must have gone for covers after she'd dozed off. But why did he sleep on the
sofa instead of going to his big king-sized bed?

Not knowing what to do in this sort of situation, Mattie decided that the easiest thing would be to simply tiptoe out. After gently tossing back the cover, she silently
eased up to her feet.

Mattie paused before she passed by Garret and gazed
down at him for a moment. When he suddenly moved
she held her breath and froze, not wanting to be caught

staring down at him. The cover slipped and exposed his chest all the way to his navel. She had the urge to pull the cover up so he didn't get cold, but she feared she'd wake him and they would have one of those awkward moments. He inhaled a breath and murmured something as if having a dream. He looked sleep tousled and sexy, making Mattie wonder what it would feel like to be lying next to him all cozy with her legs over his and . . .

What? No! Don't go there!

Mattie started to tiptoe away but then frowned when she remembered his twisted ankle. She made a mental note to check up on him later, but for now she had biscuits to bake. But when Mattie reached the door, she couldn't resist a look over her shoulder before easing her way outside.

And then she put her body into high gear, all but running over to the path winding through the woods to her cabin. Slightly out of breath when she arrived, she hurried into the bathroom, hoping for a lightning-quick shower before she had to go to the shop to begin prepping for breakfast. But Mattie paused when she saw her reflection in the mirror and realized that she still wore Garret's shirt and pants. She put a hand to her chest, thinking there was something intimate about wearing his clothing. And the vision of Garret lying bare-chested on the sofa slid into her brain, making Mattie suddenly feel warm for reasons other than her quick jaunt through the woods.

"Silly," she muttered as she slid the sweatpants down to her ankles and stepped out of them. She tugged the shirt over her head and then put her hand over her mouth when she realized she'd been drying her clothes in his dryer along with her bra and panties! Mattie swallowed hard. While she wasn't much on fancy clothes and jewelry, she did indulge in silky underwear from Victoria's Secret. Mattie envisioned Garret holding the little scrap of lace and satin in his hand and had to wonder how he would react.

"I'm sure he's seen sexy undies plenty of times," Mattie said as she leaned over to turn the shower on full blast. She stepped into the spray of water, needing a bracing shower before facing the breakfast crowd. She soaped her body, trying to find humor in the situation but failing.

After quickly toweling dry she knew she was running late but stopped to take a little time with mascara and lip gloss anyway. She peered at her reflection in the mirror and then twisted her hair into a makeshift French twist. Turing sideways, she looked at her bare shoulders and the line of her neck, remembering what Garret said about Audrey Hepburn. "Graceful," she whispered, and for the first time since she could remember she thought:

I'm pretty.

She looked at her bare earlobes and envisioned delicate little stud diamonds catching the sunlight and made the decision to get her ears pierced as soon as she found the time to go to the mall. It felt good to think about her appearance and to make improvements. She remembered that her debut was going to be at Sully's and Mattie smiled. "Look out, Cricket Creek, Kentucky. Here I come."

7

Catch My Breath

L AURA LEE HURRIED INTO RIVER ROW PIZZA AND Pasta for a late lunch, eager to hear what Mattie wanted to talk about with her. When the aroma of garlic and marinara sauce wafted her way, Laura Lee's stomach rumbled in anticipation. After a week of working for Shane McCray, she'd developed a routine of eating a light lunch after preparing his, but today she'd skipped her salad, knowing she was going to indulge in amazing homemade Italian delights. She read on the chalkboard outside that lasagna was the lunch special and she thought that sounded like a winner. She also planned to buy a slice of Reese Marino's famous turtle cheesecake and bring it to Shane, who had quite a big sweet tooth. After a quick glance around she spotted Mattie sitting in a booth over by the far wall. She made her way past square tables covered with red-checkered tablecloths. Stubbed candles dripping down empty Chianti bottles gave the dining room an authentic Italian flair that matched the old-world homemade dishes. Fresh flowers added a cheerful friendliness, and subtle piped-in music created a soothing atmosphere.

"Hey there!" Mattie said when Laura Lee slid across the red vinyl bench seat. "Thanks for comin' on such short notice."

Laura Lee leaned forward and grabbed Mattie's hand. "Are you kidding? You wouldn't even give me a hint as to what this is all about. I whizzed through cleaning Shane's house this morning. So spill, girl."

"Let's order first."

"You're killing me." She gave Mattie's hand a squeeze and then took a sip of the water that was already there.

Mattie pushed a basket of fresh-baked bread and a dish of herbed dipping oil toward Laura Lee. "Tessa brought this over and said it was on the house. I've already had two slices of that warm crusty bread, so if I reach for another slap my hand."

Laura Lee shook her head. "You know I won't slap your hand."

"Then I'll slap my own hand." She reached for another slice and demonstrated with a smack. "Ouch."

Laura Lee laughed. "So, how is Tessa? I haven't seen her in a while."

Mattie leaned forward and said in a hushed voice, "She seems really happy now that she and Mike have gotten back together. I heard that they are gonna renew their wedding vows. Can you believe it?"

Laura Lee shook her head. "I never thought that would happen in a million years, but I'm so happy for her."

"You two go way back, don't you?"

"Way back to when I was still married to Jack. We met when we were on a coed bowling team together and we became real tight." She crossed her fingers to demonstrate. "We were as shocked as the rest of Cricket Creek when Mike just up and left one day, leaving Tessa to raise Reese on her own. They seemed like the perfect little family. It just broke my heart to see Tessa so sad." Laura Lee shook her head. "And when Reese starting getting into trouble, she was at her wit's end. Good thing Tony took

Reese in up in Brooklyn and became a father figure to him."

"That must have been a tough decision for a mother to make."

"Oh, Tessa cried buckets over it, but it was the right decision." Laura Lee raised her palms upward. "And now Tony and Reese live in Cricket Creek and own this restaurant together."

"Just goes to show that no matter how dismal things look at the time, better days are always ahead," Mattie said in her typical cheerful manner.

"I think I'm the poster child for that particular insight."

"And that's why you can't give up on anything, especially love. You don't know what's written in the stars."

"True, I suppose." Laura Lee nodded, but she wasn't anywhere near convinced that she had the love from a man in her future. Just making ends meet and having a little left over was all she'd been thinking about lately. Love? Romance? She'd just have to live through the characters in her books.

"Well, if Tessa is an example, there's hope for anyone."

"I have to agree with you there." While Laura Lee hated to be judgmental, she couldn't believe it when Mike just up and left his wife and child. Even more shocking was when he suddenly returned to Cricket Creek years later. Mike had evidently gotten into some gambling debt that had threatened the safety of his family, and Tessa had somehow gathered the strength to try again. It had taken Reese much longer to get over the desertion of his father, but Laura Lee was happy to see father and son making the effort to put the past behind them. "I find her forgiveness nothing short of extraordinary." Being Tessa's friend, she knew details that others didn't, but she wouldn't break her promise to Tessa and divulge any secrets even to Mattie.

"Well . . ." Mattie took a sip of her water and shrugged.

"It just goes to show you that love really can survive against all odds. I don't know the full story, but it sure does show that Tessa's love for her husband refused to die and she had faith that he had a good reason for what he did. I know it took Reese longer to forgive his daddy, but they came in for breakfast a couple of weeks ago and Mason took them out bass fishing. Amazing, don't you think?"

"Stop giving me that there's-hope-for-you look, Mattie."

"Well, Shane McCray's super hot. He was in *People* magazine's most eligible bachelor issue." Mattie raised her eyebrows. "And you happen to be available."

"Right, like he'd settle down with his housekeeper."

"Oh, so, then, you've thought about it?"

"Not on your life." Laura Lee rolled her eyes and picked up the menu even though she'd already decided on ordering the lasagna. She wasn't about to let on that Shane made her pulse race every time he entered the room or that they had started eating dinner together on a regular basis. She just provided company for him, nothing more. To hope for anything beyond friendship would be setting herself up for a fall. And she certainly wasn't going to jeopardize her amazing job for a roll in the hay that would mean everything to her and nothing to the superstar country singer. "I thought we came here because you have something to tell me."

"Fair enough." Mattie nodded and a moment later Tessa hurried over to take their order.

"Tessa!" Laura Lee stood up and gave her friend a big hug.

"Holy cow, girl, I heard you're working for Shane McCray!"

"News travels fast in Cricket Creek."

"So it's true?" Tessa exclaimed, and when Laura Lee nodded Tessa gave her a little shove. "How cool is that?"

"Very cool," Laura Lee admitted. "I still can't believe my luck."

"Is he nice?"

"Oh yes, he's super nice."

Tessa grinned. "And super hot, I might add."

"And single," Mattie tossed into the conversation like a little time bomb.

Laura Lee slid back into the booth and shook her head at both of them. "Would y'all just quit? Shane is my employer, nothing more and never will be."

"You've always told me to never say never." Mattie wagged a finger at Laura Lee.

"I'd say that's sound advice," Tessa said. "So, have y'all decided?"

"Tessa, I'll have a slice of hand-tossed pizza with mushrooms and meatballs. Oh, and add a chef salad with ranch dressing on the side. Hold the tomato." Mattie wrinkled up her nose.

"They're good for you," Laura Lee said.

"Oh, all right, leave the tomato. You sound just like Mama wondering how a country girl couldn't like home-grown tomatoes."

Tessa grinned. "I'll go light on the tomatoes. Laura Lee."

"The lasagna sounds good and add a salad to mine too. Italian dressing, please."

"Coming right up, ladies. And good to see you two."

After Tessa left, Laura Lee turned back to Mattie. "Okay, girl, what did you want to talk about?" she asked, and noted that Mattie's mood shifted to a rare serious moment.

"Okay . . . ," Mattie began, but then looked around as if to see if anyone was within earshot, but because they were after the lunch rush the dining room was basically deserted. She toyed with the straw in her water, making the wedge of lemon swim around like a little yellow boat.

"Okay, what?" She drummed her fingertips on the table.

"Well, you know how Garret has been giving me lessons this past week on being more girlie?"

"And you're teaching him the finer points of being a

redneck? Kinda like a redneck version of *My Fair Lady*," Laura Lee said with a grin. "How is that part going?"

Mattie chuckled. "Not all that well. I need to take him shopping, but we've both been sorta busy."

"Well, you sure look cute. I rarely see your hair down and I love the slight curl."

"Beachy waves. So you like it?" While biting her bottom lip she reached up and touched her hair.

Laura Lee nodded. "And your makeup. Subtle but enhances your pretty features. Mattie, the green blouse you're wearing brings out your amazing eyes." She smiled. "I love that one side is off the shoulder."

Mattie started to talk, but Tessa brought over their salads. "Your pizza and lasagna will be out in a few minutes. Enjoy!"

Mattie stabbed a cherry tomato and gave it a wary look, but Laura Lee shook her head. "Don't you dare eat. Talk to me, Mattie."

"Okay, well, you know that part of the reason for my makeover is to draw the attention of Colby Campbell."

"Has it been working?"

Mattie nodded. "Oh yeah, for sure. I've caught him looking at me when he eats breakfast."

"So?"

"There is a complication I wasn't prepared for." Mattie gave her a deadpan stare and then caught her bottom lip between her teeth. "You see I, um . . ."

"Mattie . . . are you trying to say that you're into Garret?"

She nodded slowly. "I mean, I still like Colby and all, but, Laura Lee, all I think about is . . . is . . ."

"Garret."

"Yes!" She popped the tomato into her mouth and nodded. She winced a little bit but chewed. "Doesn't that just suck? I mean, I finally have the attention from the guy I've been mooning over for-*ever* and now that I have it, all I want is Garret."

"I don't see why that sucks." Laura Lee drizzled her

dressing over her tossed salad. "You and Garret are both single."

"Are you kidding me? I've been suffering with unrequited love for basically all my life, and it's gonna happen all over again. Why do I keep doing this to myself?"

"Why do you think that Garret can't have feelings for you? Maybe he already does."

"What?" Mattie sputtered. "The man would never, ever, ever, *ev-er* fall for a small-town girl like me."

"I think you needed one more *ever*."

"Evvvvvv-errrrr." She tried to stab another cherry tomato, but it kept eluding her until she finally picked it up and tossed it into Laura Lee's bowl. "Don't say I never gave you anything."

"Gee, thanks."

"Get real, Laura Lee, Garret dates models and famous people."

"Hmm . . ." Laura Lee tapped the side of her cheek. "Correct me if I'm wrong, but he's still single. Maybe he needs someone real like you. Someone who isn't after anything or has an agenda. I'm sure he's had that happen to him way too many times." Shane slid into her brain and she guessed he fell into that same category. But he was her employer and she wasn't about to cross that line. No, her situation was totally different. And she wasn't in love with Shane. Okay, she *did* think about him a lot, but she was his personal assistant, so he was bound to be on her mind. That was her story and she was sticking to it.

"No." Mattie shook her head hard. "No. No, no . . . *no*." She suddenly seemed to realize she was eating her salad before putting on the dressing and dumped it all on one spot without even looking. "It's a crush, nothing more because . . . because he's so different from any guy I've ever known. And he's got that whole accent thing going on to boot." She flapped her hand around like the tail of a fish. "And you know, that Keith Urban hair." She twirled her finger above her head in an animated way that made Laura Lee wonder if Mattie knew her denial was way over-the-top. "But no, Colby is the kind of man I want."

"Really? Why is that, do you think?"

"Well . . ." Laura Lee's question seemed to stump her. "Be . . . because he's like my daddy and brothers. A, you know, country boy."

"Well, now." Laura Lee gave her head a quick tilt to the side. "Seems that I remember that your favorite romance novel theme is when opposites attract."

"That's fiction. We're talking real life here. In reality two people who come from the same background and have similar interests and values are more likely to be, you know, well suited for each other."

Laura Lee just looked at her while she calmly ate her salad.

"And what I really need is for Colby to ask me out on my long-awaited date. Once I'm in his arms I'll forget all about this silly little crush I have on Garret Ruleman."

"Then let me ask you this: Why *are* you attracted to Garret? Apart from the physical things you mentioned."

Mattie toyed with a cucumber.

"Is that such a tough question?"

"No, I suppose not."

"Then why don't you enlighten me?"

"Because it's pretty obvious that my brain has taken a holiday."

"Okay, you're dodging the question."

"Well, yeah, because I thought you were going to talk some sense into my fool head. Tell me that Colby is the one to go after and to forget about this silly *thing* I have for Garret."

"Answer the question, please."

"Well, he makes me laugh all the time. I mean nonstop. And he treats me like a girl, not an annoying kid sister." She speared another cucumber but this time put it in Laura Lee's bowl. "Oh, and he listens to me like what I have to say actually matters." She looked down at the table and then said softly, "And he pays me compliments. Tells me my feet are cute and my hair is gorgeous. Said that I'm pretty. I mean, I know he's just being nice in that polite British way of his, but still . . ."

"Garret's right. You are pretty, Mattie." Laura Lee felt emotion well up in her throat. She'd seen the lovely Mattie Mayfield go unnoticed for years. Of course she knew why. Mattie always acted as if she liked being one of the boys. And her brothers swatted away any guy who so much as looked at her with the misguided notion that they needed to be protective. "It's about time someone took notice. And you need to get out more, doggone it. Hire someone other than Bubba to help you out at Breakfast, Books, and Bait so you have some free time. You work too much. You need to have fun. Take a vacation!"

"I can't!"

"Why not?"

"Because there's so much to do, especially now that Mama and Daddy have retired to Florida."

Laura Lee's expression softened. "I know your mama and daddy would want you to go out and have some fun once in a while. Things are better now, Mattie. The marina is on solid ground, right?"

Mattie nodded.

"You don't have to worry your little heart so much. And you can hire help."

"I know, but old habits die hard. Seems like if I'm not workin', I feel guilty. Mason and Danny are the same way."

"Well, squash that guilt." Laura Lee pressed her hands together to demonstrate. The marina, like everything else in Cricket Creek, struggled when the economy tanked and Mattie had to help out after school while her friends were hanging out at the mall or at Myra's Diner after Friday night lights.

"I'll try," Mattie promised.

"I'm going to hold you to it. I've been wanting a side trip to Nashville for some time now. We should do it."

"I'm in!"

"That's what I want to hear." Even now Mattie's social life revolved around events at the marina, and Laura Lee would love to see that change. Maybe somebody different, somebody worldly like Garret, could, if nothing else, open Mattie's eyes to the fact that there was more out there than the marina and her hometown. Of course she was one to talk. When was the last time she'd been on a vacation? Forever ago.

Tessa brought out their lunch. "Still working on your salads?" When they both nodded Tessa smiled. "Let me know if you need anything else," she added, and seemed to know that they were having a deep conversation. "And dessert is on the house. From the look of those serious expressions, I think you girls need something a little decadent."

"Do you have any Italian cream cake?" Mattie asked. "Reese's cake is to die for."

"We do indeed," Tessa replied, and Laura Lee could see the pride shining in her eyes when her son was mentioned. "And I think a cannoli or two."

"Turtle cheesecake?" Laura Lee wanted to know. Shane's favorite ice cream flavor was turtle, and she knew he would go nuts over the cheesecake.

"Not sure but I'll check."

"Thanks, Tessa," Laura Lee said, and then turned back to Mattie, who was suddenly staring at her pizza as if it were a foreign object. "Mattie, I'm no expert when it comes to this kind of thing and I know that Garret has a, well, reputation for being a player. At least in those magazines if they are to be believed. I don't want you to get hurt."

"He's nothing like what people think." Her eyes looked like clouds before a thunderstorm.

"Then maybe you should give the boy a chance."

"That's just it. I don't think he's, you know, into me. I know he thinks I'm funny and, well, he *likes* me and all, but I don't believe it could ever go deeper than that. I mean, he mentioned taking me to London to have his mother help with my transformation at some point. I don't know that he's serious."

"I don't see why that's so far-fetched, at least not for the world he lives in. It could be quite an adventure ... or maybe something else entirely."

"We're just friends."

"But you want more."

"If things take a romantic turn I could lose his friendship." She smacked the heel of her hand to her forehead. "Oh my God, I'm stuck in the damn friend zone."

"Then bust out of the zone."

"Nope, once in the friend zone you are doomed."

"That's just downright silly." But Laura Lee knew how she felt, so she nodded. "I don't know what to tell you and I know this sounds lame and rather trite, but follow your heart."

Mattie picked up her slice of pizza and looked at it. "But my heart is taking me down a sorry path of futility where it is sure to get broken."

"You don't know that, Mattie."

"But it's such a risk, don't you think?"

"Yes. But most worthwhile things are a risk. And, Mattie, broken hearts mend. Missed opportunities are lost forever." She reached over and patted Mattie's free hand. "Have I helped or made things worse?"

"Worse."

"So sorry, sweetie."

"No, I knew you'd be honest with me no matter what. Honesty is what I need."

Laura Lee pressed the side of her fork into the lush lasagna. "So you don't really think Garret has any romantic feelings for you?"

"Maybe I was too busy being convinced that could never happen to even consider the possibility." She inhaled a deep breath and blew it out. "I guess I'll just keep going with the lessons. I think we're making my big debut next Saturday at Sully's if I'm ready. He's supposed to be my wingman and try to get me a dance with Colby or someone else with the hope of making Colby jealous." She managed to grin. "And if I can find the time I might take Garret shopping for Wranglers instead of those designer jeans he wears and a pair of cowboy boots instead of his fancy loafers. Maybe a Western-cut shirt. We decided that a cowboy hat would be over-the-top."

"I'm with you on that. You want him to blend in, not stand out or be thought of as poking fun like he's dressed up for Halloween. Wash those Wranglers so they're not so stiff. After that he'll look like one of the local guys."

"I'm also gonna try to tone down his crazy hair, but there's not much I can do after he opens his mouth."

"Ah . . . right, the English accent."

"Yeah. He said while he lived in California he tried to lose the accent a bit, but he'd recently been to London to visit his mother for a couple of weeks and it came back full force." She laughed. "You should hear him trying to get directions from Siri on his phone. It's a riot. She can't understand him at all."

Laura Lee swallowed a bite of the delicious lasagna. The sauce was simply divine. "That's funny."

"I know." Mattie was so much more animated when she talked about Garret than when she mentioned Colby. But as much as she wanted to give Garret the benefit of the doubt, she really didn't want to see Mattie get hurt either. Garret was the son of a legendary rock star and a famous fashion model and a celebrity in his own right even if somewhat by default. Mattie and Garret were worlds apart and there was no doubt about it. A love like that would have to be strong enough to withstand different backgrounds. Garret was a world traveler and most of Mattie's travels had been journeys through the pages of her books. In spite of her earlier speech, Laura Lee did have her doubts, but that didn't mean that she didn't think that Mattie shouldn't take a chance. Even after Laura Lee's jackass husband's betrayal she loved romance. While she really did think that love had passed her by, she still believed in the beauty of happily ever after.

Mattie leaned forward. "Oh my gosh, Laura Lee, guess who just walked in?"

"Who? Garret?"

"No, Shane McCray."

Laura Lee's heart tripped all over itself, and the salad did a tap dance in her tummy. "Did he see me?"

"I'm not sure, but I think he might have."

"Oh, that's nice. You'll get to meet him." Laura Lee had the urge to rush to the bathroom to brush her hair and apply lipstick. She dabbed at the corners of her mouth, hoping she didn't have sauce on her face.

"Maybe you should turn around and let him know you're here."

Laura Lee nodded, but she didn't do it. Funny how she had started to become completely comfortable with him at his house but out in public somehow felt different. "Maybe I'll just let him spot me."

"Whatever you want to do," Mattie said, but gave her a funny look.

Laura Lee smiled but felt as if she needed to catch her breath. She told herself that she felt this way because he was not only her boss but a famous celebrity, but deep down she knew that was hogwash. She wanted to know what it felt like to be in his arms and to have him kiss her. Not that she was about to let him know how she felt. It was her little secret and she was going to keep her feelings under a lock and throw away the key.

8

You're Always on My Mind

SHANE DIDN'T THINK HE WAS HUNGRY AFTER HIS MEET-
ing with Maria and Garret at Sully's South, but he
spotted Laura Lee's van in the parking lot in front of
River Row Pizza and Pasta and his truck seemed to have
a mind of its own and he'd pulled in right beside her
vehicle. It blew him away that the mere sight of her van
could make him smile.

Because he'd always had to stay in shape, Shane avoided
carbs and when he walked inside the restaurant the aroma
of fresh-baked pizza made his mouth water. Or then again
maybe it was the sight of Laura Lee sitting in the far booth
that made his mouth water. And that was just the back of
her head. He stood there for a moment trying to decide
if he should go over with a casual greeting and then take
a seat by himself or ask to join them.

So that he didn't look silly just standing there, he reached
for a menu from the stack on the front counter and pretended to be looking it over. Of course the words didn't
even register in his brain and he thought it was quite amusing that he felt so damn nervous around her. Shane knew

he needed to rope in his feelings, but he liked the heady feeling, the rush of being so attracted to a woman.

Besides, Shane couldn't get Laura Lee out of his mind, so why fight it? But that was okay because he sure liked thinking about her. He also knew that if he didn't take it slow, Laura Lee would think he was a smarmy celebrity just in it for another notch on his bedpost. Truth be known, he never was like that and detested those who used their fame to get what they wanted, especially when it involved seducing women. Not that a lot of women didn't throw themselves at him—it came with the territory—but to him that kind of aggressive behavior was a complete turnoff.

Despite the gold and platinum records, the numerous awards and piles of money that Shane didn't even know what to do with, he remained a good ol' boy at heart and always would be. He prided himself on remembering his humble Alabama roots and never forgot where he came from. His mama, a steel magnolia through and through, would have his hide if he ever thought of being too big for his britches.

But when Shane's gaze landed on Laura Lee again, he decided that he would love to shower her with whatever she damn well pleased and then some, just to make her smile . . . and not just with her mouth but to light up the sadness that lurked in the depths of her eyes. Her upbeat, pleasant attitude might fool most people, but Shane would sometimes see her staring off into space with a bit of a lost look about her that made his heart constrict. He wanted to come to her rescue and chase away the sadness. And although he'd never been one to throw his money around, he'd just get a big kick out of taking Laura Lee on an endless shopping spree and tell her to have at it and buy whatever her heart desired.

Shane barely knew Laura Lee and yet he suddenly thought of the song "Shameless" and finally understood what Billy Joel must have been thinking when he'd written the lyrics. And Shane thought that Garth Brooks's on-his-knees version embodied what the song embraced, which was loving a woman beyond all reason.

Shane smiled, thinking he could see himself doing *anything at all to keep* a woman like Laura Lee in his life. Yeah, that could very well be him if he fell in love with her. But he had to cool his damn jets or she'd go running for the hills. Of course if she did he'd up and go running right after her. Taking a deep breath, he decided he'd been standing there long enough and needed to head her way and try not to show how jittery being around her made him. He always thought he'd say something stupid or even worse do what he'd been just dying to do for the past week, and that was . . .

Kiss her.

A deep, sweet kiss that lasted forever.

It was also funny because he hated seeing her working all day long and wanted to hire someone to do her work so she could sit by the pool and do whatever the hell she wanted. Wanting to hire a housekeeper for his housekeeper? Now, just how crazy was that? He told her she was his personal assistant, but in truth he did some of the paperwork himself or gave it to others still on his staff and told Laura Lee there wasn't much to do so she should take it easy. Although he didn't know her entire story, he did know from what she'd told him that she'd had it tough, and seeing her lounging by the pool while reading a book gave him such pleasure.

When Laura Lee suddenly turned around and waved, Shane tried to look surprised that he saw her there and headed her way as slowly as his eager legs would allow.

"Hi, Laura Lee," Shane said, and was pleased that he sounded fairly casual. "I was just, um, over at Sully's South, you know, the venue that Maria wants to be like the Bluebird Café?"

"Sure, I remember you talking about it."

"And I suddenly realized that I was hungry."

"I made a nice salad for you and left it in the fridge," Laura Lee said. "I used the leftover chicken breast from last night's dinner."

"It won't go to waste," Shane promised, and then addressed the cute little blonde sitting with Laura Lee. "Hello. I'm Shane McCray."

"Mattie Mayfield. Nice to meet you, Mr. McCray."

"Oh, please call me Shane. I insist."

"Okay, then, nice to meet you, Shane. I'd be remiss if I didn't tell you that I just love your music."

"Thanks, Mattie. Don't get me wrong, I enjoy all the new country music, but it's always a pleasure to have someone young like you tell me that they like the classics."

"Oh, I like the new stuff too, but classic is still my favorite. It's what I grew up on. And of course we're really proud of our own Jeff Greenfield and South Street Riot. And having Jeff propose to Cat Carson just before they opened for you last summer was so perfect."

"I know it sure was. And what a fun way to kick off my last concert tour."

"It was so cool of you to have them open for you. What an honor."

"He and Cat are talented. I was happy to have them." Shane smiled, appreciating the young lady's candor. "Are you Mayfield from the marina?"

"Yes."

"Your brother Mason took me bass fishing last week. He's an excellent guide, by the way."

"Thank you. Mason knows his stuff. Fished the FLW Bass Fishing Pro Tour for a while and did pretty well but had to come back to help out at the marina after my parents retired to Florida. The marina sponsored him, but when things got a little tough we had to pull back from participation when the entry fees just kept going up each year. I hope someday he'll get another shot at the big time. He's got the skills."

"Really? Well, I know some people who might be interested in sponsoring Mason. Next time we go fishing I'll bring it up and see what he thinks."

"Wow." Mattie raised her eyebrows. "That's really nice of you. Mason really is talented. He has, like, this Spidey sense when it comes to finding fish. Thank you so much. Not that I was fishing for that," she said, and then chuckled. "Pardon the pun."

Shane laughed, thinking that Mattie was as cute as a button.

"His dream was to make enough money to start up his own craft brewery," Mattie added.

"Oddly enough it's something I've considered as well. I like your brother already."

"We've already started eating, but would you care to join us?" Laura Lee asked.

Shane thought about it for a second but decided he shouldn't intrude even though he wanted to scoot in next to her. "Thanks for the offer, but I think I'll just order takeout. So don't worry about cooking dinner. We can just share the salad later if that's okay."

Laura Lee nodded. "Well, I was going to bring you a slice of Reese Marino's famous turtle cheesecake, so a light supper sounds perfect."

"Yes, it does," he said, and felt a surge of pleasure that she'd been thinking of him. "I'll just have to swim some extra laps later." Shane patted his stomach. "Mattie, Laura Lee is such an excellent cook that I have to add to my exercise routine."

"Oh, tell me about it. Laura Lee taught me some of my cooking skills. You should come over for breakfast at my restaurant the next time you go fishing with Mason."

"Her biscuits are legendary in Cricket Creek," Laura Lee said, and exchanged a smile with Mattie. Shane could tell that the two of them were close and he liked the idea of Laura Lee being a mentor for Mattie. The thought crossed his mind that she would have made a good mother.

"Well, I'd better place my order."

"Tessa should come out from the kitchen soon," Laura Lee said. "Do you want me to get her for you?"

"No . . . no, I'll just wait. Please, go back to enjoying your lunch."

Laura Lee nodded. "Oh, is there anything you need from the grocery store? I'm going to drop your boots off to be repaired and then I'm heading there after I finish eating."

"Not that I can think of, but if I do I'll send you a text message."

"Okay. I'm thinking about trying out a new recipe for salmon tomorrow. Does that sound good to you?"

"I love salmon. We can grill it by the pool if you like." He looked at Mattie. "Would you like to join us for dinner sometime soon? We'd love to have you."

"That sounds fun," Mattie said, but looked over at Laura Lee as if to see what she thought about the invitation.

"You could bring Garret," Laura Lee suggested, and then put a hand to her chest. "I'm sorry, that is if you don't mind, Shane? I should have asked before opening my mouth."

"Of course I don't mind," Shane said, and wanted to add *darlin'* and almost did. Something in her eyes said that she'd been reprimanded for speaking her mind, and it bothered him a lot. If he ever witnessed anyone talking down to her, he'd take care of it in nothing flat. "Garret as in Garret Ruleman?" Shane asked.

"Yes," Mattie answered, and gave Laura Lee what appeared to be a look of warning of some sort.

Shane could sense an undercurrent that left him curious. For some reason Laura Lee seemed to want this to happen, so Shane said, "By all means bring Garret. I've heard him play over at the studio. He's a talented musician and he's going to make a great addition to the lineup at Sully's South. I'm looking forward to working with him. Maria Sully said that he has a knack for spotting raw talent where others miss it. In fact, we could chat a bit about music," he added, knowing that Mattie couldn't refuse if it pertained to business. "Pardon me for asking, but are the two of you seeing each other?"

Mattie licked her bottom lip. "We're, um, we have, um, a bit of a project we're doing together." She gave Laura Lee another pointed look. "We're just friends, nothing more."

"Oh, well, be sure to invite Garret and I'll mention it when I see him." Intrigued, Shane wanted to know more. He wondered if he could get Laura Lee to divulge what was going on between Mattie and Garret. He was having a hard time picturing them as a couple and he'd taken an immediate liking to sweet Mattie. Although it wasn't any of his business, he'd learned in the short time he'd spent in Cricket Creek that the residents took care of their own and he made a mental note to keep an eye on Garret Ruleman. While he liked Garret, Shane knew that the young musician had a bit of a checkered past. He had to wonder if Laura Lee was doing the same thing and decided to push a little harder. "I would love for you to come over with Garret. Just see when he's available. Bring your swimsuit too if you like. I keep the water warm in the pool for evening swims." Because that was the way Laura Lee liked it.

"Thank you for the invitation," Mattie said. "I'll be seeing Garret later, so I'll ask him and let Laura Lee know, okay?"

"Sounds fantastic. I'll see you when we firm up a date. I hope it's soon. Laura Lee, I'll see you later," he said, and then walked over to the small bar area that was at the far side of the dining room. A moment later Tessa hurried his way.

"Sorry if you've been waiting. I was stirring some marinara sauce and didn't realize I had a customer."

"No problem." Shane gave her his warmest smile. He knew that she recognized him, and so many people thought that if he was put out even a little bit he might throw a fit. "I'd like a medium buffalo chicken pizza."

Tessa nodded. "Ah, one of my favorites. You get to combine hot wings flavor with pizza. It took me a while to get Tony and Reese to put this one on the menu, since they like to stick with traditional recipes. I can't wait to tell them that's what you ordered," she added, which was the only concession to letting Shane know she knew his identity. It was odd because people tended to act as if they knew him personally as if they were old friends, fawned all over him to the point of embarrassment, or acted as if he were invisible and ignored him completely. An honest reaction without overdoing it made Shane feel comfortable. He also hated when his meal was free or if he got special treatment. Leaning closer, he said, "And put Laura Lee and Mattie's meal on my tab please."

"Sure thing," Tessa said. "Can I get you a drink while you're waiting?"

A cold beer sounded good, but he hesitated because it was early in the day. He'd always watched his behavior since anything remotely questionable seemed to get caught on camera. And then he remembered that he was living in Cricket Creek and not Nashville. Nobody cared if he ordered a beer. "Well, it's not five o'clock yet, but what beer do you have on tap?" He grinned. "Go ahead and say it."

"It's five o'clock somewhere," she said with an easy laugh.

"Wish I'd gotten a hold of that song before Alan Jackson," Shane said, and joined her laughter. "But you've got a point."

"I suggest the Kentucky ale."

"Kentucky ale, huh?"

Tessa nodded. "It's a nice cross between Irish pale ale and English pale ale brewed with limestone water from Lexington, Kentucky. Would you like a sample?"

"I'm already sold."

Tessa smiled. "We're going to expand the bar area and offer a large selection of craft beers. Goes well with pizza, don't you think?"

"Absolutely," Shane agreed. He thought about the comment that Mattie had just made about her brother and smiled. He'd been researching some ways to invest his money, and brewing beer sounded like something he'd really enjoy.

Tessa put the pilsner glass down in front of him. "Here you go," she said, and waited for him to take a sip.

"Wow, this is good stuff," Shane said with a nod. "Excellent."

"Glad you like it," Tessa said. "My brother Tony is all about craft beer lately."

"Really? I think Cricket Creek needs one."

"I know that we could sell a locally brewed beer here for sure. We're thinking of adding a beer garden."

"Great idea." Shane could feel her excitement and he smiled. "With the addition of Sully's South you'll have bigger crowds up here and we're not far from the baseball stadium. I think it's something to give some thought to anyway. Hey, maybe we could do some outdoor concerts with some of the talent we discover at Sully's South."

"My husband owns some property up here too. We should put our heads together and see what we come up with."

Shane reached in his wallet and handed her a card. "My contact number is on here. Let's set something up sometime soon."

"Will do!" She gave him a bright smile. "This is so exciting! I'll go place your pizza order. Should take about twenty minutes."

"Then I might have to have two of these," Shane said with a lift of his glass. He had the strong urge to look over his shoulder at Mattie and Laura Lee but slipped his phone from his pocket and pretended interest in his messages while his mind remained on the auburn-haired woman who had somehow captivated him in a short period of time.

Although he wanted to flirt with her during the day

and especially when they ate dinner together, he refrained. Giving her the wrong impression was the very
last thing he wanted to do, so until the time felt right he
would be her employer and hopefully become her friend.
He certainly wouldn't want for her to think that he expected anything of a romantic nature from her as part of
her job description or having him throw his celebrity
weight around. He wanted Laura Lee to feel comfortable and know that he was sincere. *Slow and steady gets
the prize,* he told himself. But slow and steady was going
to be oh so hard when every time she was within reaching distance he wanted to pull her into his arms and kiss
her.

   Patience, Shane told himself, and took a drink of his
beer. He was worried, though, that while he was biding
his time someone else might beat him to the punch. The
thought of Laura Lee in the arms of another man made
his heart plummet. Two weeks, he thought to himself. In
two weeks he'd go for a kiss. With that in mind he opened
his calendar on his phone and marked the day.

9

Everybody Plays the Fool

AFTER HIS MEETING WITH SHANE AND MARIA AT SUL-
ly's South, Garret wanted to go for a run, but his
ankle, although feeling better than expected because of
his cute little nurse, was still a tad tender. He still couldn't
believe he'd been crazy enough to jump over the railing
of the deck. Of course when he heard Colby trying to get
Mattie to jump in the river he'd seen red and hadn't been
thinking straight. In truth, although he'd gotten into his
fair share of scuffles, he was usually the one causing the
issue, not coming to the rescue.

Garret had to grin. Sprained ankle or not, he damn
well knew if someone was giving Mattie a hard time he'd
do the same damn thing again, because who knew that
being the hero was so much more fun than being the villain? And felt so much better, he thought, and his smile
dimmed a bit. Living with so much anger and resentment
at his father for so long had squeezed out any chance for
happiness. What Garret was trying to prove by being a
jackass for all those years, he sure as hell didn't know, but
it certainly did feel liberating to be on a different path.

Not ready to head back to his cabin just yet, Garret

put the top down of his convertible and drove around Cricket Creek taking in the sights. Having grown up in such big cities like London, L.A., and Chicago, Garret thought he'd feel incredibly bored in a small town. When he heard his father had moved here, he had given him six months until he sold the recording studio and came to his senses. But now, driving around in his Audi convertible, he felt a sense of wonder at the slow pace, the lack of horns honking and sirens going off ever so often. At first he'd thought it odd that people waved at just about everyone passing by, including him, but now he just grinned and waved back. He found it amusing that the wave was often accompanied by a "How y'all doin'?" And Garret now knew that the correct response was "Doin' all right."

When Garret stopped for a red light he watched people strolling leisurely down the sidewalk rather than bumping shoulders in a mad dash to get wherever they needed to go. Instead of heads bent looking at cell phones or chatting with phones glued to their ear, people here in Cricket Creek actually walked in groups and talked to one another. And they were smiling. Imagine that.

From the old historical brick buildings to the flowerpots overflowing with vibrant colors, Main Street oozed small-town charm. Grammar's Bakery drew his attention, and the many antique shops reminded him of Portobello Road in London. For a minute Garret thought about pulling over to park so he could take pictures with his phone, but then with a little chuckle he reminded himself that he wasn't a tourist but actually lived here in this quaint place. Just a year ago he would have laughed his head off at the notion of residing in a town called Cricket Creek, but he inhaled the fresh air filled with the sweet scent of flowers and smoky charcoal grills coming from the park to his left. He could see the baseball field and hear the cheers after the ping of an aluminum bat connected with a baseball.

Garret had the urge to park his car and watch, wondering what it would have felt like to be a kid playing while parents cheered wildly at each little achievement. The closest he came was piano recitals when his mother insisted that he should take piano lessons. At first he'd balked at practicing, but soon discovered that like with his absentee father, music was in his blood. He picked up the guitar soon after, wanting to show off his talent to a father who was almost never there. Garret practiced, wanting to become a better musician than his father, and he often dreamed of surpassing Rick Ruleman's fame. Garret pictured himself basking in the glory of millions of fans, but he soon found out that being the son of an icon meant that critics were harsh. Garret crumpled beneath the scrutiny and played into the hands of those who wanted him to fail.

Garret drove past a place called the Dairy Bar and smiled at the long line of kids and families waiting for a cold treat on a warm summer evening. He could hear their chatter and laughter, drawing joy from the simple things in life. Young couples pushed strollers down the sidewalk, stopping here and there to chat with friends.

His own childhood had been chaotic and complicated and after his parents split up he lived in London only to be uprooted when his mother had remarried. Garret had been thrown for yet another childhood loop, feeling as if his mum loved her two children with boring banker Marcus Gordon much more than she could ever love him. There he was, all knees and elbows with a mouthful of braces, while little Sophia and Grace, a mere year and a half apart, were the picture of perfection.

Of course there were times when Garret felt like the odd man out, but he soon learned that his mother had more than enough love in her heart for all three of her children. Marcus, however, didn't deal well with Garret when he went from being a nerdy bookworm eager to please to a rebellious teenager hell-bent on causing a ruckus. Garret shook his head, thinking back to how he used to make it his job to get mild-mannered Marcus all riled up.

Garret turned onto Maple Street past the high school and drove down the tree-lined street. Residents were outside sitting on porches, mowing lawns, and strolling. After leaving London he'd been raised in huge homes, rarely interacting with neighbors. This sense of community, easy smiles, and continuous interaction must feel like having an extended family.

Garret spotted a couple of girls who reminded him of Sophia and Grace and smiled. He adored his half sisters, wishing that he could see them more often. The marriage to Marcus had lasted nearly twenty years, many of which his mother and stepfather had lived apart. While they rarely argued and were politely friendly, they grew further and further apart, staying together out of convenience and for the sake of the family. Garret found it all very sad and he was glad when his mum finally decided to end the marriage.

Becca finally moved back to London full-time after Sophia and Grace went off to college, while Marcus lived in the States. When his mum had confessed that she'd done the classic thing by marrying someone the total opposite of his father, Garret finally understood. While she and Marcus remained friendly, they were ill-suited from the start and unhappy for a very long time. Now that his father was happily married to Maggie, Garret wished that his mum could also find someone special in her life.

Garret pushed his silver aviator sunglasses up the bridge of his nose and had to wonder if his fascination with this small town had anything to do with his odd, rather disjointed childhood. He'd just bet that if he stopped the group of teenagers playing touch football over in the grass and asked if they would rather live here or have a rock star for a father, they would answer *rock star* in a split second. They would be wrong. Family life, friends who really cared couldn't be bought with money. Garret knew because he'd tried.

Garret hadn't been joking when he told Mattie that Addison had dodged the bullet by ending their engagement. But being with Addison had given Garret a glimpse of how it felt to be with someone who actually cared about him without an agenda, and he wanted that in his life. If rock legend Rick Ruleman could settle down, then there was hope for anyone, including him. That was why Garret hoped that Mattie could give him lessons on living a small-town lifestyle. He truly wanted to become part of the community. Of course he could try to subdue his accent as he did while living in L.A., but Garret was tired of pretending to be someone he wasn't. While he wanted to blend in better, he also wanted to have the freedom to finally be himself ... whatever that was, he thought with a wry grin.

Of course after his little run-in with Colby, Garret was pretty sure he had an uphill climb ahead of him when it came to making friends. Not that he bloody well wouldn't do it again!

Garret noticed the glances his silver sports car was getting and wondered if he needed to trade his Audi in for a pickup truck. He chuckled when he pictured himself behind the wheel of a big-ass four-wheel-drive monster but then decided it might be fun.

Garret turned back onto Main Street, and the aroma of smoldering charcoal from the nearby picnics stirred up hunger pangs, so he pulled into the parking lot of Wine and Diner. He'd heard that the food was amazing and he decided to order some takeout before heading back to his cabin. Cooking wasn't something he'd mastered just yet, but improving his culinary skills was on his long list of things to do to become more rounded. Garret grinned, thinking that he was much more likely to become thinner than more rounded. Even using the microwave resulted in minor explosions and overcooked rubber food.

Garret parked at a spot near the entrance so he didn't have to put too much stress on his ankle. Once inside, he was immediately glad he'd stopped. The interior was as the name of the restaurant indicated, a blend of an old-school diner and a modern flair. The thought went through his head that he'd like to eat here with Mattie and then he shoved it aside. Mattie Mayfield was hell-bent on getting the attention of Colby, and he'd best remember that their little arrangement was for mutual benefit and friendship, nothing more. Of course his memory took an extended holiday every time he laid eyes upon her.

"The hostess is off duty, so you can seat yourself," called a lady from behind the counter at the far end of the restaurant. The stools were the old-fashioned kind that spun around, making Garret wonder if he might just eat here and enjoy the atmosphere. But dining by one's self rather sucked, so he walked over to her and sat down, barely refraining from taking a little spin. But just as he got to the counter, a little boy ran past Garret, nearly knocking into him.

"Ben! Get back here this minute or I'll tell your mama," said the same lady who'd greeted Garret. "Hey there, would you do me a favor and catch him?" she shouted to Garret. "I'm supposed to be watching him for his mama and he's quicker than lightning and squirms away like a greased piglet."

Garret was hesitant to apprehend the little chap, but he also didn't want to have him scoot out the door and into traffic, so he hurried over and scooped him up.

"Put me down," Ben demanded, and indeed had the squirming thing down pat.

"You little booger," the lady said, and held her hands out for Ben to come to her. "Come here to Auntie Myra."

"No," Ben said, and wrapped his chubby arms around Garret's neck. "I don't want to take a nap, Auntie Myra!"

"Mama's rules, Benny."

His answer was to cling to Garret tighter.

"I say, little chap, I think you must mind Auntie Myra. And naps are actually quite nice."

"You talk funny," Ben said, and pulled back to give Garret a curious look.

"Ben, be polite."

"Well, *you* smell like strawberries," Garret said.

"I know." Ben grinned and showed Garret a fistful of slightly squished strawberries. "Want one?"

"No, thanks," Garret said, but Ben wasn't having no for an answer and smashed one into Garret's closed mouth.

"Benjamin McKenna!" Aunt Myra exclaimed, and tried to tug Ben away from Garret, but he clung like a little monkey to a tree. "I'm gonna tell your daddy," she threatened, and that seemed to give Ben pause, but after a second he went back to force-feeding Garret. "Ben, stop smashing strawberries in his face."

McKenna ... it suddenly dawned on Garret that the little rascal was the son of former baseball great Ty McKenna, who was part owner of the Cricket Creek Cougars, the local pro baseball team in town. Maggie had told him about the baseball stadium built by baseball great and resident hero Noah Falcon a few years ago when financial woes hit Cricket Creek hard. He remembered now that Addison's uncle, Mitch Monroe, was a silent partner in the baseball complex along with several other developments in and around Cricket Creek. The small town certainly had drawn quite a few heavy hitters along with Garret's father.

"I think you might be getting yourself into a spot of trouble, Ben," Garret added, but Ben didn't seem to care. Garret could relate and had to chuckle. He couldn't remember when he'd held a guy so small, and he found the little chap quite amusing.

"Don't want a naaaaap!" Ben wailed, putting extra emphasis on the *p*.

"Well, it's way past your naptime anyway," Aunt Myra grumbled. "So just come with me so we can get a bath and wash up for supper."

"Don't want peas or cawits, just sta-waw-baa-wees."

"I'll let your mama deal with that battle," Myra said, and was finally able to pry Ben from around Garret's neck.

"So sorry," Myra said, and then laughed. "Oh goodness, you have strawberries all over your face."

Ben looked at Garret and giggled. "You look silly."

"I get that a lot," Garret said, and reached down onto the counter for a napkin from a silver container. He tugged a few napkins loose and started wiping his face.

"What's your name?" Ben wanted to know.

"Garret."

"Ga-wit, you wanna play?" Ben asked, and Garret felt an odd pang of longing that he couldn't explain. Other than his sisters he had never been particularly fond of being around children, but he thought Ben was completely cute in a rascally little way.

"Ben, Garret came into the diner to get a bite to eat, not to play."

"I wanna eat wiff him." Ben pointed at Garret.

Garret thought it might be fun to eat with little Ben, but Aunt Myra didn't look too pleased about his request. Besides, they might just end up skipping peas and going straight for dessert. Addison had once told him that he suffered from the Peter Pan syndrome, and although he was trying hard to grow up, he often found it difficult. "I would love to eat with you, Ben, but I'm getting takeaway."

"Takeaway?" Ben angled his curly head in question. "What are you gonna take away?"

"My dinner."

Myra looked at him kind of funny too. "Oh, you mean takeout," she said, and chuckled. "The takeout, I mean *takeaway* menu is on the back. Oh, and dessert is on the house for your trouble. Ben's mama is owner of Wine and Diner and I was in charge of Ben while she baked strawberry pies. I'll pack a slice for you."

"May I trouble you for two slices?" he asked, thinking of when Mattie came over later for their joint lessons. "I have a friend coming over later. I'll be happy to pay for it."

"Sure thing and don't worry about it. Do you know what you want or do you need a minute or two?"

Garret glanced at the menu. "Oh, wow, you have shepherd's pie?"

"We just added it last week. My niece Jessica makes it from scratch from an authentic recipe. You won't be sorry."

"Brilliant. Add a side salad please."

"Salads are yucky," Ben informed him. " 'Specially maaaters." He made a face.

"Maters?"

"Tomatoes," Myra translated.

"Ah, I used to think so too, but I like them now," Garret said. "But I'm with you and strawberries are the very best."

"Want more, Ga-wit?" Ben extended the hand that held the remaining red pulp.

"No, you may have it. I'll wait for your mum's pie."

"Mum . . ." Ben giggled. "You're funny."

"Thank you, Ben. I like being funny. I think you're funny too."

Myra tipped her head to the side. "Oh, wait. You're Garret Ruleman. I just heard that you recently moved here. Well, welcome to Cricket Creek! We're all fond of your father. Nice guy and likes to give back to the community."

"Thank you. I'm working with him at the record studio."

Myra shook her head. "This little old town is suddenly chock-full of interesting people, and I do believe you qualify for that category."

Garret grinned. "Don't believe everything you've read about me."

"No worries." Myra waved a hand in his direction. "I make up my own mind about people." She looked at little Ben. "And children are a good judge of character, and you seem to have Ben's vote in your corner already. So welcome!"

"Thank you, Myra. I'm sure you'll see me here quite often. I've heard that the food is fantastic."

"Why, thank you. Make yourself comfortable. I'll be out with your *takeaway* in a jiffy."

"Thanks," Garret said, and when he did a little spin on the stool, Ben tossed his curly head back and laughed. Garret liked the sound and he was a bit sad when the little chap went toward the kitchen with his auntie. When the double doors swung open he watched Ben scramble out of Myra's arms and rush over to his mum, who bent down and braced herself for the collision.

Garret settled back and read through the menu that was full of comfort food but also had a nice selection of healthy options. He smiled when he saw "stone soup" along with a sidebar of the fable about feeding the hungry. For every bowl of stone soup ordered, Wine and Diner pledged a dollar to the local food bank. He thought about Mattie's charity for literacy at her shop and couldn't help being impressed at how people in this little town looked after one another. No wonder his father decided to settle down here! And Garret did feel a sense of pride that his father was obviously respected as one of the community who gave back. Garret considered the comment Myra made about his father being such a nice guy. There was a time when long-haired, leather-clad, hard rocker Rick Ruleman would have been called anything but *nice*.

Garret had been blown away when his father recently confessed that his years as a hard-core rocker had been an act that was just short of a total sham. Garret never would have guessed that his father's music genre of choice had always been bluegrass and blues, and that his first record was supposed to be a ballad. When the head-banging version that his record label had insisted upon became a huge hit, the stage was set and he'd been pigeonholed into performing hard rock for the rest of his career.

Garret understood. His own bad boy image still followed him around and was so hard to shake. He too had been living a life totally different from his true self. Garret blew out a sigh. What he wanted now more than anything was respect for his musical talent, but after acting the fool for so many years he knew that day might never come.

A moment later Myra came pushing through the double doors, carrying a big plastic bag. "Here you go, Garret," she announced with a friendly smile. "When Ben wouldn't stop talking about feeding you strawberries, Jessica decided you deserved an entire pie."

"Thanks, but little Ben wasn't a bother. I found him quite charming."

"Well, you've got a friend for life."

"Good to know." Garret chuckled, thinking that might be a first.

"Just follow me over to the register and I'll ring you up."

Garret noticed that the dinner crowd was starting to file into the restaurant and he was glad he'd decided to head back to his cabin. Although it was widely known that he was on friendly terms with Addison, Garret was well aware that he was still cast in the role of villain by many. Mattie was going to have to do a bang-up job of repairing his image and teaching him how to fit into small-town life. "Keep the change and put it in the stone soup charity."

"Thanks, Garret. And, again, welcome to Cricket Creek. We're glad to have you."

"Next time I come in I want to dine with Ben," Garret said. "Just hold the salad and we might eat dessert first."

Myra laughed. "You're gonna fit in just fine," she said as if somehow knowing it was going to be a bit of a challenge. "But don't go changin' that accent of yours. Girls around here are going to go gaga over it."

"Well, Mattie told me that my American accent sounds like a bad impression of John Wayne, so I think I'd better stick to my English one with a bit of California tossed in."

"Oh, you've met cute little Mattie Mayfield," Myra said, and gave him a long look.

"I bought the cabin next to the marina. We've become . . . friends."

"Well, now . . ." Myra nodded slowly. "I haven't seen her in a coon's age. Bring her in for dinner sometime soon. Feisty little thing, but her smile can light up a room, don't you think?"

"You must know her well. I'll do that," Garret promised, and that seemed to please Myra. He'd been warned by Maggie that matchmaking was like a sport here in Cricket Creek, and if he wasn't mistaken by the gleam in Myra's eye, that was exactly what she was trying to do. Fat chance of that happening, Garret thought. Mattie had her sights set on Colby. The best he could hope for was friendship, and Mattie was probably much better off with a good old boy like her brothers. While Colby had acted like a jackass last night, Garret figured that the big clod was a good guy or Mattie wouldn't be interested in him. Coming between what Mattie had wanted for so long would just be shitty on his part. And he was over being the bad boy. Being the hero felt so damn sweet and he'd decided to do his best to keep it that way.

Dominick the swashbuckling pirate would toss her over his shoulder and have wild sex with her, Garret thought with a laugh. But then he pictured himself doing this with Mattie and had to turn the air-conditioning in his car up on high. Although he was attracted to her, Garret couldn't remember when he'd had so much fun talking to a woman. He'd shared some of that with Addison, but he'd been too self-centered back then to realize that friendship was every bit as important in a relationship as sex. That being said, he did wish she would have stayed the night at his place so he could have seen her sleep rumpled and sexy in the morning. And when he'd found her lacy bra and panties in the dryer, he couldn't chase the image of her wearing them from his brain.

After Garret arrived at the cabin he opened the bag filled to the brim with delicious-smelling food. "Holy cow," he said when he lifted the lid on the shepherd's pie and decided to text Mattie and invite her to come over early to share the huge dinner. He told himself that it was just because he had so much food and not that he was trying to spend a bit more time with her. He stared at his phone and waited for the answer. When she accepted he blew out a sigh of relief and then shook his head. "Back off, Ruleman," he muttered, and opened the bottle of bourbon he'd bought because Mattie said that was what she preferred. After pouring two fingers into a cocktail glass, he added some ice and gave it a sip. "Nice," he said, and let the smooth Woodford Reserve slide down his throat, leaving a trail of warmth in its wake. All he had to do was keep his hands to himself and teach her the finer points of being feminine.

Easy enough.

"Right. . . ." He took a bigger swig of the bourbon and sighed. Who was he fooling?

But Garret liked the feeling of this newfound integrity. He wasn't about to fall back into his take-what-you-want way of living. He would just have to power his way through dinner and then teach her how to entice Colby into asking her out on a date. The thought had him staring into his glass as if the amber liquid held all the answers.

Garret inhaled a deep breath. Flicking his wrist, he made the ice clink against the glass.

Surely he could do it. He took another sip.

But he damn well didn't want to.

10

Luck Be a Lady

"Yoo-hoo, Mattie?" Laura Lee called. "Are you in your bedroom?"

"Yeah, come on back here," Mattie shouted, and then angled her head at the mirror. She gave her reflection a critical once-over. She wasn't used to wearing dresses except for special occasions and she felt silly going to Garret's for dinner and her how-to-be-a-lady lessons this dressed up.

When Laura Lee entered the room, she gave Mattie a low whistle. "Well, now."

"I think I'm going to change into jeans. I feel silly."

"What you should feel is beautiful, because you are! Don't you even think about changing, Mattie Mayfield! Lavender is such a good color for you." Laura Lee came up beside her and smiled into the mirror.

"That's what Violet told me. Laura Lee, I have to admit that I had such fun trying on dresses today at her shop. Of course, it helped that she kept *ooh*ing and *aah*ing at every single thing I tried on."

"Oh, sweetie, you'd be pretty wearing a darn paper sack. You're cute in jeans, but you are simply stunning in a dress." She reached up and touched Mattie's hair. "And the French twist is nothing short of elegant."

"I looked up how to do it online. It was actually very simple."

"Garret is going to be blown away."

"But I feel silly. Like I'm way over-the-top."

"But it's part of your lessons. He told you to get dressed up like you were going out, right?"

Mattie nodded. "But I guess that's the problem. This is just for the lessons. Laura Lee, I think I've wanted him to kiss me since the moment I met him. How crazy is that?"

"Not crazy at all."

"It's so frustrating. And we talked and talked last night about everything under the sun. He's so easy to be around."

"Because you like him."

"And he listens like he cares."

"I'm sure he does care, Mattie."

"I could have wrung his fool neck when he jumped over the railing to come to my rescue."

"But you liked it, right?"

Mattie smiled. "It was like a scene from a romance novel, for sure. Except the rescue didn't end with a hot, steamy kiss but a sprained ankle instead."

"Maybe it should have. Perhaps you should have encouraged him a bit."

"I guess I'm not so good at the whole flirting thing."

Laura Lee arched one eyebrow. "Hmm . . ."

"I know that look. What?"

"I'm just . . . thinking."

"Thinking what?" Mattie asked, and then she got it before Laura Lee could answer. "Wait. Are you suggesting that I ask Garret to teach me . . . things like kissing? How to be, like, se-duc-tive?"

Laura Lee widened her eyes and put a hand to her chest. "Child, I would never suggest such a thing."

"Right." For a moment Mattie believed her, but when Laura Lee's lips twitched she gave herself away. "Wait.

Should I?" She shook her head but felt a little thrill slide down her spine. "No . . . no, I couldn't."

Laura Lee lifted one shoulder. "Do you dare?"

"Did you just dare me?"

"I do believe I did." Laura Lee pressed her lips together and shrugged.

"You know I can't refuse a dare."

Laura Lee chuckled. "It's the Southern way, right?"

"How would I even go about voicing such a proposition? Oh God, my heart is just racing simply thinking about it." She closed her eyes. "No. No, I can't do it."

Laura Lee put her hands on Mattie's shoulders. "Open your eyes, Mattie." When she did Laura Lee met her gaze in the mirror.

"Risk it for the biscuit?" Mattie whispered, and caught her bottom lip between her teeth.

"A kiss is a powerful thing. I'm thinking that if you do kiss Garret you'll know if there are fireworks or if you simply have a passing crush."

"I don't care that he's a celebrity of sorts, if that's what you're thinking."

"Are you kidding? I know you better than that, Mattie. But he is different and oh so charming. That in and of itself is exciting in a way you've probably not experienced before."

Mattie nodded. "I know. I've already thought of that."

"Look, I know that you've set your sights on Colby for so long that this sudden turn of events has to be somewhat emotional, sort of like giving up on a dream."

"Before I even gave the dream a fair chance," Mattie admitted softly. "Laura Lee, I've thought about all this. It's just that Garret seems to always be on my mind these days instead of Colby. I can't wait for the day to end so I can get to my lessons with him. When the door opens at Breakfast, Books, and Bait, I hope it's him walking in. When he texted me to ask me to dinner before our lessons, my heart thudded so hard I thought if I looked down it would be doing one of those beating-out-of-my-chest things you see in a cartoon."

Laura Lee laughed. "Sorry, but I just imagined that in my head."

"And I had to force myself not to answer *yes*, lickety-split with capital letters and, like, ten exclamation points and seem too eager. So I typed *yes* real fast and then waited for a minute or two before I hit the send button."

Laura Lee started laughing again. "Forgive me, but that's so cute and funny at the same time. You know that you brighten my days, right?"

Mattie turned around and gave Laura Lee a big hug. "You deserve bright days. And that whole ship-sailing thing you said is a big bunch of bull. You need to listen to some of your own advice."

"Oh, Mattie," Laura Lee said, and then had to dab at a tear. "I'm much better at giving advice, I'm afraid."

"Then practice what you preach," Mattie said, and felt emotion well up in her own throat. She sniffed hard.

"Don't you dare cry and mess up your makeup! Which, by the way, looks lovely too. Understated and classy. The soft coral lipstick is perfect."

It was Mattie's turn to laugh. "It's amazing what you can learn online. I just joined Pinterest and I swear I could play on there all day long." Inhaling a deep breath she turned around and smoothed down the skirt on her dress. "Maybe I'm more girlie than I ever imagined."

"You look spectacular. The dress is simple but time-less. The slope of your neck and shoulders is so very feminine. But enough talk. You need to get your pretty self over there pronto."

"I'm suddenly really nervous." She put a hand to her tummy.

"I think it's called excited. There is a difference." Laura Lee took Mattie's hands and squeezed. "Oh my, so cold."

"Told you!"

"Look, you need to see this through but take it slow

and don't let your emotions run away with you. And call me tomorrow and give me all the details. Okay?"

Mattie nodded. "All right, I'm off."

Laura Lee gave her a quick peck on the cheek. "I'm going to call your mama later tonight."

"Oh, don't go tellin' her any of this. She'll be planning my long-overdue wedding and knitting baby booties."

"No . . . no, I wouldn't do that. I just want to tell her how things are going with my new job. Miranda was so thrilled for me. Your mama is such a dear friend. Well, all except for the whole up-and-moving-to-Florida part."

"I know. I miss Mama too, but she and Daddy earned a permanent vacation as they call it. They vowed to return if we ever provide grandbabies."

"Sounds like something Miranda would say."

"Yeah, well, that's not looking too promising at the moment. But truthfully Mason and Danny put their social lives on the back burner and put their heart and soul into saving the marina. Daddy had to get away from the stress or have a heart attack. We could have sold out to all the new development in Cricket Creek, but we wanted to save our family business and I'm so glad we did. This is my home."

"Sweetie, I'm well aware of that. But remember that the marina is thriving now. It's time for you and your brothers to go on with your personal lives."

"I know. But I don't have any regrets."

"We all make mistakes, but having no regrets is the only way to live your life. Just live and learn."

"Hey, you should go down to the beach for a visit. Mama would love it."

"I will after I've worked for Shane long enough to ask for some time off." She smiled. "Although working for him sometimes feels like I'm on vacation. He lets me use his pool and workout room that's state-of-the-art." She flexed a muscle. "At this rate I'm going to be in the best shape I've been in a long time. Plus, he likes to take walks in the evening."

"Interesting . . . ," Mattie said, and gave Laura Lee a pointed look.

"Don't go there. I'm not about to mess up the best job I've ever had by doing something stupid."

"I think you're not following your own advice once again."

"Shane McCray is my employer. My situation is way different than yours, not to mention he's simply lonely with just moving here. He's trying to keep his residence on the down low to keep the paparazzi away or I'm certain he'd find something better to do than hang out with me," she said firmly, but judging by the high color in her cheeks, she was trying to convince herself.

"If you say so," Mattie said lightly.

"I know so," Laura Lee insisted, and then took a step back. "Okay, sweet pea, get yourself over there and enjoy your evening. Time's a-wastin'. I'll walk out to your truck with you."

"I was gonna walk."

"And get all wilted? Not on your life," Laura Lee insisted.

"I guess you're right. It just seems silly to drive such a short way, but I will take your advice."

"Good girl," Laura Lee said, and followed her out the door.

"Say hi to Mama for me. Tell her I'll call her tomorrow after the breakfast rush."

"Will do," Laura Lee said, and gave her a wave.

As Mattie drove away she could see Laura Lee standing in the gravel driveway, watching her progress. It occurred to Mattie that Laura Lee would have made such a wonderful mother, and it was such a shame that her jerk of an ex-husband didn't know what a gem he'd had and tossed it all away. Laura Lee never complained, but Mattie could see the sadness lurking in her friend's eyes every so often. Mattie hoped and prayed that someone in this town would have the sense to take notice and sweep Laura Lee Carter right off her feet. If Shane

McCray were the one it would be such a sweet fairy-tale ending.

A couple of minutes later Mattie arrived at Garret's cabin and parked her blue Ford Ranger next to his fancy little sports car. She wondered if he knew that the shiny silver car wouldn't do all that well in the winter. They tended to get more ice than snow, but it could get pretty nasty on occasion. She decided she needed to alert him to the fact. Random thoughts, but her mind always started racing when she was nervous. And she'd probably talk his ear off if she wasn't careful. And just how did she go about asking for her underwear?

"God," Mattie whispered when she finally mustered up the nerve to actually grab her purse, open the door, and step out of her truck. "This just might be an epic fail." She swallowed hard, trying to calm the butterflies that felt like the size of bats in her stomach. When she opened her mouth, would one fly out? That would be a deal killer, she thought with a nervous giggle.

After one step toward the front porch she stopped to smooth her skirt. Mattie took one more step and then reached up and checked the status of her French twist. Was she trying too hard? No! The French twist was an assignment of sorts just like the dress. She shook her head, thinking at this rate she'd get to the front door by morning.

Okay, she'd made it. Raising her fist, Mattie rapped lightly on the door and for a crazy second considered running away before Garret had the chance to answer like the knicker-knock prank she and her friends did as children. The thought made Mattie laugh, dissolving some of the anxiety of standing on the doorstep of a man she shouldn't fall in love with because it would cause nothing but heartache. And yet she didn't think her life would be complete unless she kissed him . . . just one time.

Laughter still lingered on her lips when Garret opened the door. "Care to share the joke?"

The joke is on me, Mattie thought, but said, "Sure, but

you have to invite me in first." She expected him to step aside for her to enter, but he simply stood there blinking at her. "Garret?"

He seemed to snap out of it. "Oh, right . . . come on in, Mattie."

Mattie entered the cabin, brushing past him so closely that she could feel the warmth of his body. Whatever that aftershave he was wearing was, it made her want to sigh. Probably something that cost a million dollars an ounce. The damn stuff should be outlawed. Her bare arm grazed the soft cotton of his shirt, causing a tingle that awoke the butterflies from their brief slumber. When she put a hand to her stomach Garret looked at her with concern.

"Are you all right?"

"I'm nervous," Mattie admitted.

"About what?"

Mattie hesitated for a second while all the things she was jittery about ticked through her brain. "About asking you for my underwear," Mattie finally replied, and he burst out laughing. When in doubt choose humor, she thought with a grin.

"And what if I want to keep them?" he shot back.

"I dunno. What do I get in return?"

"What do you want in return?" The low, teasing tone of Garret's voice slid down Mattie's spine like a pat of butter on her griddle, and when he took a step closer she almost asked for the long-awaited kiss. Wait. Was he flirting? Or just playing the teacher?

"A glass of wine will do for now."

"I have bourbon," he offered, and it pleased Mattie that he must have bought it just for her. "Woodford Reserve, in fact."

"Nice, but tonight I'm going to be a lady." She did a little spin in her dress, making the skirt billow slightly before coming back to caress her legs.

"I do believe that ladies drink bourbon."

"I know that Southern ladies do."

"Well, then, it's your choice. I do have a nice merlot that'll go well with the shepherd's pie I have keeping warm in the oven."

"How about starting with bourbon on the rocks and then have the wine with dinner?"

"Brilliant. Would you like to go outside in the fresh air? It's shaded back there now. Dinner will keep for a bit if that's okay."

"Sitting outside would be delightful," Mattie replied in her best ladylike tone. She gave him a serene smile, thinking that this was easier than she thought. "Oh, and when I had lunch with Laura Lee we ran into Shane Mc-Cray and he wanted to know if you wanted to have dinner at his house sometime soon."

Garret looked a bit surprised but then nodded. "That sounds quite nice."

"You don't have to pick me up or anything," she added, not wanting him to think that she thought of this as a date.

"No, I'd rather pick you up, Mattie, if that's okay with you."

"Sure. Just check your schedule and let me know when you're free." She tried so hard to sound casual, but it pleased her to no end that he wanted to pick her up like a real date.

"I will. Perfect. Now let's get your drink."

Yes! She could use some liquid courage. Mattie followed Garret into the kitchen and watched him fuss around getting her glass and filling it with ice. He added a generous pour of bourbon and handed the glass to her.

"Good stuff, this Kentucky bourbon of yours." He filled his empty glass and raised it in a salute before tapping his rim to hers. "Cheers!"

"I wouldn't steer you wrong," Mattie said, and then took a sip. "Smooth, right?"

"Absolutely."

"It makes me cringe when people add a mixer to something this special."

"I'll keep that rule in mind and I must agree. Good whiskey should be savored. Now tell me more."

"What do you want to know?"

"Does bourbon have to be distilled in Kentucky?"

"Okay, well, Kentucky makes over ninety-five percent of the world's bourbon, but by law bourbon doesn't have to be distilled in Kentucky." She gave him a sideways look and tapped her chest. "But I for one won't buy bourbon that isn't distilled here."

"Ah, loyal. I like that about you."

"Thank you."

"Do you know a lot about it, then?"

"I do." Mattie grinned. "I've been on the bourbon trail. I went with Mason and Danny a few times."

"Sounds like a fun trail to be on. Is it like a pub crawl?"

"No, silly boy. The bourbon trail is a bunch of bourbon distilleries, eight, I think, that got together and created a tourist trail where you can visit each one and learn how fine bourbon is crafted. You get a passport and get a stamp for each one you visit. If you hit them all you get a T-shirt in the end."

"Did you fill your passport?"

"I did indeed." She pointed to the bottle sitting on the counter. "Woodford Reserve is on the trail. So, what else do you want to know?"

"What's the difference between bourbon and any other whiskey?"

"Well, since you asked . . . there are strict rules that must be followed to be called bourbon."

He looked at his glass with interest. "Carry on."

"Bourbon got its name in the seventeen hundreds when the whiskey was shipped down the Ohio and Mississippi rivers all the way to New Orleans from Bourbon County. At the time Kentucky was still part of West Virginia. Because it was shipped in white oak barrels with Bourbon County stamped on them, the whiskey became known as Bourbon, although *some* would argue that the name came from Bourbon Street in New Orleans." She rolled her eyes.

"Ah, I take it you don't like that version."

"I like to keep it in Kentucky."

"Fair enough." Garret gave her a nod. "Tell me more."

"Really?"

"Yes. Did you forget that I enjoy trivia?"

Mattie grinned. "I like trivia too, so this could go on forever. Take me to a museum and I read everything, even stuff I'm not interested in. Well, I take that back. I'm interested in pretty much everything."

"Ah, Mattie, the long-suppressed nerd in me is swimming to the surface. I am the same way. I read anything that's put in front of me, even cereal boxes. And now romance novels," he added with a grin. "So please, carry on."

"All right, then, since you really want to know."

"I do," he said, and gave her a smile that made her forget what she was saying. "I thought I loved scotch, but you just might have converted me to bourbon. I love the color."

Ah, *color*, she thought as her brain came to her rescue. "Well, the long trip down the river aged the whiskey, giving it the mellow flavor and pretty amber color. Although bourbon doesn't have to be made in *Kentucky*, to be recognized as true bourbon it must be made in the United States. Back in the nineteen hundreds Congress declared bourbon as America's native spirit." She grinned. "Are you sorry you asked now?"

"Not in the least. In fact, you might get weary of answering my questions. Plus, I enjoy listening to your sweet Southern drawl."

Mattie felt a blush warm her cheeks.

"So, what makes bourbon so special if it *is* made in Kentucky?" Garret took a sip of his drink. "And this is special." He tilted his head and gazed at her with interest.

Mattie cleared her throat. "Well, the limestone water for one thing. Limestone naturally filters out nasty-tasting minerals, especially iron."

"Interesting. And then what?" He scooted a little bit closer, making it hard for Mattie to concentrate on the subject. The heady scent of bourbon mingled with his spicy aftershave, and her thinking power came to an abrupt halt.

"Um . . ." She searched her brain and then took another sip to hide her confusion. "Well . . . oh yeah, grains, mostly corn with rye, wheat, and malted barley, are ground into a mash and cooked with limestone water. After the fermentation process the liquid is actually a beer until it's condensed into the white dog."

"White dog, huh?"

"Yeah . . . it's the clear liquid right off the still." Was it her imagination or was he staring at her mouth? Wait. She was staring at *his* mouth. She shook her head, trying to focus.

"And then?" Her gaze locked with his, and time seemed to stand still.

"Oh . . . and . . . then . . ." *And then I kiss you.* "It's aged in, um, charred American white oak barrels, only one time and nothing else is allowed to be added."

Garret raised his glass and looked at the amber liquid. "Ah, I love the purity."

"I think it has to be aged for at least two years. Longer gives it a darker flavor." She arched one eyebrow. "And a bigger price tag."

"Thank you, Mattie. Now I will appreciate bourbon even more."

When he turned around to refresh the drinks, she got to admire his very nice butt. "Oh my gosh, you're wearing Wranglers!"

"I'm just a good ol' bourbon-drinking boy," he sang, making her laugh.

"Not hardly, but you're getting there."

"A work in progress, then." Garret turned around and pressed the glass into her hand. "You're not the only one taking notes. I had to wash them twice, though, before wearing them. They were stiff as a board."

Mattie laughed and then took a sip of her drink.

"So, what do you think of my shirt?" He pointed to the Western-cut short-sleeved shirt that showed off his biceps. The thought went through her head that the mother-of-pearl snaps would pop open easily. When she failed to answer he frowned. "Not good? I knew I should have waited for you to go shopping with me."

"Oh!" She clutched the glass harder. "No, I think light blue plaid is a good color for you. All you need is some cowboy boots and you'll be good to go."

He looked down at his loafers. "Then we should take a road trip to Nashville to go shopping. I need to head there soon to do some talent scouting anyway."

"Sounds like fun."

"Are you free in a couple of weeks on a Sunday perhaps?"

Mattie wondered if he meant sometime in the distant future or was simply making polite conversation.

"I know that your restaurant isn't open on Sundays," he explained, "but if you're busy or like to relax . . ."

"No, Sundays work for me."

"Then it's a date," Garret said, and although Mattie knew he meant the term *date* loosely, she still got a little thrill hearing him say it.

"Shall we?" he asked, and nodded toward the back deck.

"By all means," Mattie replied, and then turned toward the door. She took a sip of her bourbon but nearly choked when she felt Garret's palm at the small of her back. The touch, although featherlight, somehow felt intimate. As they walked Mattie noticed a slight increase in pressure, the movement of his thumb, and it was all she could do not to toss her fine bourbon over her shoulder, grab him by his Western-cut shirt, and drag him against her for an endless kiss.

When they reached the sliding door, Garret removed his hand, making Mattie long to grab his wrist and put his hand back where it belonged . . . touching her.

"Nice evening," Garret commented, and Mattie nodded. Her voice, if she found it, would surely come out breathless, so she took another sip of her drink and looked out over the cove. "You should take me on the bourbon trail sometime," he continued casually, and Mattie had to wonder if he was feeling any kind of reaction to her nearness at all. When she only nodded again he frowned. "Everything okay, love?"

Mattie managed a smile and a nod. She followed him over to the railing and they stood there looking out over the marina.

"So, has the ham bandit struck again lately?"

Mattie knew he was trying to strike up a conversation and she felt awkward not saying anything. After inhaling a breath she said, "No, Rusty is too busy being in love."

Garret turned and leaned one hip against the railing. "Come again?"

"There's a little beagle mix named Abigail that belongs to a couple who rents a slip for their ski boat. Rusty follows Abigail all the way to the dock and watches wistfully when they pull away. Ham has been the last thing on his mind. In fact, I felt so sorry for him that I offered him a chunk yesterday."

"Poor lovesick fellow. Does Abigail return the affection, I hope?"

"I don't think so or maybe she's just playing hard to get."

Garret gave her a sideways glance. "Is that going to be your tactic with Colby?" he asked in a light tone, but his gaze seemed to sharpen while he waited for her answer.

"Do you think that's the way to go?" Mattie asked, trying not to sound disappointed. "I mean, I guess he has to notice me first before I play hard to get, don't you think?"

Garret reached over and trailed a fingertip down her cheek. "What makes you think he's not noticing you?"

Mattie shrugged. She had noticed Colby looking her way since Garret had started with his lessons. "Maybe he is a little bit." She held her thumb and index finger an inch apart.

"Well, there's not a man on the face of the earth who wouldn't notice you in that dress, Mattie. You look lovely tonight." He took a sip of his drink and glanced away. "If I took you out on the town you would most definitely turn heads. Stop traffic, even." He looked down at his drink and said, "And Colby would all but swallow his tongue."

Mattie remained silent.

"Don't you believe me?"

"I suppose." Mattie dug deep for the courage and then after a heart-pounding moment she said, "Well, then, you need to step up the lessons and include, um, seduction."

"C-come ... again?" Garret stood up straight and looked at her as if she'd asked him to train her as an assassin.

"I want you to teach me how to be ... you know ... sexy."

"Mattie, you are sexy, love."

"Well, I guess I mean I want to know how to *act sexy*." She swallowed hard and then said, "How to ... entice. Flirt. I want to be irresistible." She inhaled a deep breath and looked up at him beseechingly. "I want to know how to *kiss*."

"Kiss? I'm sure you know how."

"No, I want to kiss like an expert. Can you help me, Garret?"

11

Sooner or Later

ARRET BLINKED AT MATTIE FOR A FEW SECONDS. OVER the years he'd gotten himself into some pretty damn stupid situations, but this particular scenario ranked up there with the best of them. But seriously? Giving a girl he was falling for lessons in how to entice another man was about as horrible as it got, and he'd had his share of horrible. After all the crappy things he'd selfishly done, perhaps this was karma rearing its ugly head. Ha, he should have known it would happen sooner or later.

"Garret?"

Garret had once wanted his own reality show, but his acting skills were suspect. Still, he tried to act pleased and put a smile on his face. "Oh . . . uh . . . sure. We could work that in, I guess. So, when would you like to begin?" Like never perhaps? Never worked really well for him.

"My daddy used to say that there's no time like the present."

"The . . . present. Like in . . . now." He pointed down at the deck.

"Yeah."

Garret jabbed his thumb toward the cabin. "Not, like, after dinner maybe?"

"No . . . now." She took a sip of her bourbon and waited. "Now is fine."

"Okay. Yeah, now is a good time as any to start. I'm just going to refresh my drink. You . . . you okay with yours?"

Mattie looked down at her glass. "Yes, I'm nursing mine. But you go ahead. I'll just think of a few questions."

"Would you like pen and paper?"

"Mmm . . . no, I think I have them all right up here." She tapped her temple. "I'm going to have a seat on the swing. I'll be waiting for you."

Garret opened his mouth, closed it, and then nodded. "Right. I'll be back in a jiffy." When he turned around he winced. Jiffy? Who said jiffy these days? God . . . Garret took his sweet time walking toward the kitchen, trying to remember when he'd been this damn flustered. After putting a few more cubes of ice in his glass, he added a generous pour of bourbon but then told himself to go easy or he was going to get smashed. Maybe he needed to get smashed to get through this lesson.

Garret sighed. He really did want to go to Nashville to shop for boots and to take Mattie on the bourbon trail or wherever the hell else she wanted to go. He wanted to take her to London and . . .

Oh God.

Meet his mum.

When had he ever wanted to take a girl to meet his mum? Addison, *maybe*. That was about it. And in truth, he'd adored sweet Addison and she taught him a life lesson about what love is really all about.

But he'd never felt tied up in knots like *this* around a girl *ever*. Jittery . . . sweaty palms. Ew, were his palms really sweaty? He wiped his palms on a dish towel, checked his breath, and sniffed under his arms. Dear God, he felt edgy . . . no, hyper . . . What the hell was this crazy-ass feeling?

Love?

Wow . . . *love*?

Holy shit.

Was it possible to fall for a girl this quickly? No. Yes. Apparently so.

Garret grabbed the edge of the sink and drew in gulps of air. There was no denying it. Well, he could deny it, but it would be a big fat lie. He was completely captivated by Mattie Mayfield. He knew it the moment he'd opened the door and tried to act completely casual when he wanted to press her up against the wall and kiss her senseless. But if he let on, if he told her or even gave *an inkling* of how he truly felt, the lessons would end and she would be out of his life.

Wait . . . maybe during these so-called lessons she might fall for him too? Garret scrubbed a hand down his face. Right . . .

Garret shook his head and had to find some humor in the situation. "Karma, you are such a bitch." He took a sip of the cold bourbon and a thought hit him that had him shaking his head. He actually wanted to call his father and ask what the hell he should do about this situation he'd gotten himself into. Dinner at Shane McCray's. And soon he was supposed to take Mattie to Sully's for her big reveal. And perhaps the following Sunday to Nashville. Maybe if he kept her occupied that damn Colby chap wouldn't stand a chance.

But a local bloke like Colby is what she wants, Garret told himself, and pushed away from the sink with a sad groan. He was what she'd dreamed of all her life, and he'd promised to help her achieve that goal. Maybe he should just carry on with the lessons and squash his feelings for her. Or at least do a bloody good job pretending. A true hero would want her to be happy even at his own expense.

Right?

"What makes you think you're a fucking hero, Ruleman?" he whispered.

Garret thought of Mattie's sweet goodness and of the

trust she was putting in him and knew he had to do the right thing for once in his damn jaded life.

Putting a smile on his face, he knew he had to go back out there onto the deck and do as she asked. It was just so ... weird.

But he could do it. He would show her how a touch, a look, a lingering glance could drive a man crazy. He added another splash of smooth Woodford Reserve to his glass and paused to put on some soft rock piping through the outdoor speakers to set the mood.

"Hey there."

Seemingly lost in thought, Mattie looked at him with surprise.

"Sorry I took so long, but I was checking on ... dinner."

"Oh, do we need to eat?"

"No, it's keeping warm." Garret sat down next to her, making the swing glide back and forth. He noticed her bare feet that barely reached the deck. "You're such a little pixie."

Mattie groaned. "I hate being short. It's so annoying not to be able to reach things, and jeans are always miles too long."

"It's cute. So are your feet."

"Oh, sorry, but I toss my shoes off whenever possible. And those were pinching my toes a little bit."

"No worries. Your little toes make me smile."

Mattie looked down at her toes and laughed softly. "I'd go barefoot all the time if possible. I guess that's not what a lady is supposed to do, though, right?"

"You don't have to exactly be a lady, Mattie, just soft and feminine. Bare feet are both of those things. In fact, if you want to put those cute feet up on my lap I'll give you a foot rub."

"But ... I thought I was doing the, you know ... seduction."

"I'm not trying to seduce you, merely soothe your aching feet."

"Oh . . ." She blushed in the waning sunlight and he thought it was the sweetest thing.

"You might just want to express that your feet are tired from working all day and if I were Colby I'd offer to give you a foot massage."

"You say massage funny."

"Part of my charm, right?"

"Definitely."

"Oh, so you find me charming, do you?"

She pulled a face and waved a hand in his direction. "Right . . . ," she scoffed, but her comment made Garret chuckle. Maybe she liked him more than she was letting on. Denial is always a big sign. Perhaps there was hope for him yet.

"You *told* me that you liked me, remember?"

"A moment of insanity," she said, but grinned. "Let's just begin the lessons."

Garret nodded. "Okay, so darkness is falling and I put on some mood music coming through the outdoor speakers. Now you should touch me . . . just barely. Brush up against my leg or graze my arm lightly. Make like it was an accident or that you don't even notice. But I'll notice . . . or, you know, I mean Colby will notice."

"Simple enough," she said, but failed to touch him.

"Go on. . . ."

Mattie nodded but didn't move. "I . . . I feel awkward. You know what's coming."

"Okay, it can be part of conversation. Say something and then touch my arm."

"I . . . it's . . . oh, I can't!"

"All right, then, let me demonstrate." Garret turned just slightly toward her and said, "So, I heard that Rusty is in love," and put a hand on her arm for just a second and then leaned in next to her ear. "Do you want to tell me about it?"

Mattie giggled but then sobered at his pointed look. "See, I suck at this. I will never get married and have babies, and my parents will never come home from Florida." She raised her hands skyward.

"I think you're overreacting just a tad."

She nodded. "I tend to do that. Sorry." She folded her hands in her lap and twiddled her thumbs.

"It's okay." He nodded but he thought it was funny and cute. "Right, now do it. Say something and then touch me."

"Did you say punch you?" she joked, and lightly punched his arm.

"Mattie . . . get with the program, love."

"I'm just nervous. I don't know what to say."

"Make conversation. Like the bourbon trivia earlier. That was fantastic."

"Right." She licked her bottom lip as if in thought and then tilted her head and said, "Did you know that the Cricket Creek Cougars are in first place in their league?" She reached over and briefly put her hand on his forearm.

"I didn't know that. We should go to a baseball game," he said, and then smiled. "Excellent work, Mattie. You also led into getting a date to go to a game."

"I did!"

"So we should go." When her eyes widened a bit he quickly added, "You know to, like, a practice date."

"Oh, right, sure. To practice. Good idea." Mattie nodded and then put her hand back on his arm and gave it a light squeeze. "So, do you like baseball?"

"I do, in fact." When Garret nodded she rubbed her hand over his hand.

"I do too." She leaned closer so her arm pressed against his side and then pulled back. "How was that? Too much? Not enough?"

"Good." Garret swallowed hard. "You're getting the hang of it."

"Sweet!" she said, and put her hand exactly where it was before and left it there longer. Her small hand felt cool against the heat of his skin. She didn't seem to realize it and that made her touch all the more enticing. "So there's hope for me yet?" Her eyes lit up and he wanted to kiss her so badly that it felt like a physical ache.

Garret put his drink down, turned toward her, and nodded slowly. "I do believe so."

"Yes!" She fist-pumped so hard that the swing lurched forward, putting her off balance. When she put her hand on his thigh for support, she left it there and then gave him a shy smile. "Is this where I should swoop in for the . . . kiss?"

"Yes." Garret's heart thudded. "By all means . . . swoop."

"So, do I, like—"

"Do this?" Garret pulled her to him and captured her mouth with his. Her lips were so soft, so warm. He felt her little start of surprise, but then she melted against him and put one hand on his chest. The swing rocked back and forth and he put his arm about her waist, pulling her closer.

Her light floral scent filled his head and he tasted the bourbon on her tongue. He'd anticipated this kiss for days, but the reality of having her in his arms was even better than he'd imagined. Garret deepened the kiss and longed to pull her onto his lap, but he wanted her to be in control and to take the lead. But when her tongue touched his Garret felt a jolt of desire that carried more punch than the fine Kentucky bourbon.

Mattie didn't need lessons. She was a good kisser in a natural, organic way. She explored his mouth and ran her tongue over his bottom lip back and forth, and to his utter surprise she suddenly swung her leg over his waist and straddled him, barely breaking the contact of their mouths. Her hands clutched his shoulders and she moved against him . . . just slightly but enough to drive Garret wild with wanting her. Her hands moved to his cheeks, caressing his stubble as if liking the abrasion against her palms. With a soft moan she slid her hands upward and threaded her fingers through his hair. She slanted her mouth, taking him deeper. He felt her breasts against his chest, making him long to tug the strapless dress down to her waist and feast his eyes on her breasts before taking her nipples into his mouth.

She pulled back and Garret thought the kiss was over, but she tugged at his shirt, popping the first few snaps open, and then put her hot mouth at the bottom of his neck. She kissed him lightly and he could feel the tip of her tongue tasting his skin.

A hot tingle traveled down his spine and he became completely aroused. Garret knew she could feel his erection pressing against her panties and he wanted to slip his hands beneath the skirt of her dress and cup her ass. The memory of the silky wisp of lace he'd pulled from his dryer filled his head and he nearly groaned. Her fingers tugged at his shirt, popping the snaps to reveal more of his chest, followed by the teasing heat of her mouth.

"You smell so good." Her shoulders moved up and down as if taking deep breaths.

"So do you." This little lesson was getting out of control, but Garret was powerless to stop it. He didn't want to stop it.

And then she suddenly pulled back.

"How . . . how was that?" Her voice was velvety soft but husky. Sexy as sin. Her dress had somehow slipped lower, revealing the soft swell of her breasts. Was she wearing a strapless bra or nothing at all?

"G-good." He cleared his throat, trying hard not to press his mouth to her bare shoulder. "Excellent, in fact."

"Really?"

"Truly."

"Then you must be a good teacher."

"Well . . ." Garret rubbed the pad of his thumb over her bottom lip. "I'll take credit, but in truth you have a natural sensuality about you that's completely enticing."

She played with the collar of his shirt. "Sitting on your lap wasn't too much?"

"Does it look like I'm complaining? I mean, I'm sure

that Colby wouldn't complain. The move was unexpected, which made it all the more exciting."

"I'm usually a doer first and a thinker later." She looked at his mouth and then her gaze locked with his. "Gets me into trouble sometimes."

"So, what do you want to *do* right now, Mattie Mayfield?"

"I want to kiss you again." She dipped her head and pressed her warm mouth against his and kissed him with a light, teasing, barely there pressure that made Garret long to pull her closer. The swing tilted back and forth in a gentle simulation of the act of making love, making Garret want to scoop her up and take her into his bedroom and make sweet, sweet love to her. She deepened the kiss just a bit and when she lightly nipped at his bottom lip, Garret couldn't suppress a groan. When she slid her hands into the open part of his shirt and explored his chest, Garret nearly gave in to the desire to tug her dress down and do some exploring of his own. But he refrained.

Just barely.

Did she know she was driving him wild? She was a heady combination of sex and innocence and he'd never wanted a woman in his arms . . . in his bed . . . more than he wanted Mattie Mayfield.

Just when the remaining shreds of Garret's restraint were about to take a flying leap over the back deck, Mattie pulled back. She tilted her head slightly and looked at him as if wondering what to say. "Thank you, Garret."

Okay, *that* was unexpected as well. He put his hands around her waist and waited for her to explain. "For what?" he finally asked softly.

"For giving me the confidence boost that I sorely needed." She placed her palms on his cheeks. "For making me feel pretty . . . and desirable." When her eyes misted over, Garret felt a tug of emotion unlike anything he'd ever experienced before.

"You are pretty and desirable."

"Well, I guess I've never really *felt* that way."

"Well, feel it and believe it."

"I'm trying." She smiled and then after planting a light kiss on his lips scooted off his lap. She stood up and walked over to look out over the marina.

Garret followed her over to the railing of the deck and stood beside her while she gazed out over the water. After a moment he reached over and took her hand. She slanted a glance at him but didn't pull away.

They stood there for a few minutes, holding hands, while the evening breeze cooled the heat of the day. In that small space of time Garret knew he wanted to help Mattie in any way he could and to make her happy. For the first time in his life he felt the need to put someone other than himself first. They had become friends and although he wanted her to become more, he valued her happiness so much that if she wanted Colby he wouldn't stand in the way.

After a few more minutes of which Garret was dying to know her thoughts, she squeezed his hand. "I guess we should eat dinner."

Garret nodded, but before they turned to head inside he leaned over and gave her a soft kiss on the cheek. "Thank you too, Mattie."

It was her turn to look surprised. "For what?"

"I've always been a selfish piece of work looking out for number one. I had people in my life who were there simply for what they could provide, nothing more."

She put a hand on his arm. "Garret, I think you're being way too hard on yourself."

"I wish I could say that you're right." Garret chuckled without much humor. "I should have had one of those foam fingers telling everybody I was number one."

Mattie looked at him with those beautiful, sincere eyes of hers. "Not to make an excuse for you, but I think that selfish or self-destructive behavior can be the result of other things going on in a person's life. My brother Mason was on that path for a while. He had his sights set on being a top-notch pro fisherman on the FLW Tour and he resented having to put his career on hold to come back and work the marina. My father's health was failing and Mason really had no choice, but he took his anger out on anyone crossing his path. Thank goodness he's snapped out of it. But it took losing a girl he loved and even some of his closest friends before realizing he needed to get his act together and mend some fences."

"It had to be hard to give up on his dream," Garret said, and thought about how he'd wanted to follow in his father's footsteps but was never taken seriously.

"Oh, no doubt. But we all wanted to save this marina. It's more than our livelihood. It's our home."

"Do you have dreams, Mattie?"

"My mother thinks I need to set my sights higher, but I love what I do and not everybody can say that," she answered, but there was something in her tone that suggested that she might want more out of life. She shrugged and then added, "I mean, I guess I would like to travel and see some of the places I've read about, but sometimes it's kinda hard for a small-town girl to take that big a step." When he nodded she said, "Garret, maybe some of the issues you had in the past were that the people surrounding you didn't value you as much as they should have. Your life might appear charmed to some, but I suspect it was difficult."

"I guess I always felt as if I had something to prove."

"When you feel good about yourself, then you don't have to prove anything, you know?"

Oh, Garret did know. But he'd never thought about it in Mattie's terms, only beat himself up about things he'd done. He'd questioned his talent when critics were harsh. "I once thought I wanted to be a superstar like my father. A legend. But I've found that I really like scouting for new talent and being a studio musician at My Way Records." He chuckled. "I told you I was a closet nerd. I spent most of my adult life chasing after a dream I really didn't want. Now I just want to be valued for what I can do as Garret Ruleman and not try to outdo my father."

"Good plan."

"You're right, Mattie. I've got nothing to prove." He looked up at the sky and shook his head before turning back to her with a grin. "Wow, it felt really awesome saying that."

"High five!" Mattie raised her hand and smacked his palm so hard that he shook it while laughing.

"Are you ready for some dinner?"

"Yes! I am famished."

"Well, then let's go inside and polish off the shepherd's pie." He wanted to pull her into his arms for another kiss but offered his arm and she accepted it with a smile.

"You're right. We do make a good team, don't we?" Mattie asked lightly, but her gaze seemed to search his face for some sort of answer, but the problem was that he didn't know the question.

"That we do," he agreed, and her smile faltered just a bit.

"Colby will take notice of you, Mattie. And if he doesn't he's a complete fool. Actually he's a fool for not doing so already."

She nodded, but there was a bit of a frown on her face. He wanted to bring her smile back and hear her laughter.

And of course he wanted her in his arms.

"Will he be at Sully's Tavern on Saturday night, do you think?"

"Most likely. It's where people go on Saturday night here in Cricket Creek. And I'll be your wingman, Garret. Girls are going to be tripping over their feet to get close to you."

Garret forced a smile. "I can't wait."

"Yeah, it will be such fun," she said brightly, but then quickly looked away. "I think I'm ready for that wine," she said when they stepped inside the cabin.

"Me too," he said with a smile, but realized that something had shifted. Perhaps the kiss had shaken her up too? Or maybe she felt guilty that she wasn't kissing

Colby. Garret wanted to know but didn't have the courage to ask either of those questions. One thing he did know for sure was that he cared about Mattie and the very last thing he wanted to do was screw up her life. So he would pull back and play this cruel little game of pretend and hope that it wasn't going to drive him stark raving mad.

12

Sunshine on My Shoulder

*L*AURA LEE SLID THE PERFECTLY CRIMPED HOMEMADE potpie into the fridge, ready to pop into the oven later that evening after Shane arrived home. She cleaned up the mess she'd made of the state-of-the-art kitchen and then blew out a sigh. The house gleamed with spotless, polished beauty. A dust bunny wouldn't have the nerve to show itself. The pantry was bursting with groceries, and Shane's clothes were all laundered and neatly folded on his bed.

Tapping her cheek, Laura Lee tried to think of something else she could do to earn the large sum of money Shane paid her every Friday. She could head up into town to Grammar's Bakery for the butter cookies that he had taken a liking to. Or she could drive over to the Beer Barn for some of the Kentucky bourbon barrel ale she'd introduced him to last week. Although he'd jokingly said that he was packing on weight from her cooking and never-ending treats she showered upon him, Laura Lee thought the man looked damn good. When he'd come in from his run this morning shirtless and sporting a fine sheen of sweat, she acted casual but just about swallowed her tongue.

Although Laura Lee knew Shane was off-limits, she did appreciate that he'd awakened the longing for her to be in a man's arms once more. After Jack cheated on her she'd made a promise to never give a man the power to hurt her or to take advantage of her *ever* again. But when she'd felt the intense urge to run her hands over Shane's sculpted chest, she decided that she shouldn't give Jack the power to ruin what was left of her life. Maybe her ship was still in the harbor after all.

Laura Lee looked around the house, hoping to see a speck of dust or a fingerprint somewhere, but she knew that the entire house was simply spotless. And Shane was a very neat man, leaving her even less to do than if he were a slob.

Finally she decided to go out onto the back deck in the sunshine and give Mattie a call to hear how her dinner with Garret had gone last night. After pouring a glass of sweet tea she opened the sliding door and settled onto a cushy lounge chair. She picked up her cell phone but paused to take in the view. The glistening water in the pool did look inviting and she had a swimsuit in her van. But she still felt a little bit guilty lounging around as if she owned the place.

"Hmm . . ." Laura Lee decided that she could hose down the deck and then maybe head up to purchase some pretty hanging baskets from Gabby, the cute little owner of Flower Power up the road in Wedding Row. While there she could stop in River Row Pizza and Pasta and see what delectable dessert Reese had made for the day. Laura Lee smiled. And now that she was making such good money, she just might pop into Designs by Diamante, the lovely jewelry store where she'd only been able to window-shop before now.

Laura Lee tilted the glass up to her lips, making the ice cubes clink together. Because Shane liked sweet tea she made sure there was always a fresh pitcher in the fridge. While she considered thinking of his favorite things as her job, Laura Lee found caring for him rewarding in ways she didn't fully understand.

"Oh boy." Knowing that she needed to change her train of thought, she called Mattie, who thankfully answered right away.

"What's up, Laura Lee?"

"I called to ask you that question, sweet pea. Give me the lowdown on your dinner with Garret last night," she requested, but was met with a long pause. "Do I have to come over there and pry it out of you with a can opener?"

"Oh, Laura Lee . . . ," Mattie murmured in such a sad tone that Laura Lee sat up straight and put her glass of tea on the table beside her chair.

"Sweetie, talk to me."

"Well, I asked Garret to teach me how to be all sexy and everything."

"And?"

"I kissed him, and yes, before you ask, there were fireworks. . . ."

"Really?"

"Yeah, and not just little firecrackers, but, like, Fourth of July lighting-up-the-sky fireworks."

"Oh wow."

"I know! It's all I've been thinking about all day long. I couldn't sleep last night, which is part of my problem. I'm walking around in a fog. I burned a batch of biscuits this mornin' and forgot to start the coffee!"

"Oh, Mattie."

"Can you believe it? Rusty wouldn't even eat one. I had to toss the entire batch in the trash."

"So now what? I mean, you're supposed to do this thing with Garret to attract Colby at Sully's. How are you going to pull that off without giving yourself away?"

"Um, yeah. I dunno! I offered to be his wingman too! And my goal is supposed to be to capture Colby's attention with the hope of getting a dance and maybe a date. God . . ."

"Are you still going to do that?"

"I don't think I have any choice."

"Mattie, maybe you need to see how it would feel to kiss Colby. You've waited so long and I think that if you don't you'll never know."

"That's one of the reasons I couldn't sleep. I don't want to screw things up by not going after what I always wanted for something I can never have."

"There's no reason you can't have Garret if he's the one for you, Mattie."

"Really? Well, for starters I don't know that I'm sophisticated enough for a guy like him. I mean, I know he *likes* me, probably because I make him laugh. And I do value his friendship. But I don't think I should hope for anything more than what we have now."

"A romantic relationship that has the foundation of friendship is the strongest kind, sweet pea."

"But I keep thinking that he might get bored with the likes of me eventually and just up and leave. A city boy like him just might get tired of living in the slow lane in Cricket Creek too."

"Well, I know you love it here, Mattie, but there's nothing that says you have to stay in Cricket Creek all your life."

"I can't begin to even imagine living anywhere else. This marina is dear to me and . . ." She trailed off as if searching for more reasons.

"And what? All I'm saying is keep an open mind. I can tell you from firsthand knowledge that life might not turn out anywhere near how you envisioned or expected. I mean, here I am, sitting on Shane McCray's back deck."

Mattie laughed. "I know. That is pretty sweet."

"It is. I feel so guilty. Everything I do feels like fun and not work."

"Soak it up. You sure do deserve a break."

"Well, I should try to find something to do before Shane gets back from his meeting with Maria Sully and Rick Ruleman. Oh, I think Garret is also going to play a part in the development of Sully's South. Shane told me that Garret is an amazing musician and hasn't gotten the credit he deserves. It must have been hard being in the shadow of his famous father."

"We actually talked about that. Garret really seems to be coming into his own."

"Sometimes it takes a while to find ourselves," Laura Lee said. "I'm not sure I have yet," she added with a laugh.

"Well, then go do it," Mattie said, and it was good to hear the cheer back in her voice. "And I'll see you at Sully's tonight, right?"

"I think so."

"Oh, come on. You need to see me put my skills in action."

"All right. I'll be there."

"That's more like it. See you soon."

After ending the call Laura Lee took another sip of her tea and looked up at the light blue sky dotted with fluffy clouds. She thought about hauling the hose up to clean the already clean deck and then decided she should take Shane up on his offer and use the pool. He wouldn't be home for hours and in truth there wasn't anything pressing to be done. When was the last time she'd lounged by a swimming pool and soaked up some sunshine?

Before she could lose her nerve she scrambled to her feet and hurried through the house and out the front door to her van. Sliding open the door, she found her beach bag with her swimsuit, floppy hat, lotion, and a Nora Roberts romance she'd been reading. Still feeling as if she was somehow playing hooky, she went into the bathroom and slipped into the navy blue tankini and then paused to look in the mirror. She checked out her butt and then adjusted the straps of the top, thinking that since starting her cleaning business she'd become pretty doggone fit from all the physical work. Using the weights in Shane's workout room had helped to define her arms a bit too.

Laura Lee pulled her hair up into a bun and then slathered sunscreen all over but then frowned when she realized there was no way to get her entire back. After doing the best she could, she picked up her bag and then decided to refresh her sweet tea before heading out to the pool.

Whistling lightly, she headed into the kitchen and then dropped her beach bag and let out a horror-movie-worthy scream.

13

Slow and Easy

SHANE HEARD A SCREAM JUST AS HE STARTED THROUGH his front door. "Laura Lee?" His heart pumped double time and he ran through the entrance in search of her. He knew there wasn't much crime in Cricket Creek, but if someone was attempting to hurt her, there would be hell to pay. "Laure Lee!" he shouted this time when he failed to see her.

"Over here," she whispered, and he spotted her flattened against the wall with wide eyes and a look of stark fear on her pretty face. He also noticed that she looked damn hot in a bathing suit. When he started to come closer she shook her head. "No! Don't move."

"What's wrong?" Shane asked, truly worried.

When Laura Lee nodded her head forward just slightly, Shane followed her fear-filled gaze.

A black snake was curled up on the white tile floor directly in front of the fridge. And it was small. "That little bitty thing?"

She nodded. "It's a snake," she whispered, and he thought it amusing that she felt the need to tell him that.

"It's harmless," Shane said in a reassuring tone, but

when he moved the snake raised its head and its tiny forked tongue appeared. Laura Lee whimpered and pressed her back harder against the wall. Seeing that she was really frightened, Shane felt his humor vanish and he hurried over to her side. "Hey, it's okay." He took her hand and squeezed. It was ice-cold.

"I'm so sorry. I am deathly afraid of snakes."

"There's nothing to be sorry about. A lot of people are scared of snakes. I once had a roadie who was big enough to wrestle a bear but would cower in the corner if he spotted a spider."

"I can relate. I think I'd rather face a bear too."

Shane squeezed her hand again and then without thinking brought her fingers to his mouth and kissed her on the knuckles. He inched closer to her and could feel the slight tremble in her body. "I'll go over there and take the snake outside."

"No!" She held his hand in a viselike grip. "It might bite you!" she still whispered.

"Well, we can't stay up against the wall forever."

"I was thinking that I might just have to do that."

Shane chuckled. "Listen, I'm a country boy. I've picked up many a snake in my day. I'll be fine."

"Absolutely not." Laura Lee shook her head firmly. "I won't let you," she said, but then gave him a sideways glance and the hint of a grin. "Oh, I forgot you're the boss, not me."

Shane wanted to tell her that she could order him around all she wanted and he wouldn't mind one little bit. He also felt it very sweet that she was so concerned for his welfare. "How about if I get a broom and just sweep it out the front door?"

"Do you think that would work?"

"Yes."

"Okay, the broom is in the laundry room off the garage. I'd go and get it, but as silly as it seems I am completely frozen with fear of that tiny little guy."

"No worries. I'll get the broom. But, Laura Lee?"

"Yes," she whispered.

"You have to let go of my hand."

"Right," Laura Lee said, but the snake chose that moment to slither across the tiles to hover in the corner beneath the cabinets and she refused to release his hand. "I almost peed in my pants."

He tried hard not to laugh. "Do you want to come with me?"

Laura Lee glanced at Shane again. "No! What if he goes somewhere and hides? I'll have to keep an eye on him."

"He's more afraid of you than you are of him."

"That's not even remotely possible."

Shane chuckled. "I'm sorry. I shouldn't laugh."

"Yes, you should. I'm a grown woman. This is totally ridiculous."

"I think it's cute," he admitted.

"You're just being nice," she whispered, and he thought it funny that he was talking in a normal tone but she still felt the need to keep her voice down as if the snake would hear. "This is my entire fault! I'm sure he came in through the back door when I went out there to call Mattie. I should have been more careful."

"I'm not sure he could have gotten up onto the back deck, Laura Lee, but who cares if he did? You've got nothing to be sorry for," he insisted in a gentle tone. He had to wonder if her ex-husband always placed blame upon her and if that had sucked the life out of someone so sweet and caring. He didn't even know the guy and he wanted to punch him in the face. "Now stay here and I'll be right back. I'll take care of the snake for you."

She nodded and gave him a small smile before letting go of his hand.

Shane found the broom and dustpan and hurried back. He had to smile at her intake of breath when he walked across the kitchen and swept the scared little snake onto the dustpan.

"Oh, don't hurt him!"

"I won't." The snake wiggled a bit, making Laura Lee shriek, but to her surprise she followed Shane out the front door.

"Make sure you get him into the woods so he can find his family."

Shane finally had to laugh. "You're very concerned for something you detest."

"I don't detest him. I'm just afraid of him." She walked a safe distance from the dustpan. "I would never hurt him."

"I don't think you could hurt anything or anyone."

"Unless they were trying to hurt someone I loved. Then I'd have to show off my karate skills."

"You know karate?"

"No, so it would be kind of a problem."

Shane laughed so hard he almost dropped the snake. He gently put the snake at the edge of the wooded area to the side of the garage. The little guy slithered away as if happy to be back in his element. "All done," Shane said when he reached her side. "You can breathe a sigh of relief."

"Oh ..." Laura Lee put her hands over her face. "I feel so silly."

Shane put the broom and dustpan in one hand and then reached out and pried her fingers from her face. "Well, don't, because you shouldn't. Please."

"Okay." She looked at him and when he took her hand she didn't protest. "Thank you for being so nice to me," she said, and then looked away as if embarrassed that she said such a thing to him.

Shane paused when they reached the front porch. "Why wouldn't I be?" When she only shrugged he said, "Did you think I was going to be an arrogant jerk because of my success?"

"No. . . . Oh, maybe, I guess. I didn't know what to expect."

"Listen, because I was blessed with a good voice and get paid piles of money doesn't make me any better than anyone else. I'm just a man, Laura Lee. Lucky that I got a break. Not everyone who has talent gets discovered. That's one of the reasons I'm looking forward to working with those trying to break into this crazy business."

"I'm sure that you worked hard for your so-called lucky break."

"I paid my dues and then some." Shane looked at her and she reminded him of the sweetness that Patsy possessed. "And maybe I'm not as lucky as you might think."

Laura Lee's eyes widened in surprise. "Do you want to talk about it?"

Shane had never talked about his divorce on a deeply personal level with anyone, not even his parents. But for some reason he wanted to open up to Laura Lee, so he found himself nodding. "I do, in fact. I'll change into swim trunks and grab a pitcher of sweet tea."

"I'll do that part."

"No way. I'm giving you the day off. We're just two friends talking. Okay?"

"Okay," she said, and although she smiled Shane saw the play of emotion cross her face. He knew she must be thinking that she shouldn't get this close to him or perhaps risk her job, and he hated it. There were so many times when he wanted to be friends with employees, but they never completely let their guard down with him in the way he'd see them interact with others, especially on the road. He'd often walk up to a group of people laughing and the laughter would immediately die down when he approached. Fame came with a huge price tag. So he was not only her employer but a famous one to boot. A double whammy to overcome.

"I'll meet you out by the pool."

"I'll just grab my beach bag."

"You have plenty of sunscreen?"

"Are you kidding?" She smiled. "I'm a ginger. We always lather up with powerful sunscreen. And even then I'll have freckles pop out all over the place." She wrinkled up her nose.

"I like them."

"My freckles?"

"Yes, your freckles." She seemed so surprised that he reached over and pulled her in for a quick hug. "There's a lot to like about you, Laura Lee," he said when he really wanted to say that there was a lot that *he* liked about her. But he had to be careful. He didn't want Laura Lee to think that he expected anything from her or would take advantage of her in any way, so he started walking toward the house. "I'll meet you poolside," he said, and had to grin when she took a rather fearful look around. "I don't think the little snake has any brothers or sisters lurking about."

"I was more interested in a mother or father slithering about. What if there is a whole family?"

Shane laughed. "I think you're fine."

"See, the operative word there is *think*."

"Well, then I'll keep a look out for mama and papa snake. In the meantime go out to the pool and relax. I'll bring some snacks too," he said, and when she looked as though she was going to protest he shook his head. "You're off the clock, Laura Lee. Let me wait on you for a change," he insisted, but when she appeared so uncomfortable he shooed her with his fingers.

"But—"

"Don't even bother to protest. You already go way over and above the call of duty. I don't think I've ever been this pampered in my entire life."

"Are you serious?"

Shane thought about that for a moment, but it was true and he suddenly knew why. "The difference between you and anyone else is that you do things for me because you're being thoughtful. Most others do things for me with an agenda or because it was part of their job description. You might be doing your job, but you also care."

"Guilty as charged." Laura Lee smiled as if she knew it was pointless to deny that she cared about him. And then as if shy about her admission, she turned around and walked toward the back deck. He watched her go, admiring the sway of her hips and long, slender legs. For a split second he wondered what it would feel like to have those legs wrapped around him and he pushed that thought from his mind. But he shook his head, thinking that she must have been an amazing wife. Who in his right mind would have mistreated a woman like her and put such sadness in her pretty eyes? The thought brought out a masculine protective instinct that had him clenching his jaw. In that moment Shane vowed to make Laura Lee laugh and to chase the sadness as far away as possible.

As promised, Shane brought a tray of veggies and dip, fruit, crackers and cheese, and the pitcher of tea out to the pool deck. He paused, though, when he looked at Laura Lee stretched out on a lounge chair. One endless leg was bent, giving him a side view of her elegant body. She wore a wide floppy hat that looked both cute and classy, and he thought that she looked as if she were in an ad in a glossy magazine for something cool and delicious. He actually longed to put the food down and snap a picture with his phone.

"Gorgeous day," Shane said when he walked past her to put the tray on an umbrella table.

Laura Lee looked up from her book at him and smiled. "Oh, I was thinking the same thing. The sky is so blue and the slight breeze feels refreshing."

"It's a perfect day to be outside."

"Oh, would you look at the nice display of snacks?"

"You keep us well stocked." Shane walked her way and put the tray within reaching distance.

"Thank you." She plucked a green grape from a bunch and popped it into her mouth. He liked her deep rose shade of lipstick with just a hint of shine. She had full, lush lips and Shane had the urge to feed the grapes to her, one by one.

"I even put ice in a tray beneath the food to keep it from spoiling," he said, trying to derail his train of thought.

"I'm impressed!"

"Comes from many years of consuming catered food. I often had to eat at odd hours, usually late at night after shows. Your home-cooked meals are so much better." Shane inclined his head and wished he could see her eyes behind the bold black sunglasses she wore. He'd bet she'd never guess how elegant she really did look lounging gracefully on the chair. While as a celebrity Shane had become used to women staring him down, he wondered if Laura Lee found him to be attractive.

Sexy?

Shane sure did wish that she wasn't his employee so he could flirt with her and see where it took them. But he knew that at least for now he'd have to settle for friendship. "Would you like me to bring you a plate of food?"

"No, thank you. You don't have to do that. I'll come over there and sit in the shade and have a snack," she replied, and then stood up.

Shane joined her and they sat in companionable silence for a few moments.

"If you've changed your mind and don't want to talk about personal things, it's perfectly okay. I do want you to know that anything you do tell me goes nowhere."

"I believe you, Laura Lee," Shane said, and in truth it had been difficult for him to confide in many people for that very reason. "I've learned over the years to be a good judge of character and I feel as if I can trust you completely." He brought over two plates of food and put them on the small table between the lounge chairs.

She swiped a carrot stick through the ranch dip. "Thank you."

Suddenly feeling more comfortable than he'd felt in a long time, Shane stretched his legs out and crossed his ankles. "For the food?"

She nodded. "And for placing trust in me. So, do you still want to talk about something?"

"Yes, I do. I want to tell you a little bit about me if you're interested."

"Of course I am."

"Okay, then." After taking a swig of tea, he looked out over the pool and said, "I married my high school sweetheart. A girl I completely adored."

"What happened?"

"It was simple. Patsy couldn't handle me being on the road all the time. And I couldn't blame her. We'd known each other since we were kids. Do you know the George Strait song 'Check Yes or No'?"

"Of course."

"We were like that," Shane said, and then chuckled. "I really did send her a note that said something like that."

"Oh, Shane, that's so sweet."

Shane looked her way. "We were friends and then sweethearts and we were inseparable."

"Until you went out on the road and were separated all the time."

Shane nodded. "It didn't help that after I won *You Can Be a Star*, my career took off like a rocket. Funny thing is that I entered at Patsy's insistence."

"She must have believed in your talent."

"Yes, she did. But neither of us was prepared for what was to come and come so quickly. To her credit she tried, but in the end she just couldn't take it. Patsy wanted the white picket fence with two kids and a dog, and I was no longer that person."

"I'm so sorry." Laura Lee took a drink of her tea and then asked, "Do you wish you'd given up your career so you could have stayed together?"

"Oh, at times . . . sure." Shane looked down at his glass and then over at her. "When I was lonely on the road, not even remembering what city I was in that night. And lots of folks, even those who claimed to be my friends, thought that I dumped my hometown girl because I wanted someone with more flash. Or that I'd been cheating on her. Just because I became successful didn't mean that I changed my values. I let stuff slide off my back, but rumors like that really hurt."

"Did Patsy really think you would step out on her while you were gone so much?"

"I guess it must have crossed her mind. In the end it just wasn't the life for her. By the time we knew our marriage was on the rocks, I'd become huge . . . a franchise. So many people were depending on me to put food on the table, and I couldn't turn my back on those who'd worked so hard to make me the success I had become." He inhaled a deep breath. "And there was the music. Not only is it in my blood, but I know what music means to people."

"Oh, I hear ya." Laura Lee nodded. "Music got me through some tough times, for sure. A certain song can take you back to memories that just soothe the soul." She angled her head and looked at him. "You know we all envy celebrities and as you can imagine I've struggled financially, so the envy goes beyond fame to the money too. I guess just about everyone at least dreams about what it would feel like to have adoring fans."

"I get that. And I'm not going to be one to complain about a life that has been blessed in so many ways. And that's why I want to give back."

"But no one knows that it cost you your marriage?" Shane shook his head slowly. "Nope."

"Is that why you never remarried?"

"Partly. I didn't want to face pain like that ever again. I poured a lot of the heartache into my songs."

"And you didn't want to put someone else through the pain either."

"Yeah, I mean, there are those out there who can find a way to combine a demanding career like mine and be happily married, I suppose. It just isn't easy."

"I guess not." She seemed to digest this. "Well, so, now that you're retired do you think you'll . . . you know . . ."

"Look for love?" Shane gave her a steady gaze. "I guess I was so caught up in the daily demands of my career that I let the rest of my life sort of just slide by. Now here I am, fifty-eight years old, wishing I had someone special to spend time with." Someone like her.

"I'm sure you'd have ladies champing at the bit if they knew. We could have a ball in Cricket Creek and find you a wife. You are considered country royalty," she said with a laugh. "If the boot fits?"

Shane knew she was joking, but he wanted to tell her she could be his Cinderella. "What about you, Laura Lee? Think your Prince Charming is out there?"

"I don't know. I've been too busy getting my life back in order to think about dating." Laura Lee took her floppy hat off and put it in her lap. "Mattie has been after me about getting out there, but I told her that my ship has sailed."

"Oh, come on, you don't really believe that, do you?"

"I suppose so. Or at least I did." Laura Lee shrugged. "But Mattie girl is hell-bent on proving me wrong. In fact, I'm going out to Sully's tonight."

Shane felt a hollow pang hit him in the gut at the thought of her dancing with someone. "You know, I haven't been out on the town in ages. Would you save me a dance if I end up at Sully's?"

"I thought you wanted to keep on the down low for a while."

Shane tried to act casual. "Eh, an evening at the local honky-tonk shouldn't cause too much commotion. I'll hover in the background."

She laughed. "I can't imagine you in the background anywhere, but if you go to Sully's make sure you say hi, okay? And I owe you a drink for saving me from the deadly snake from hell."

"I do believe I'll take you up on that," Shane said, feeling much better about the situation. "Would you like to jump in the pool for a swim?"

"I am getting hot," she answered, and glanced at the water. "But you promise to keep your clothes on, right?"

Shane put the heel of his hand to his forehead. "I will never forget the look on your face. It was almost worth the embarrassment I suffered."

"I'll never let you live that down. And if truth be told

I think I was much more embarrassed than you. I wanted to tell so many people, but your skinny-dipping escapade is safe with me."

"Thank you," he said, but thought that skinny-dipping might be a whole lot of fun. "Are you ready to get in?"

"Yes." She licked her bottom lip and then said, "But I have to ask you to do something for me."

"Name it," he said, and meant it.

"Well, I need some lotion on my back. I got everywhere else, but I couldn't reach below my neck."

"Sure," Shane said casually, but the thought of rubbing his hands on her bare skin made a bead of sweat pop out on his temple.

"Thanks," she said, and then topped a cracker with a slice of cheddar cheese. After she polished it off she walked over to her beach bag and pulled out a bottle of lotion.

Shane walked over to where she sat on the end of a lounge chair. Her swimsuit was modest by today's standards but revealed a good portion of her back. The curve of her neck was so alluring that he longed to place a kiss on her bare shoulder. "I'll get you all lathered up." He squirted a generous amount on his palms and then started to slather the white cream onto her bare skin. He tried to be casual and used a light touch, but he still felt a jolt of desire that had him wanting to drag her up against his chest. To his complete horror he suddenly had an . . . God . . . erection that was impossible to hide in his swim trunks.

"All done," Shane said briskly, thinking he needed to take a running dive into the pool before she noticed the tent in his trunks.

"Thanks. Would you like me to do you?"

Would I ever!

Shane nearly groaned. "I . . ." He was about to protest, knowing that having her hands caressing his back would contribute to his, well, growing problem.

"You know I'm going to insist," Laura Lee said, and

before he could say another word she got up and took the plastic bottle from him. As he predicted, having her hands rubbing the warm lotion over his back had him closing his eyes and trying to think about anything other than how amazing it felt to have her touching him. He started reciting the alphabet backward, but nothing could counteract what she was doing to him. And it seemed to be taking days for her to finish. "There, all done," she said brightly, and when she stood up to put the bottle back in her bag, Shane jumped up and dove into the deep end of the pool.

The silky water felt delicious against the heat of his skin and he swam underwater for a moment and hoped to cool his ardor. When he surfaced he watched Laura Lee tentatively entering at the shallow end. The sunshine glinted off her auburn hair and she looked so pretty that he couldn't help staring. "It's colder than what I thought," she said as she waded in up to her knees.

"Dunk beneath the water and get it over with." Shane wanted so badly to swim over there and pull her into his arms. He wanted her to wrap those long legs around him so he could carry her around, letting the water lap around them.

And he wanted to kiss her.

Instead he swam over to her and said, "Come on in, the water is refreshing once you get used to it."

"I'm one of those wimps who has to enter inch by inch," she said innocently, but Shane was again thankful that the bottom half of his body was hidden from view.

"Oh, really?" His answer was to give her a playful splash, to which she squealed in protest. She flicked water at him with her foot, laughing when she doused him square in the face but almost lost her balance. "You wanna play, huh? I think someone needs to be dunked."

"Don't you dare!"

Shane wouldn't do that to her in a million years, but he loved the sound of her laughter and vowed to keep making her laugh and smile until she let her guard down. "I won't. I promise," he said, but the look she gave him said she wasn't sure. "I can turn the heat on in the pool if you like."

"Oh no, you don't have to do that!"

"No, I will," he insisted. He wanted her to be comfortable and enjoy the day.

"No . . . oh, here I go!" Her eyes widened and she held her nose and then dipped beneath the water. She immediately popped back up and laughed. "It's all good now."

"That was so brave!"

"I know! I think I'll do it again," she said, but before going under she gave him a big splash.

Shane had to laugh. He thoroughly enjoyed her company. Laura Lee made something as simple as taking an afternoon swim so much more fun. He knew without a doubt that he wanted this sweet woman to become much more than his employee. But he needed to gain her trust first. After her painful past he knew he should hold back until the time felt right.

The problem was that every minute he spent with her felt right.

Going slow wasn't going to be easy. But Shane had waited a long time to let someone special back into his life. He looked at Laura Lee's smiling face and knew that she was well worth the wait.

14

I Only Want to Be with You

WHEN GARRET REACHED MATTIE'S CABIN HE LOOKED at the digital clock on his dash and noticed that he was nearly fifteen minutes early. With a short chuckle he shook his head, thinking that for a guy who usually arrived late, this just might be a first. How did that even happen?

Garret knew how. He was eager to see Mattie and he'd come from a recording session at My Way Records to see her straightaway. He'd hoped to have a chat about Mattie with his father, but his dad had been in a conference with Jeff Greenfield about Jeff's upcoming tour, so he didn't get the chance.

Garret stepped out of his car and looked over at Mattie's cabin. A cheerful wreath entwined with sunflowers hung from the front door. Plump hanging baskets overflowing with colorful flowers twirled slightly in the breeze, and a whimsical wind chime made of forks and spoons played a tinkling song of summer. Two lazy-looking wooden rocking chairs sat to the right on a long porch made for relaxing. He could picture himself strumming his guitar there late in the evening while fireflies flickered all around.

Looking past the cabin, Garret could see the lake appearing still and serene in the background. Cattails poked their heads skyward and swayed slightly to the left when the gentle breeze kicked it up a notch. He noticed that the dock behind Mattie's cabin had a boat roped to it and Garret wondered if it belonged to her. He envisioned himself rowing her about on a warm summer evening such as this.

On the opposite shore he could see the collection of smaller log cabins that added to the picture-perfect scenery. To the right a field of wildflowers abundant with a riot of color seemed to go on forever before butting up to the woods leading back to the marina.

Bees buzzed, frogs croaked, and crickets chirped. As if on cue a big yellow butterfly landed on one of the terra-cotta potted plants Mattie had perched on each step up to the porch landing. Garret felt as if he had fallen into a Disney movie and wouldn't have been surprised if the Seven Dwarfs suddenly marched past him.

Amid all the serenity Garret was surprised when he was hit with a sudden flash of nervousness in his gut. Could someone like him ever fit into a laid-back lifestyle like this? Oddly when he thought about his past he almost felt . . . undeserving.

Garret looked down at his Wrangler jeans he'd worn for Mattie. Without the stiffness they felt better now and he had to grin when he thought of the commercial with the football player advertising the extra room in the crotch area. The short-sleeved cotton twill dress shirt he'd chosen was also Wrangler and he had to say that he rather liked the country-meets-city design. He'd gone online to find cowboy boots in Cricket Creek and had ended up shopping at a local feed supply store that had a large selection of all sorts of boots and work shoes. Plain brown with a bit of trim, they were perfect and surprisingly comfortable, he thought. He'd actually tried on a few cowboy hats and although he thought he looked rather cool, he felt silly and opted not to go that route. He had to admit that the whole cowboy thing had a certain charm . . . but did he pull it off?

After living mostly with his mum in London before she remarried, moving to America had been an adjustment. Kids his age in L.A. wanted to look and dress like everyone else, and Garret was different. He wore his hair longer and his clothes were colorful and on the hippie side. Whenever he spoke he was made fun of or mocked. Garret never did understand why kids thought that if you had an accent they had to try to imitate it. He worked hard at trying to fit in. Most of them had no clue who his aging rock star father was, so not even that helped with his desperate need for friends.

Of course now everyone thought his accent was cool or charming, but he was finally getting to the point in his life where it no longer mattered if he stood out or fit in. Garret just wanted to be himself. So now here he was, having a flashback of how it felt to be the nerdy kid with the odd clothing and funny accent made even worse by a mouth full of braces.

Why the hell was he playing dress-up? Maybe he should be carrying a Halloween bag and asking for candy. He was about to hop in his car and head to his cabin to change into his own clothes when the front door to the cabin opened and Mattie walked out.

"Are you going to stand there all day or come up and knock on my door?" Mattie asked with a tilt of her head and her hands on her hips. God, she looked pretty.

"I think I'll stand here all day," Garret said, but then grinned. "A moot point now that the door is already open."

"Well, then I'm going to have to march over there and drag you inside for a cold beer."

"A cold beer?" Garret pushed up from the car fender and walked toward her. "Now, that's an offer I can't refuse."

"Will you just look at you?" Mattie gave him a once-over, followed by a low whistle.

"Be honest. Do I look like Woody from *Toy Story*?"

She tossed back her head and laughed.

"I'm serious."

"You're missing the hat."

"Mattie!"

"Well, I think you look amazing . . . like a classy cowboy."

"For real?"

"Turn around and let me see your butt."

When he didn't do it she tapped her foot.

"Oh, you're serious."

"Um . . . yeah."

Garret turned around and then looked at her over his shoulder. "Well? How's the bum situation?"

"Lookin' mighty fine."

"Sweet."

"You haven't said one darn thing about how I look." She stepped to the edge of the porch and turned in a little circle.

"You haven't given me a chance. Come down here and let me have a look."

Mattie wore a faded denim skirt that hit a few inches above the knee. A gauzy white peasant blouse came to the edge of her shoulders and had lacy see-through sleeves cinched at her wrists. Small silver hoop earrings and a silver necklace with a peace sign charm gave her a hippie vibe that Garret found adorable. Because of his mother he always paid attention to clothes, and Mattie wore this outfit well. She finished off the look with red cowboy boots that hit midcalf. She wore her hair down but flipped up at the ends with her bangs swooped over to the side. "Well?" She caught her bottom lip between her teeth and waited for his approval.

"Vintage?"

"Yes." Mattie gave her hair a little toss and raised one shoulder. "Everything is from Violet's Vintage Clothing Shop on Main Street up in town. I like it there better than going to the mall. Violet helped me put the outfit together. I had such fun!"

"You are absolutely adorable." He took a step closer.

"You really think so?" She smiled at his compliment.

"No."

Her smile faded. "Oh."

Garret took a step closer. "You're more than adorable. You look super sexy too, Mattie. If you had go-go boots on instead of your cowboy boots, you'd look like Dusty Springfield from back in her heyday. Dusty was the ultimate queen of mod. And she was a tiny little blond pixie like you. You probably don't know who Dusty is, but she's still an icon in England."

"Ah ..." Mattie wagged a finger at him. "Now, there's where you're wrong. I have a huge collection of vinyl records from the fifties, sixties, and seventies, including a couple of her albums. 'I Only Want to Be with You' is one of my favorite songs of hers. Oh, and 'Son of a Preacher Man.'"

"Really?"

"There's more to me than meets the eye, Garret."

He grinned. "Well, I like what meets the eye. I'm going to have to beat the boys off with a stick."

"You're supposed to encourage them, not beat them away."

"Right," Garret said, but he really wanted to chase them all away and have her all to himself. "That was the plan." A horrible plan. "And one bloke in particular," he said lightly, but the words felt hollow in his chest. Perhaps he should suggest a practice kiss, but that would be torture as well. "Did I hear you say something about a cold beer?"

"You did indeed." She waved in the direction of her front door. "Come on into my humble abode."

Garret followed her inside, eager to see her home. But when he stepped inside he pulled up short. "Wow ..."

Mattie flicked a glance at him. "Was that a good wow?"

"That was an I'm-blown-away wow," he explained as he looked around. Garret had envisioned homey, country, or even rustic, but not ...

Not this.

"Mattie, there's nothing humble about your abode." As

with most log cabins, the layout was open with vaulted ceilings and an upstairs loft. "And much larger than I thought."

"The outside is deceiving." She gave him a shy smile, but he could see the pride shining in her eyes. "It's been a work in progress for several years. And most of what you see was purchased at antique stores, thrift shops, estate sales, or repurposed from odds and ends that nobody else wanted. I'm not beyond Dumpster-diving. See that chandelier?"

Garret looked up. "A weather vane?"

"Rescued from a Dumpster. I had Mason add the circle at the bottom and the lights that look like lit candles."

"I am totally impressed."

"About the Dumpster-diving?"

Garret laughed. "Sounds like an adventure. I want to go with you next time around and search for treasure."

"I'll remember that, but you might be sorry what you asked for."

"Don't let the accent fool you. I'm hardier than I look. But seriously your home is amazing. Would you mind giving me a tour?"

"Not at all." She waved her hand in an arc. "Well, this is the main room." A fieldstone fireplace filled one side of the room, and floor-to-ceiling windows showcased a view of the lake. The décor might have been purchased at secondhand shops or saved from a Dumpster, but it was nothing short of elegant. A jewel-toned Oriental rug graced the gleaming hardwood floor in the center of the room, creating a splash of vibrant color in contrast to the cream-colored leather sectional sofa facing the fireplace.

Garret walked over to see if the leather felt as buttery soft as it looked. "Gorgeous," he said, thinking that he'd love to snuggle up next to her and hold her close.

"I know." Mattie nodded. "I bought it from Ty Mc-Kenna after Jessica had baby Ben. The light color doesn't go well with a messy toddler."

Garret grinned. "I met the little rascal when I got the

takeaway from Wine and Diner. Nearly knocked me over and then force-fed me strawberries. But we bonded and he wanted to have dinner with me as long as it didn't include peas or carrots."

Mattie laughed. "Ben is hysterical," she said, and then motioned for him to follow her. She pointed to a large glass-topped dining table that took up the side of the room. "Another purchase from Ty McKenna. I wanted a table big enough to have my family over for dinner." She headed to an arched doorway that led into a spacious kitchen. Stainless steel appliances gleamed in contrast to the cherry cabinets, and a large granite island filled the center of the room. The far wall was made of fieldstone with a baker's rack positioned in front but allowing the wall to show through.

"This is a nice little nook," Garret said with a nod to the table in front of doors that opened to the far end of the outdoor deck. He could see another smaller bistro table outside. "Do you take your morning coffee out there?"

"Only on Sundays when I don't have to be at the restaurant. But I do eat dinner out there occasionally."

"By yourself?" Garret didn't really mean to ask the question, but he thought it a bit sad to think of her dining alone.

"Mostly," she said, and he watched a shadow fall across her face, making him wish he hadn't asked such a stupid question. "But after dealing with the public all day long I don't mind the solitude," she added quickly. But something in her eyes said that she was sometimes lonely. He could relate. "I cook for Mason and Danny sometimes too. But lately we've all been busy with the summer season at the marina. In the spring and fall we have fishing tournaments. Winters are much more laid-back." She walked over and opened the fridge. "I forgot all about the beer I offered." She reached in and pulled out two longneck bottles. She popped off the caps and handed one to him.

"Oh, Kentucky ale. I have to say that I'm growing

fond of all things Kentucky," he said, and then took a long pull from the bottle. He wanted to add *especially you*, but refrained. He thought it, though, and smiled.

"This one is actually Kentucky bourbon barrel ale. The beer is aged in the bourbon barrels we talked about earlier."

"I can taste it. It's really nice."

"And you'll feel it," she said with a smile. "Along with the flavor comes an extra kick."

"Sneaks up on you, I would imagine." He looked at the label on the bottle and took another swig.

"It's my favorite."

"I can see why."

"Would you like to see the rest of the cabin?"

"Absolutely." Garret nodded, thinking again that this interior wasn't what he'd expected from the feisty little breakfast cook. "I need to have you come over and help me decorate my place. You definitely have an eye for this sort of thing. Did you study interior design in school?"

"No, I have a boring ol' associate degree in business that I got mostly by studying online," she said with a wave of her hand, and seemed a little bit shy at the compliment. "I just know what I like."

"Me too," Garret said, but he wasn't talking about the furnishings. "You'll have to show me your record collection later, if you don't mind."

"Not at all. It's nice to have someone else show interest. My brothers are mostly country music and bluegrass fans, but my tastes go way beyond what's popular at the moment. And there is just something so cool about playing a record. I know I didn't grow up in that era, but it just—I don't know—makes me relax somehow. And of course I love finding a pristine collection at a yard sale or thrift shop. How anyone could part with them is a mystery to me."

"I know I wouldn't part with my collection." Garret thought again that they had more in common than what he'd first thought.

"Well, obviously music is in your blood, Garret. I've been told that you're an amazing musician."

"Would you like to sit in on a session sometime?"

Mattie stopped in her tracks and put her hand on his arm. "Really? Oh my gosh, I would just love it!"

"Then you shall," Garret said, and he had to wonder if she touched him because of the lessons from the other night or if she simply wanted to have the physical contact. That thought reminded him that she was interested in Colby, not him. They were friends, not lovers, and that status wasn't likely to change. But that realization didn't keep Garret from wishing that instead of going to Sully's they could stay at her cabin, sit in front of the fireplace, and listen to her record collection. "I'll have to take you to the Groove in Nashville," he said.

"The used record store?" she asked with raised eyebrows. "I've been longing to go there!"

"There are quite a few shops around town. We could take a little tour if you'd like."

"I would like that a lot. But I have to warn you that you'll have to drag me out of the store. When I'm browsing through records I get in a zone and have to look at everything," she said, and gave his arm a squeeze.

"Well, then that'll make two of us," Garret said. "So closing the shops down won't be a problem," he promised, and when she smiled it took everything in his power not to pull her into his arms for a much needed kiss. He felt such a connection to her on so many unexpected levels, making him want to know everything about Mattie Mayfield. He also knew that it was going to be difficult to even look at another woman tonight . . . and even harder to see her dancing in the arms of another man.

15

Let the Sun Shine In

ATTIE WISHED THAT THEY COULD FORGO THE EVENING at Sully's and spend the night at her cabin spinning records and talking. And now that she was walking toward the other side of the cabin with the master suite, Mattie felt her heart start knocking against her ribs. If she was honest she wanted to do much more than talk. But she couldn't be honest, because giving in to her feelings would mean ruining the night and risking their friendship.

"This is my bedroom," Mattie announced. She was going for a breezy tone as she waved her arm in an arc, but her voice decided to betray her and come out husky and suggestive. She also realized that her hand was pointed directly at the queen-sized wrought-iron bed that she'd painted white. The down-filled comforter was accented by plump satin and lace pillows in various shapes and sizes. The antique vanity, accessories, and dresser were all white as well, giving the room an ethereal look and feel that she found soothing.

"This is simply gorgeous," Garret commented as he looked at the bed. "It looks like you sleep on a fluffy cloud."

"It's the only room I wanted finished in drywall so I could paint the walls white. So you like it?" She was surprised at how much she wanted his approval.

"Yes, except you can't eat Cheetos in bed," Garret answered, making her laugh.

"True." But then again if she had him in her bed she wouldn't waste time eating snacks. Warmth filled her face at the thought and she turned around from the bed so fast that she nearly spun in a complete circle. She led him to the master bath located behind pocket doors that popped open when tugged. From the pristine tile floor to the antique linens neatly draped on a three-tiered rack, the entire room also gleamed in pure white accented with a smattering of cream trim here and there.

"So, what do you think?" Mattie watched him take in the large antique claw-foot bathtub perched on a large square pedestal at the back of the room.

"Wow," Garret said, and walked over to the tub. He ran his hand over the smooth curved edge. "This is just brilliant. So, do you take long bubble baths and have candles lit all around?" He looked over at the white wicker stand topped with several fat, stubby candles, all of which were slightly burned down. The light scent of vanilla filled the air.

"When I get the time I take a long soak and read. But most days I use the shower in the smaller bathroom across the hall." She pointed in that direction.

"Pity not to get to take long soaks more often." Garret shook his head and continued to look at the tub, making Mattie wonder if he was picturing her with her hair pinned up while taking a sexy bubble bath. Then again maybe he just thought the old-fashioned tub was cool. Mattie had a sudden vision of the two of them in the tub together and had to take a sip of her cold beer in an effort to cool off.

Garret turned and gave her a long look. The spacious bathroom suddenly seemed to shrink to the size of a closet. "Ah, Mattie . . ." He shook his head slowly. "I knew I was right."

"What?" Mattie asked, trying to sound feisty, but the doggone breathless thing happened again. She cleared her throat and took a sip of beer to try to hide the hot thoughts that started flashing into her head. Washing his hair; soaping his back.

Oh, and then slowly sliding her wet body against his, rocking against him while the water and bubbles surrounded them like a warm, fragrant cocoon. Pretty soon she was going to melt into a puddle that could slide right down the drain.

"You're a hopeless romantic," Garret stated softly. He reached over and picked up a lock of her hair just briefly and then smiled.

"So, did you expect a rifle over the hearth and deer heads on the walls?" she tried to joke.

"No." Garret didn't crack a smile but simply shook his head. "And I'm guessing nobody really sees this side of you."

She lifted one shoulder. "Of course my family comes over, but they think I did all this by looking at magazines. My brothers actually poke fun at my white bedroom, and boy, they complained when I bought the tub at an estate sale last year. That thing weighs a ton and they grumbled the whole time they carried it in here," she said.

"But this is who you really are," he said, and when she glanced away he reached over and tilted her cheek back to face him.

"Yeah," she answered in a barely there voice. "I like pretty things."

"Me too," he said, and let his gaze lower to her mouth.

Mattie's heart raced when she realized that he wanted to kiss her. Or at least he seemed to be thinking about it. But then again maybe this was part of the game they were supposed to be playing. But for her the game was becoming all too real. "And you're not that badass person that you tried to sell to the entire world, are you, Garret?"

"No."

"Then who are you?"

"Well, now." He tilted his head to the side. "I dunno, really. I suppose I'm just now trying to figure that part out. Rather silly to be living a life that's a lie, don't you think?"

"Yes. Incredibly silly." Mattie longed to reach over and rub her thumb over the tawny stubble on his chin and then cup her palms against his cheeks. What would happen if she was honest and told him of her deepening feelings for him? But was she really falling for Garret? Or were her feelings simply a tangled-up reaction to how much male attention he gave her? Attention that she'd craved as long as she could remember.

She was growing so weary of playing the role of the tomboy kid sister.

"Are you okay? Did I say something wrong, love?"

"Of course not." Mattie gave him a smile that she hoped looked real. "I think I'm just a bit nervous showing up at Sully's all dressed up like this. I'm usually in jeans and a T-shirt with a logo on it."

"You will turn heads, you know."

"You are so good for my ego."

"I'm only telling you the truth."

Mattie allowed herself to lean in and give him a quick kiss on the cheek, but even that light touch ignited a hot sizzle of desire. In about one more second she would completely lose control and pull him into her arms for a long kiss instead of that unsatisfying peck on the cheek. Mattie shook her head, thinking that she always considered those ripping-clothes-off-each-other love scenes that she read about were pure fantasy. Oh, but she suddenly longed to tug Garret into her bedroom and shove him onto her bed. She'd push the pillows to the side in one fell swoop and make wild, crazy love to him until she fell back exhausted, unable to move. Mattie turned away before he might see in her eyes what she was thinking, but Garret reached out and took her hand.

"Why did you shake your head? I'm not just playing

the role, Mattie. When I give you a compliment, I'm sincere."

Mattie inhaled a deep breath. He wasn't making her plight any easier.

"You believe me, right?"

"I do." She shook her head and felt emotion well up in her throat.

"Good." He gave her hand a squeeze but then fell silent.

"Let's go take our drinks outside onto the back deck and watch the sun sink low in the sky. What do you say?" She willed him to read her mind and take control, because if he did kiss her or, *dear God*, want to make love to her she just might be powerless to stop him. She wanted to be in his arms more than she wanted to breathe.

But that would change everything in a heartbeat. The thought frightened her.

Still, she held her breath and waited.

Garret licked his bottom lip and paused long enough to give Mattie hope. "Mattie, I spent most of my adult life doing selfish things for all the wrong reasons. For the first time in my life I can look at myself in the mirror and not cringe at the memory of what I'd done the night before. And quite frankly sometimes I couldn't even recall what I'd done. I was reckless. Careless. The stories in the tabloids all held a grain of truth."

"We've all done things we've regretted, Garret."

"Yeah, but my bad behavior was on a regular basis and I got to the point where I didn't even care anymore. I was simply lost without any sense of direction. Mattie, I was so far gone that I was willing to get married simply to create a reality show."

"*Was*, Garret. You're not that guy any longer. Give yourself some credit for making changes in your life."

"Moving to this town and being around you has helped me become a better person. It feels good to do the right thing."

"And what is the right thing that you think you're doing?" Mattie asked even though she was pretty sure of his answer.

"Do you want me to be honest?"

"Yes," Mattie replied, even though she wasn't sure she wanted to hear his explanation.

Garret looked at her with serious eyes, and her heart took a plunge. This wasn't going to be good. "I want to pull you into my arms and kiss you senseless and then take you into that white bedroom and make sweet love to you all night long. I want to fall asleep in that big bed that looks like a cloud and wake up next to your beautiful face."

Her heart sprang upward and bounced to its rightful place but beat wildly. "And would that be so wrong?"

"Yes." Garret reached over and cupped her chin. "Because you're in love with someone else. Someone who is completely right for you. I came swooping in here and turned your orderly world upside down."

"I think my orderly world needed a bit of shaking up." Mattie wanted to tell him that she couldn't possibly be in love with Colby because she thought of Garret constantly. "In more ways than one." Lately she'd been bored with fixing the same breakfasts and had been thinking about making some changes at the restaurant. But the locals loved it there, and change could chase people away. She didn't want to disappoint her older customers who came in every day. Her restaurant was more than just food and she knew it. "Change is scary, Garret, but can be a good thing in the end. You just have to be willing to embrace it. Look at the changes you're making."

"I wouldn't be good for you, Mattie."

"You can't know that."

"I wouldn't want to hurt you or come between what you've wanted for so long." He sighed. "I already have and I hate that."

"Really? Well, sometimes you have to be like Rusty

and risk it for the biscuit." She tried for a smile, but it trembled at the corners.

"That's just it. I don't want to steal you away and then break your heart. It's one of the few things I've been consistently good at."

"That's all in the past! You're starting with a clean slate here in Cricket Creek."

"Yes, but, Mattie, breaking your heart would shatter me as well."

"Then you must already care," she said with the hint of a challenge.

"I won't deny that."

Mattie leaned against the edge of the pedestal sink for support. "I'm a big girl, Garret. Why don't you let me decide what risk I'm willing to take?"

Garret closed his eyes and swallowed. After taking a deep breath he looked at her. "Because we both know that you need to see where this thing with Colby will take you. He's more than taken notice of you, Mattie. You've wanted this for so long and I'm damn well not going to ruin it for you. That wasn't the plan."

"But honestly, Garret, I would much rather stay here with you tonight."

"And I would be powerless to keep my hands to myself."

"I wouldn't want you to."

He raised his hands to cradle the sides of his head. "God, you're killing me."

"Then—"

"No." He reached over and put a gentle fingertip to her lips. "I wouldn't feel right, Mattie. I know I'm different from any guy you've ever known. What happens when the novelty wears off?"

"Do you think I'm that shallow?" She felt a stab of hurt. "That you're like some shiny toy that I'll grow weary of and toss away?"

"No. *God no*. I think you're that innocent."

"Innocent? Why? Because I'm from a small town? That's not fair."

"No, I didn't mean it that way," he said, clearly becoming frustrated. "You have this big heart and see the good in people."

"And what's wrong with that?"

"Nothing! I'm just undeserving!"

"That's totally ridiculous!" Mattie sputtered, but she studied his face for a moment and she finally understood. "Are we still being honest?"

He nodded. "Of course."

"This isn't about me at all. You're the one who's afraid, Garret."

"Of hurting you? Yes."

"No. Okay, yes, maybe. I'll give you that because I can see it in your eyes. But the real problem is that you truly believe that the novelty *will* wear off."

"Okay, yes! I am. And then you'll wish you hadn't blown your chance with Colby. I won't . . . no, *can't* start a relationship with you until you know that you're not in love with *him*. That would be unfair to either of us."

"So, let me get this straight. You're going to push me into the arms of another man?" Mattie felt tears well up in her eyes. "That's just . . . plain stupid."

"Yeah, I do stupid really well." Garret shoved his fingers through his hair. "Sometimes it seriously sucks to be me." He gave her a wry smile and then reached over to cup her cheek once more. "I've seen the way you look at him, Mattie. You get this . . . this *dreamy* look on your face. And I remember how you defended him even when he tossed you into the damn river!"

Mattie shook her head, but she knew that Garret spoke the truth. She had to know or she would never have closure. It really wouldn't be fair to Garret. Would it? "So, what do we do now?"

"We go to Sully's and carry on with the plan," he insisted in a rather sullen tone that tugged at her heart.

Mattie inhaled a deep breath. She wanted to shake

some sense into him, but she could see in his eyes that he was going to stubbornly dig in his heels and she felt powerless to stop him.

She suddenly had all the clarity she needed. It felt as if she'd just opened the curtains, allowing the sun to shine in. She soaked up the warmth, the light, and tilted her head to the side. "Okay."

"Okay . . . what?"

"There's only one way I'll stick to this so-called plan."

He hesitated and then said, "Go on, then."

"You have to go out onto the back deck with me and finish our drinks."

He looked relieved and gave his bottle a glance as if he'd forgotten he was holding it. "Fair enough."

"And then you have to kiss me." Mattie watched the look of surprise pass over his face, closely followed by hesitation.

"No," he answered barely above a whisper. "Hell no," he said more firmly.

"Why?" Mattie clung to the edge of the sink, not sure where she was channeling the bravery to do this, but she lifted her chin. "Give me one good reason."

"I just gave you a whole list of reasons."

"I said a *good* reason." She pushed away from the sink. "Because I'm sorry, but they were all bullshit."

"They were all valid!" He took a step backward as if needing to put distance between them, but Mattie quickly closed the gap.

"Really? Go on. What were they again? Oh, right, that I'll get bored with you. You're really not a boring person."

He looked at her as if trying to remember the reasons he'd given her.

"It's just one little bitty kiss."

"No . . . a kiss needs to be spontaneous, not something we're walking out there thinking about doing."

"That's funny because I've been thinking about it all day long. I want to know how it feels."

"You already know."

"You're right. I do. And that's why I don't want to kiss Colby. I want to kiss you. But just forget it, okay?" Mattie brushed past him, feeling angry and all twisted up inside. She didn't want to go to Sully's. She didn't want to flirt with Colby. And she sure as hell didn't want to be a wingman for Garret.

"Mattie!" Garret said, but she didn't turn around.

Mattie walked almost blindly out to the deck and stared unseeing out over the lake. The sun, now a big orange ball, sat low in the horizon, sending streaks of purple and red dipping into the water like finger paint.

Mattie set her bottle down and leaned against the railing. She waited to hear Garret's footsteps and she hoped he would come out onto the deck so she could kiss some sense into him, but when he failed to appear sadness washed over her in waves.

She heard the sound of his car start and knew he was gone. She'd done what she'd feared the most and had chased him away. A fat tear slid down her cheek and she slashed at the wetness, angry with herself for ruining their friendship. And now she felt silly for trying to force him to kiss her. "God!" And now she felt . . .

Exposed.

Empty.

Lonely.

And pissed!

Mattie thought about calling Laura Lee but didn't want to ruin her night. Later she'd text her to say that she wouldn't be coming to Sully's after all. But at least she knew now that Colby was just a longtime crush. She didn't want to give him a shot or a chance. Colby wouldn't want to shop in thrift stores or listen to her collection of old vinyl records. He would find her white bedroom frilly and chuckle at her claw-foot bathtub. And he wouldn't be caught dead reading a romance novel even as a dare. Colby was like a clone of her brothers . . . a great guy . . . and Mattie supposed she was drawn to him because he felt safe. Familiar. Colby would always hold a special place in her heart.

But she wasn't in love with him.

And she didn't need to kiss him to know it. Mattie blew out a sigh. Yes, it was like letting go of a dream, but truthfully this knowledge gave Mattie a sense of freedom. She could at least thank Garret for that and move on with her life. She loved this town dearly. She loved her family and working at the marina.

But she'd felt restless lately. She wanted . . . more. Something fresh and exciting. Something challenging. But what?

Mattie stood there for a few minutes hovering between clarity and confusion, and the night she'd been anticipating all week long now seemed endless and dreary. After a few more minutes she decided to get out of her special outfit and pull on some sweats. Maybe she'd read more of the Stephen King novel just to take her mind off Garret. But then the scary clown popped into her mind and she shivered. Okay, maybe not.

Perhaps she'd just climb into her cloud of a bed, pull the covers up to her chin, and have a good ol' noisy cry. She sniffed when her nose already tickled with tears. Or maybe she'd take a long soak in her big bathtub with a giant glass of wine and a steamy romance novel. No, that would just be depressing. Ah, she'd dig through her favorite movies and find a funny one to watch. No . . . she didn't feel like laughing. Mattie waited for at least one of those suggestions to grab hold and capture her interest. But nothing sounded remotely appealing. There was only one thing she wanted and he'd walked out the door.

Mattie lifted her shoulders and let out a long-suffering sigh. She picked up her beer and then walked over to a lounge chair and decided that for now she'd finish drinking it even though it had grown rather warm, but she didn't care. She'd watch the last of the sun dip beyond the trees while she sat there and brooded.

"No!" In the end, however, she decided she wasn't

one to cry in her beer like the lyrics of one of Shane McCray's much loved songs. "Oh, hell no!" Mattie declared so loudly that nearby birds took flight from the trees. Nope, she'd head on over to Sully's anyway and at least try to let friends and music lift her spirits. And Laura Lee was expecting her.

Mattie looked down at her red boots and had to admit that it would be fun to watch the reaction when she entered Sully's all dolled up. Ha! Maybe she'd flirt up a storm and then stick her nose in the air at all the guys who'd ignored her over the years. "How do you like me now?" Mattie said, and then nodded. Yeah, she liked that plan the best of all. She stood up and brushed herself off.

Now it was high time to put the new plan into action.

16

Crazy

$\mathcal{L}$AURA LEE TAPPED HER TOE AGAINST THE HIGH-TOP chair while she listened to Myra Lawson belt out a pretty darn good rendition of Patsy Cline's "Crazy." The once-a-month karaoke night at Sully's always drew a big crowd, and tonight the honky-tonk bar was hopping. Myra, always a big ham, stood up from the stool where she sang, grabbed the mic, and raised one hand up in the air while she brought the song home. As she drew out the word *you* she pointed to her husband, who watched with a huge smile on his face. When the last drawn-out note ended, Owen put his fingers to his mouth to give a shrill whistle of appreciation while Myra took a deep bow.

Laura Lee had to smile when Owen jumped up to give Myra a big hug when she returned to her table, causing the crowd to erupt with a second round of applause. Although Myra was a bit older than Laura Lee, they'd been friends for as long as she could remember and it did her heart good to see Myra so happy. Myra, who was a generous soul, took in her niece Jessica when she had been a pregnant teenager. The entire town watched sweet little curly-haired Madison grow up to be a respected play-

wright and teacher at the nearby college and she was now
happily married to a local boy. Jessica started her life all
over again, eventually married baseball superstar Ty
McKenna, and had beautiful baby Ben.

Myra and Owen had married just a few years ago and
Myra didn't have to tell anyone that Owen adored her,
because it showed plain as day on his face. Mattie spoke
the truth. Love could happen at any time and at any age.
Laura Lee just didn't know if she was brave enough to
risk heartbreak a second time in her life. Now that she
had the amazing job with Shane McCray, she reminded
herself again that she didn't want to do anything to mess
things up. But as soon as she thought of Shane she got a
fluttery feeling in her stomach and wondered if he was
really going to show up tonight.

And would they dance?

She shouldn't.

People would talk.

But she'd promised.

Laura Lee looked over toward the front door when it
opened, but it was Colby who looked over and spotted
Mattie's brothers playing a game of darts. They waved
him over and handed Colby a beer from a silver bucket.
Laura Lee looked down at her cell phone, hoping to see
a message from Mattie saying that she had arrived. What
would everybody think when Mattie walked in with Garret? With her new look she was sure to turn heads. Laura
Lee took a sip of her lemon-drop martini, thinking that
her little town sure did have some drama going on and
tonight could kick some local gossip into high gear.

A moment later Laura Lee's cell phone pinged and
then showed a text message from Mattie stating that she
had just arrived. Laura Lee replied that she was at a
high-top table near the back of the room across from the
main bar. She took another sip of the tart martini and
then licked some of the sugar from the rim. Pete Sully
mixed a mean martini and if she had another one she'd
have to use the shuttle that Pete's son, Clint, provided on

the weekends. The only other taxi service was Bubba Brown and he fell asleep early, failing to respond enough to cater to the late-night crowd.

A moment later Laura Lee saw Mattie walking through the front entrance and she watched with interest when Colby looked over and spotted her. His jaw, bless his heart, dropped, along with the jaws of several other men who looked Mattie's way. Mason elbowed Danny and it was funny because Laura Lee could see the sudden look of brotherly pride, followed by a quick glance around at the guys who were staring. Mattie waved their way but kept walking with an air of confidence that Laura Lee hadn't seen before. After pausing to buy a beer, Mattie made her way toward the table, and every guy she passed turned around for a second lingering look.

Well, good, Laura Lee thought. It was about damn time!

When Mattie reached the table Laura Lee scooted from her chair and gave her a quick hug. "Don't you just look simply gorgeous? I simply love that peasant blouse! Did you get it at Violet's?"

"I did. Don't you just love the lace sleeves?" She plucked at one and smiled.

"I do! Tongues are hanging out, let me tell ya."

"Oh, go on with you. . . ."

"I'm serious, Mattie. And Colby is one of them, girlie. In fact, don't look but he's craning his neck your way right now," she said, but when Mattie failed to show much interest she had to ask, "Is everything okay, sweet pea?"

Mattie shrugged and then slid onto the chair. She took a swig of her beer and set the bottle down with a solid thunk that spoke volumes. "That's a loaded question."

"Well, then unload on me."

"In a minute."

"I was beginning to worry when you were gonna get here. And where is Garret, by the way?"

"I dunno," she answered glumly.

"I thought he was coming with you tonight."

"We kind of had a . . . I don't know. I guess a fight."

"Oh, sweetie." Laura Lee put her hand on Mattie's and squeezed. "About what?"

"Garret thinks I'm in love with Colby."

"Are you?"

"No." She shook her head firmly. "Laura Lee, all I do is think about *Garret*. But he has this stupid notion that he's just a passing thing for me and once the novelty wears off he thinks I'll go back to wanting to be with Colby."

"His theory does have some merit if you think about it."

"I'm not thinking. I'm tired of thinking! I'm *feeling* and I know what my heart is telling me, just like you said." She tapped her chest. "But for the sake of argument I guess I'm going to sashay over there and flirt with Colby and see where it takes me. I'm gonna prove Garret wrong once and for all."

Laura Lee leaned closer and lowered her voice. "So, did Garret indicate that he has feelings for you?"

"Yes! Isn't it so damn crazy for him to want me to throw myself at another man? I mean, what is he thinking?"

"Um, that he might get hurt. Everybody envies the rich and famous and in truth I think that they are the most fragile people of all."

Mattie picked up a couple of peanuts from the dish of mixed nuts. "Weren't you the person that said that you have to risk getting your heart broken? That broken hearts mend but opportunities are lost forever?"

"Yes," Laura Lee said softly, and Shane popped into her head. She wished that she could be brave and take her own damn advice. She took a sip of her martini. "They surely do."

Mattie groaned. "So, then, what should I do?"

"Well, fate is helping because I think Colby is trying to make it over here your way." She watched Mattie crunch the peanut and swallow hard. And then her eyes widened. "What?" Laura Lee asked.

"Well, what are we gonna do if Shane and Garret show up here tonight? Let the girls have at 'em?"

"Oh boy. I don't know. Could get interesting."

"Yeah." Mattie nodded slowly. "It would indeed. And he sure looks fine in Wrangler jeans and cowboy boots. Add the accent and the girls are going to be tripping over themselves getting to him. I've created a sexy British beast."

"Well, I say that if they come in here we should stake our claim on our men."

"Is that the lemon-drop martini talking?"

"Most likely." Laura Lee shrugged. "But hey, why the hell not?"

"Do you think we're out of our league with these guys?"

"Of course." Laura Lee nodded but then straightened her spine and grinned. "But I like a good challenge. Don't you?" The thought snuck into her brain that she would be risking the job of a lifetime, but she shoved it aside. "We might get shot down at the stroke of midnight, but for now let's get our Cinderella on. Are you with me, Mattie?"

"You're some kind of crazy."

"I know. I don't know what's gotten into me."

"It's called vodka."

"Well, it feels good. I'm tired of living life on the sidelines. Let's get into the game. What do you say?"

"Just how are we going to stake our so-called claim?"

Laura Lee tapped her fingernail against the rim of her glass. "I haven't thought that far ahead. I guess we need a strategy."

"Well, think fast because Colby is walking this way. Now what do I do?"

"I don't know! This is all new territory for me," Laura Lee tossed back the last of her drink but then grabbed Mattie's hand. "But I'm willing to blaze some new trails. Hurry, let's go to the ladies' room and talk this thing out."

"Girl code. Good idea. Let's roll."

17

Fame

SHANE PULLED HIS TRUCK INTO ONE OF THE FEW VACANT spots in the parking lot of Sully's Tavern and then killed the engine. He tried to remember when he'd last been out on the town on his own and couldn't. While he never really had what he could call an entourage, he was always surrounded by people centered on the music business. Being out on his own felt like a fresh taste of freedom.

Shane hoped that when he entered Sully's he'd be left alone to go and locate Laura Lee, but he doubted that would be the case. By staying out of the limelight his fame would eventually fade at least somewhat, though being a celebrity would follow him around for a lifetime. Shane gripped the steering wheel and blew out a sigh. Maybe this wasn't such a good idea after all, because if he went inside and found Laura Lee dancing with another man he didn't know how he was going to handle it. But not knowing really sucked too. "Damn. This is a fine pickle you've gotten yourself into."

What would Laura Lee do if he was honest and told her that he was falling for her? Shane groaned and hit his hand against the steering wheel hard enough to smart. He kept going over the same ground in his head and came up with the same damn answer. He should go slow and not risk pushing her away. He just couldn't stand waiting any longer! Screw the whole two-week waiting period! He removed the keys and opened the door. It was time to make a move.

After getting out of his truck, he heard the sound of gravel crunching and looked over to see Garret Ruleman walking his way. "Hey there, Garret. What's up?" Shane extended his hand to the young man.

"Not much, Shane."

"Been in the studio much this week?"

"Not really. I've been mostly listening to demo tapes with my dad. Oh, and Jeff Greenfield is thinking about cutting a Christmas album with Cat and we've been discussing with them what songs to choose."

"They are such an amazing duo, but I respect that Cat wants to take a backseat to Jeff's career so they can start a family. It helps that she's such a talented songwriter, so she can fill that creative void while she raises her children. I'm sure she'll be happy to be part of Sully's South too. She'd be amazing at a roundtable."

Garret nodded. "Yeah, it's a tough business to be in and have a family. I think I would rather stay in the studio than go out on the road. My dad was gone all the time and it sucked."

"It can be damn draining and a grind. You're a talented musician. All the good stuff happens in the studio anyway. I wish you'd been around when I was still recording."

"Thanks. I would have been honored. Do you miss it yet?"

Shane mulled that over for a moment. "Yeah, I miss the music and the fans but not the long hours or constant touring. I'll come out of hiding here and there for a special event or charity work, but for now I just want to kick back and enjoy the rest of my life. And I'm looking forward to being a part of Sully's South. I'm glad you're on board with it too. It must be rewarding discovering new talent, especially when it comes to songwriting."

Garret nodded. "I have to say that it is."

"Oh, and hey, did Mattie tell you I want to have you two over for a barbecue and a swim at my place?"

"Yeah, she did," Garret replied, but then fell silent, making Shane curious as to why he suddenly seemed so sad.

"Mattie is such a sweet girl," Shane said, and looked at Garret to see his reaction.

"No doubt," Garret agreed, but then glanced down at the ground.

"I thought that Laura Lee said something about you two coming out together tonight. Is Mattie in there already?" He angled his head toward Sully's.

"I don't really know for sure," Garret replied, but something in his expression told Shane that he wanted to know if Mattie was indeed inside. He could relate.

"But let me guess. She's why you're here."

"Am I that transparent?"

"Son, you've got girl trouble written all over your face."

"Well, damn . . . ," Garret said, and then chuckled. "Really?"

Shane laughed. "No, but it was a damn good guess." He clamped a hand on Garret's shoulder. "You can tell me to mind my own business, but if you want to talk about it, I'll listen. And then keep my mouth shut. You got my word."

"Seriously?" Garret asked, and looked as if he wanted to talk about it.

"Absolutely." Shane propped his boot up against his bumper and rested his forearm on his knee. "Shoot."

Garret drew in a deep breath. "Mattie and I had this sort of plan. I was supposed to help her find her girlie side so she could entice that Colby bloke into asking her out on a date. She'd been trying to get his attention forever and I offered to help in exchange for Mattie trying to help me fit into the Cricket Creek social scene."

"Ah, that explains the boots and Wranglers."

"Right."

"And you've fallen for her instead."

"Good guess again?"

"Actually this time it's written all over your face. Keep going."

"Now Mattie claims she's into me and not Colby after all," he said with a frown.

"Um . . . so, isn't that good news?"

"I dunno." Garret shoved his hands into his jeans pockets. "I mean, what if she's got it all wrong and I'm just a . . . you know, a curiosity? I mean, as a celebrity you must understand where I'm coming from."

"Oh, believe me. I do." He glanced toward the neon sign and then back at Garret.

"Whoa. Wait. . . . Who are we talking about? Is it Laura Lee?"

Shane nodded slowly. "Guess I got girl trouble written all over my face too."

"Lovely lady."

"Yeah, and I know that if I dare make a move she'll think I'm a smarmy celebrity taking whatever I want without a care. And she's my housekeeper and personal assistant, so I'm guessing she worries about jeopardizing her job."

"I'm sure she does."

"So, what the hell do I do?"

"Well, it's a fine mess we've got ourselves in, mate."

Shane chuckled. "You damn well got that right."

"So, what now?" Garret rocked back on his heels and waited. "I mean, what if we go in there and Mattie and Laura Lee are dancing with some other blokes?"

"That's when we start throwing punches," Shane said, and then laughed when Garret looked horrified. "I'm kidding."

"Good, because I've spent way too much time on the

cover of tabloids. You, on the other hand, have this sterling reputation. Kind of funny that we're hanging out together."

"Well, are you ready to head on in there and cause a stir?"

"No time like the present," Garret said, and they fell in step together. "Do we have a smattering of a plan?" he asked when they reached the front door.

"I guess we locate our ladies, buy them a drink, and ask for a dance."

"Like the local blokes."

"Yeah, like the local blokes," Shane said, and had to laugh. "Normal dudes."

"All right, then. Let's go give it a go," Garret said, but then put a hand on Shane's shoulder. "Let's exchange phone numbers in case we find ourselves in a bit of a spot."

"Smart thinking," Shane said, and reached in his pocket for his cell phone. "Because I'm afraid it's bound to happen."

They typed numbers into each other's phones and then looked at the door for a second. Music and laughter spilled out from inside. For the locals it was just another Saturday night. For Shane it represented the new beginning of the rest of his life. Or at least it felt like it.

"You ready, Garret?"

"As ready as I'll ever be."

"Let's do it." Shane pushed the heavy door open and of course as soon as they entered, the crowd started to buzz. After nearly thirty years of fame, he still wasn't comfortable with the attention. No one knew how to treat a celebrity. Shane found that people either were too friendly or went the total opposite way and completely ignored him. Men got pissed when their dates or wives gushed all over him even though he did his best to be polite but keep his distance. Shane had learned to take it all with a sense of humor and did his best to put those around him at ease. And now that nearly everyone had phones with cameras, having his picture taken was inevitable. He didn't mind posing if asked but found it rather disconcerting to have his picture taken without his knowledge or permission.

"Do you see them?" Shane asked, but Garret shook his head. "Well, I guess we should make our way through the crowd and try to find them."

"And then what?" Garret asked. "Right, do the local bloke thing."

Shane shrugged. "Yep, I guess we do what any other guy would do. Buy them a drink and ask for a dance."

Garret nodded. "Simple enough, I suppose. So why am I so damn nervous?"

"Beats my whole hand, but I am too," Shane agreed, but then chuckled. "It's weird but I like the feeling. Makes me feel almost normal, you know?"

"I get what you're saying. Tonight we're just a couple of blokes out on the town."

"You got that right." Shane went over to a galvanized tub and bought two beers from the cute bartender who tried hard not to act flustered. He handed one to Garret and then tapped his bottle to Garret's. "Let's roll."

18

You're the One That I Want

OF COURSE THEY WEREN'T JUST A COUPLE OF REGULAR blokes and although everybody at Sully's was trying to act cool, within a few minutes Shane had a crowd of fans surrounding him. People recognized Garret, but he wasn't adored like the country superstar and after a few minutes he drifted from Shane's side and went in search of Mattie.

While Garret weaved his way through the packed bar, he finally spotted Mattie sitting with Laura Lee at a high-top table near the back of the room. When Mattie looked his way Garret started to wave, but she quickly averted her gaze in the way that people do when they don't want to acknowledge someone. His heart sank, but of course he understood. She had spilled her guts to him and he'd pushed her away. No, not just pushed her away but into the arms of another man. Garret took a swig of his beer. At the time his actions made perfect sense, but right now he had to wonder if he'd lost his damn mind. All he'd wanted to do was the right thing and ended up hurting her feelings anyway. By the time he'd gone back to her cabin, she was already gone, so he decided to come here in an effort to set things straight. And now she wouldn't even look at him!

But just when Garret decided to hell with wanting her to find out if she was still in love with Colby, the damn guy started strolling Mattie's way.

And she smiled.

When Colby reached her table Mattie stood up and gave him a hug and then gestured toward an empty chair for him to join her. Colby nodded, gave Laura Lee a kiss on the cheek, and then sat down. Damn! Garret stood there rooted to the spot while wondering what the hell he was supposed to do. Should he casually stroll over there and join them? Buy them a round of drinks? Ask Mattie to dance?

No . . . that would be tacky.

Well, the decision was made for Garret when a moment later Colby offered Mattie his hand and tugged her up on the dance floor. As if on cue someone started singing a fairly decent Elvis cover of "Can't Help Falling in Love." Feeling a hot flash of jealousy, Garret wanted to storm onto the dance floor and cut in. Instead he turned away.

So, at this point he could finish his beer and leave or act as if seeing Mattie dancing with Colby didn't bother him and then ask a girl to dance just to get Mattie's reaction. Or maybe he should just let the whole thing play itself out. If Mattie was still into Colby, then Garret had just saved himself a great deal of heartache. Yes, this was for the best.

But it sure as hell didn't feel like it.

Instead it felt as if some other bloke was dancing with *his* girl. Only Mattie wasn't his girl. *She should be* went through Garret's head, but when he stole a quick glance at the dance floor Mattie tossed her head back and laughed at something Colby said close to her ear. Feeling a bit sick, Garret decided he needed some fresh air and headed out to the back deck.

The cool evening air felt refreshing. Garret took a

deep, cleansing breath and walked over to the railing to gaze out over the river off in the distance. Thankfully the deck was deserted, most likely because of Shane's presence inside. Music and laughter drifted his way, but he tuned it out while he tried not to think of Mattie slow-dancing with Colby.

With a long sigh Garret looked at the beer that no longer appealed to him and decided he should just call it a night and save himself the agony of watching what he'd already feared unfold before his eyes. Mattie wanted Colby. But just as he was about to make his escape via the side entrance, he heard footsteps coming his way.

Garret turned sideways to see Laura Lee standing next to him. "Good evening, Laura Lee," he said with as much enthusiasm as he could muster, which was almost none.

"Are you going to let that happen?" Laura Lee jabbed a thumb toward the bar.

"Let what happen?" Garret took a swig of his luke-warm beer and winced.

"Mattie and Colby."

"She's making her choice. I knew that it wouldn't be me. Not that I blame her."

"Oh, would you just listen to yourself?" She fisted her hands on her hips and tilted her head sideways.

Garret turned and leaned his hip against the railing, trying his best to appear casual. "Laura Lee, Colby is the kind of bloke she wants."

"Oh, really?" Laura Lee pressed her lips together for a second. "Is that what she told you?"

"No—"

"Then why are you standing out here?"

Garret pushed up from the railing and stood up straight. "Because I've spent my entire adult life not giving a crap and taking what I wanted regardless of the consequences. Hurting people left and right." He shook his head. "And Mattie is the last person in the world I want to hurt."

"Because you're in love with her."

Garret refused to answer and he didn't look Laura Lee's way because she would see the truth in his eyes. "Don't you get it? Our plan from the beginning was to get Colby to finally notice Mattie. It was never my intention to come between them. Look, I might be dressed in Wranglers and boots, but we both know that I'm different than the blokes around here."

"Maybe Mattie wants a different *bloke*. Garret, let me ask you something. Have you seen her cabin?"

"Yes," he replied, wondering where she was going with this.

Laura Lee tilted her head to the side. "And was it what you expected?"

"No, not at all," he replied. "She has exquisite taste and a variety of interests that I didn't expect."

"Garret, I believe that Mattie has facets of herself that she has yet to discover and explore. And I think you are the person who could help her blossom."

"I don't know . . . when it comes to relationships I've been known to do more harm than good," he said with a mirthless chuckle.

"Really? Well, that's interesting because you've already had a positive impact on her life. She's taken an interest in how she dresses and did you see her hair tonight? Garret, you've already started the process of helping Mattie become the woman hidden beneath the surface. Why stop now?"

"Because she's gotten what she wants."

"No, she hasn't. Mattie wants you."

"I've seen how she looks at Colby."

"Me too and she looks at you differently. Garret, she always had that dreamy look on her face when she looked at him because that's all it ever was. A crush. Schoolgirl puppy love for her older brother's best friend. What she has with you is *real* with a solid foundation of friendship."

"How can you be so sure?"

"Because I know her and love her like a daughter."

"If that's true, then she'll come to me," Garret said firmly. "That's the only way I'll have her. I'm all through with taking what I want, Laura Lee." He gave her a slight grin. "Even though that's not what Dominick the shirt-less pirate would do."

Laura Lee angled her head and then smiled. "Ah, from the historical romance novel you read. I do believe that you're true hero material, Garret Ruleman."

"Not hardly. My past isn't so pretty."

"Ah, but those are the best heroes, Garret. The re-formed rake. The bad boy with the heart of gold. The hero who loves the heroine so much that he has the mis-guided notion that he has to give her up or isn't worthy of her love. Take your pick, although I think you're a little bit of all the above."

"I think you're getting fiction confused with reality. At any rate you're giving me way too much credit."

"Or perhaps you're not giving yourself enough credit. You've proven your worth tonight, so don't even try to argue with me." She poked him in the chest but then leaned in and gave him a light kiss on the cheek.

"And that's why I'm leaving," Garret said.

"Have it your way, but keep an open mind."

"Fair enough. Oh, and by the way, there's someone inside who wants to have a dance with you. And he'd be very pleased if you'd go in and rescue him from his fans." Garret watched the play of emotion on Laura Lee's pretty face.

"Shane's my employer, Garret. I won't cross that line."

"Then quit."

"Quit the best job I've ever had? Are you crazy?"

"I get that question a lot and the answer is always yes."

Laura Lee shook her head.

"Well, then at least dance with Shane. It will make his night."

"I hardly think so," she scoffed, but then glanced toward

the bar. "But I did promise to save a dance for him," she conceded. "And I keep my promises."

"Then promise me *you'll* keep an open mind when it comes to Shane. He can always get another house-keeper."

"Not one as good as me," she boasted.

"I don't doubt that one bit," Garret said, and then gave her a hug. "You're a good woman, Laura Lee. Shane couldn't do better than you and I'm not talking about cooking and cleaning. Remember that, okay?"

"I will."

"Promise?" He raised his eyebrows and waited.

"I promise," she said, lifting her palms upward.

"Good, now go in there and give the man his dance."

"Okay!"

Garret watched the spunky redhead walk back inside and then headed over to the steps leading to the parking lot. He walked toward his car with his hands shoved in his pockets and his head down. The wind had suddenly picked up and he could smell a hint of rain in the air. As if confirming his suspicion, he heard the rumble of thunder in the distance. As he walked Garret mulled over what Laura Lee said to him and wondered if she was right. He did know that Laura Lee cared about Mattie endlessly and wouldn't do anything to cause her any pain, and so for some reason she must believe in him. "Ha," Garret said with a shake of his head. "Imagine that," he mumbled, and the thought lightened his mood if only a little bit.

"Can you give a girl a ride home?"

"Mattie?" Startled, Garret looked over to see her standing in the shadows by his car, and his heart felt as if it flipped over in his chest.

"The new, improved Mattie Mayfield at your service. Now open the car door. It's going to rain and I don't want my beachy waves to get wet." She pointed to her head. "I know I look effortlessly tousled, but it took me an enormous amount of time to curl my hair."

"How did you get out here?"

She looked down at her boots and then back at him.

"Okay, silly question." He walked over to stand next to her.

"Even in the dark your silver sports car stands out among all the pickup trucks," Mattie said with a wave of her hand. "I watched you walk outside and it was either go look for you or karaoke the Dixie Chicks song 'Earl' with Myra."

"I would have come back in to hear that," Garret said. "Are you any good?"

"I can't carry a tune in a bucket."

"What does that even mean?"

"That I pretty much suck."

Garret laughed. "Even better." He clicked his remote to unlock his doors and walked over to her. "So, why are you really out here, Mattie? You seemed pretty happy dancing with Colby." The question made his heart beat faster.

"I was."

Garret felt a flash of hurt. "Is that what you came out here to tell me? Did you kiss him too?"

"I thought that's what you wanted me to do."

"Is that a yes, then?"

"No."

"Why not?"

"Because I don't want to kiss Colby. I want to kiss you," she said, and before Garret could say anything more Mattie rose on tiptoe and wrapped her arms around his neck. "I was happy dancing with Colby because it was making you jealous."

"Ha!"

"Am I right?"

"Okay, yes. Guilty as charged. In hindsight pushing you into the arms of another man was a poor suggestion."

Mattie's eyes turned serious. "No . . . you were right. I

needed to sort out my feelings so I could prove you wrong once and for all."

"And did you?"

"Yes, I want to be with you. Now just shut up and kiss me, Garret."

"Gladly." Garret cradled her head with his hand and slanted his mouth across hers. He kissed her slowly, savoring the texture of her soft lips, the taste of her sweet mouth, and the erotic touch of her tongue to his. When she leaned against the door of his car, Garret pressed his body intimately to hers, loving when her soft curves melted against him. Garret poured all his pent-up passion into the kiss, licking across her full bottom lip and nibbling before plunging deeply yet again. When fat raindrops started to fall he didn't care. Nothing mattered more than having Mattie in his arms.

"It's raining," she said breathlessly.

"I don't care."

"Me neither," she said with a low breathless laugh. "Proving you wrong is so much fun."

"Then keep doing it." The rain pelted against Garret's back, but he barely felt it. Bending down, he kissed her neck, cupped her breast. He wanted to lay her over the hood of his car and make love to her while the rain and the wind raged all around them, but getting caught kept him from suggesting that fantasy. "I want to take you home and make love to you in your white cloud," he said in her ear.

"Then what are you waiting for?"

"For you to ask me."

"Take me home and make love to me, Garret."

Moments later they were in his car driving as fast as Garret could go in the pouring rain.

"Since when did my cabin get one hundred miles away from here?" Mattie asked with a laugh. "You need to get a truck so you can take the off-road shortcut."

"I'll do it anyway."

"And get us stuck in this sassy little sports car? No way."

"Good point." Garret laughed and felt an almost giddy sense of pure joy. He had the strong urge to tell Mattie that he loved her, because in that moment he knew that he really was hopelessly in ass-over-teacups love and he wanted to shout it to the world. No one else had ever made him feel this damn happy and for no other reason than that she was sitting next to him.

"What?" she asked when he fell silent. "I can hear you thinking."

"You have good ears." Garret glanced her way before putting his attention back on the winding road. "You make me smile."

"How?"

"Just by being with you. We could be digging a ditch and I'd still be happy as long as you were by my side."

Mattie leaned her head back against the headrest and laughed.

"Okay, that wasn't exactly Hallmark quality but you get what I mean."

"No . . . I love it," she said softly. "And I completely understand because I feel the same way, Garret."

"Thank God."

"That I feel the same way?"

"Yes, that . . . but thank God we've finally arrived at your cabin."

"You covered the one hundred miles really fast," she said with a laugh. "I'll race you to the front door!" With a squeal she scrambled from the car and ran laughing through the rain. She fumbled with her keys until he took them from her and opened the door.

"I'm soaked!"

"Then we better get you out of those wet clothes, pronto."

"Excellent idea!" Mattie made a mad dash for her bedroom and Garret followed in close pursuit. She paused to click on a small decorative lamp, casting the room in a soft glow.

Wet clothes landed with a plop against the hardwood floor. Mattie and Garret fell against the mountain of pillows, kissing and caressing, skin sliding against warm wet skin. "I've wanted to feel your naked body next to mine, but the reality of it is blowing me away. I can't believe that you're in my arms, Mattie."

"Better than digging a ditch?" she asked, and then kissed his shoulder.

"Way better," Garret said, and then pulled back to look at her. He'd waited for this moment and wanted to slow down as much as his passion would allow. She was in a half-sitting position, leaning against the pillows. Her hair, still damp and slightly curled, looked like spun gold against the stark white bedding. "God, you're beautiful." He traced a fingertip over her cheek and then down her neck until he reached the valley between her breasts. She remained still and allowed him to look his fill.

"Am I?"

"Yes." He cupped her full breasts. "Perfection," he said softly, and looked into her eyes.

She swallowed hard, but her gaze didn't waver. "Thank you."

Garret rubbed his thumbs over her nipples until her breath caught and she arched her back. Leaning down, he kissed one breast and then the other and then sucked a nipple into his mouth.

With a soft moan she threaded her fingers through his hair. "Oh God, that feels ... mmm ... amazing," she said, making Garret smile. He knew that making love to Mattie would be organic and natural.

"I love how you taste and how you feel, Mattie." Garret explored her skin, lightly caressing her everywhere. She urged him on with little gasps and sexy groans. Her hands moved to his shoulders and then slid down his back.

"The feeling is mutual. Oh, but I want ... ," she said, but sucked in a breath when his fingers trailed over her mound and then slid inside her wet heat.

"This?" He moved his finger in slow circles and watched the play of emotion on her face. She closed her eyes and her breathing became shallow through slightly parted lips.

"Yes . . . ," she said. "Oh yes."

Garret increased the pressure just slightly, dipping his fingers in and out. She felt so warm and silky against his hand and looked so utterly gorgeous while in the throes of passion. He longed to lick her, to taste her, but he couldn't tear his gaze away from her face. He plunged his finger deep and then touched her with a barely there caress until she arched her hips in a silent plea for release. Still, Garret held back, wanting her to be wild with desire for him. When she opened her eyes he replaced his finger with the pad of his thumb and she climaxed with a soft and oh so sexy throaty moan.

Garret rolled to the side, almost painfully aroused, and dug into his wallet for a condom. He quickly sheathed himself and then slid his body against hers. Garret looked at her flushed face and then kissed her parted lips before entering her in one fluid, gentle stroke. "God, you feel so good."

"I love having you inside me."

"It's where I belong."

"Mmm . . . yes." She wrapped her legs around him while he made slow and steady love to her, bringing her back to the brink of an orgasm. "Oh, Garret."

"Mattie . . . beautiful Mattie." Garret kissed her and then stroked her faster, deeper, and when he felt her climax he found his own sweet release. A hot wave of pleasure washed over him unlike anything he'd experienced before and he knew why. What they'd just shared went beyond sex. His heart thudded with the knowledge and he had trouble not telling her, because he wanted her to know how much he cared for her. He didn't know how to verbalize what he was feeling other than professing his love for her, but he was so afraid it was too soon and that Mattie might not believe him, so he somehow remained silent. Instead he rolled to the side and held her close, hoping that she might feel his love through the beat of his heart.

As if in response to his silent admission, she placed a flutter of light kisses on his chest and then rested her head on his shoulder. After a few moments he said, "Mattie?"

"Yes?" she responded in a lazy, satisfied tone. She started tracing her fingers over his skin in small circles.

"I . . . I want us to be together."

She stopped drawing circles and raised her head. "You want me to be your girlfriend?"

"Yes, love, my girlfriend. I want us to be exclusive. Do you . . . do you want to?"

Mattie laughed.

"Um, that wasn't the response I was hoping for," he said with a frown.

"No!"

"No?" Garret felt crestfallen.

"No, I meant you're just so doggone cute. And when you say gar-el in that English way of yours, I just melt."

"Wait. I'm confused. So, is that a yes, then?"

"Yes!" She leaned down and gave him a quick kiss, but he held her there and kissed her thoroughly. "Well, now I get to stake my claim. Every girl in Sully's had her eye on you tonight."

"Really? I didn't know. Maybe I spoke too soon, then," he said, and was rewarded with a playful shove.

"Surely you noticed."

"Mattie, love, I only have eyes for you," he said, and trailed a fingertip over her bottom lip. "I know it sounds like a cheesy line, but I'm telling you the total truth."

"Garret, I believe you." She smiled. "I understand because I feel the same way." She kissed him softly, sweetly. "Will you stay with me tonight?"

"And sleep on this white cloud?"

"Yes."

"Do I get to take a bubble bath in your big tub?"

"Absolutely."

"That just sealed the deal."

"And since tomorrow is Sunday I get to sleep in."

"And I'll fix you breakfast."

"Really?"

"As long as you're okay with toast."

Mattie laughed. "I'm totally fine with toast with a side of Garret Ruleman."

"Mmm . . . and you shall have it. And you know the best part?"

"What?"

"We still have all night ahead of us."

"Oh so true."

"I'm going to go to the bathroom and then we must get beneath the covers," he said, and she gave him a sleepy nod.

"Don't be too long."

"I won't," he said, and gave her a quick kiss on the forehead.

Garret padded across the hardwood floor and entered the big bathroom. He marveled at this unexpected turn of events and then gazed at himself in the mirror. "Don't screw this up," he said to his reflection. "Mattie Mayfield is a gem."

When he reentered the bedroom Mattie had turned the bed down and was beneath the covers. When he scooted in beside her she sighed and snuggled close. "Mmm . . . I like having you in my bed," she said in a sexy sleepy voice that had him immediately aroused.

"And I like being in your bed. You know I usually suffer from insomnia, but I think tonight I'll sleep like a log."

"Because you're sleeping on a cloud?" she asked with a low giggle, and looked at him with half-lidded eyes.

"No, love." Garret brushed a lock of hair from her face and then shook his head. "Because I'll be sleeping next to you."

Mattie kissed him and then asked, "Have you always been this romantic?"

"Never. But you are my inspiration."

"Oh, Garret . . ." She sighed and then placed her hand on his chest. "You are so good for me. . . ."

"And you for me." Garret put his hand over hers and waited until he heard soft and steady breathing. "Sweet Mattie, I love you so." He knew she was asleep and he couldn't wait for when the time was right to say those words directly to her. But he told himself to take one step at a time. He wanted her to feel how much he adored her before he said the words.

Garret smiled, thinking that he couldn't wait to tell his mum that he was in love. She'd want to meet Mattie straightaway, so he'd have to start making plans for a trip to London in the near future. Garret thought that it was pretty crazy that he'd traveled all over the world and met the girl of his dreams in a small town in Kentucky.

Garret turned sideways and pulled Mattie close. With a sigh he brushed her hair to the side and then kissed her shoulder. She murmured something and sighed. After a while Garret closed his eyes and thought for the first time in his life everything felt so right and he was going to do whatever it took to keep it that way.

19

I Could Have Danced All Night

$\mathcal{L}$AURA LEE SQUEEZED THE HANDLE ON THE GARDEN hose, sending a gentle spray of water onto the potted plants dotting Shane's pool deck. When she was unhappily married her garden had become her sanctuary and had brought her much needed peace. Nourishing the plants and watching them thrive kept her feeling alive and somehow connected to the earth when her world had been crumbling all around her. Laura Lee had cultivated flowers that attracted butterflies, bees, and hummingbirds so she could enjoy the beauty of nature; she'd been adding some of those same plants around the pool and deck area at Shane's. While he'd given her permission to purchase whatever she wanted, Laura Lee enjoyed taking clippings and growing plants from seeds.

She hummed "We're All Alone" while she watered not only because she adored the Rita Coolidge classic but because she'd slow-danced to the love song with Shane on Saturday night. She'd managed to keep busy yesterday doing nonstop chores at her own house in an effort to keep the man off her mind, but as soon as she spotted Shane coming in from his morning run, all she could think about was dancing with him. The memory of swaying in his arms made her so hot and bothered that she considered turning the hose on herself!

Laura Lee looked at the tranquillity of the pool and sighed. Perhaps she'd take a refreshing dip after she finished making Shane's lunch. Even though he wasn't supposed to be home until late in the afternoon, she thought he might like a light chicken wrap or a tossed salad before dinner.

While she watered the growing collection of plants, Laura Lee thought she might start an herb garden in the bay windowsill in the kitchen so she could garnish his food with fresh organic seasonings. She tried to tell herself that she did so much because Shane paid her an insane amount of money for such an easy job, but she knew she simply wanted to please him. "Making him happy is my job," she said, trying to justify her need to impress him at every turn.

But she damn well knew better.

Of course, Laura Lee was doing pretty well hiding her growing feelings for him. At least she hoped so. "And then he had to go and give me the slow dance of all slow dances," she muttered.

Laura Lee knew that she shouldn't dwell on Saturday night, but her blasted brain refused to listen. She closed her eyes and relived the heady feeling of having her hand tucked in Shane's while they glided across the dance floor cheek to cheek. And on top of everything else he'd smelled divine. When she got home she'd realized the lingering scent of his aftershave had clung to her blouse and she'd refused to wash it like some sort of love-struck fool.

"Because that's what I am," she whispered, and then shook her head so hard that her ponytail swung back and forth. And not only could Shane dance like a dream, but when he'd started singing along with the song, goodness, she'd, well, nearly swooned. Seriously how much could a girl take, for Pete's sake?

Laura Lee closed her eyes and relived the evening

one more time before sternly telling herself to file the memory away once and for all. Her fantasy was fueled by the fact that after Mattie and Garret left, Shane had stayed by her side for the duration of the night. And to make matters worse Shane talked to people about her almost as if they were a couple. At one point Laura Lee actually wondered if he was doing so to get her used to the idea because perhaps that was what *he* wanted as well, but then she quickly discarded the notion as sheer folly. She also warned herself to stop having dinner with him nearly every night, but she could never find the will to refuse.

"Tonight," she said firmly. "Tonight I will come up with an excuse to have his dinner warm and ready but then go home where I belong." The thought, however, made her feel a bit sad. With a frown she realized that she'd been watering the pot of purple and white petunias too long and abruptly turned the hose away. Earlier she'd put a load of towels in the washer and then realized she'd forgotten to add detergent! And the entire reason for her scatterbrained behavior stemmed from daydreaming about her super-sexy boss.

And he wasn't just sexy. Shane McCray was kind and giving. He received constant requests from charities and he made a generous donation to each and every one either with money or donations of signed CDs and memorabilia. And the man made her laugh! She shook her head, thinking that she felt more at ease with Shane, a huge celebrity, than she'd ever felt with her ex-husband. For just a moment Laura Lee allowed herself to fantasize what it would be like to be Shane's woman. What would it feel like to kiss him?

To make love to him?

Oh, it had been so long since Laura Lee was intimate that she wondered if she still knew how to satisfy a man. And at fifty-five was she still attractive? She was in decent shape, but still . . . "Oh, stop!" she shouted skyward.

"Stop what?"

Startled, Laura Lee spun around and squirted Mattie directly in the face. "Oh, sorry!"

"Eeeeek!" Mattie shrieked, but in her good-natured way simply laughed while wiping the water from her cheeks. "That went up my nose!"

"I'm so sorry," Laura Lee said again, but she was having a hard time not laughing. "You did sneak up on me, you know."

"No, I didn't. I called your cell phone, but you didn't answer, so I thought I'd come over and see if you were here. When you didn't come to the door I took a chance and came back here, since your van was in the driveway. You seemed to be in a world of your own. Who were you talking to?"

"Myself." Laura Lee pointed to a towel draped over a chair. "I didn't mean to douse you, Mattie."

She shrugged as she patted her face dry. "Well, it's hot out and you cooled me off a bit. Do you have a minute? I have something to tell you." Light danced in her eyes, telling Laura Lee that the news was going to be good.

"Sure." Laura Lee put the hose down and gestured toward the umbrella table. "Have a seat, dear heart."

Once they were in the shade, Mattie said, "Um, Garret and I are, well, sort of dating."

Laura Lee felt a flash of joy. "Sort of?"

"No . . . well, we are." She put her hands up to her cheeks. "Is that crazy or what?"

"Oh my gosh! That's wonderful news!" Laura Lee jumped up and gave Mattie a quick hug before sitting back down. "So, how did this come about?"

"Well, I have a feeling you played a part in it, you little matchmaker."

"Who?" Laura Lee put a hand to her chest and then looked over her shoulder. "Oh, wait. Do you mean me?"

"Don't even try to act innocent. Yes, you." Mattie gave her a long, knowing look. "Garret gave me a ride home Saturday night."

"And?" Laura Lee drew out the word. "You have to tell me more than that little tidbit."

"We . . . we kissed." She lifted one shoulder, and her cheeks turned a pretty shade of pink, suggesting that they did more than just kissing. "We spent the entire day together yesterday doing nothing. Just hanging out, you know? Watching movies, sitting by the lake. I didn't even know I knew how to loaf around like that, but Garret said he was an expert and taught me how," she said with a laugh. "He said that he had loafing down to an art."

"Good! You need to know how to kick back and relax. It's healthy."

"I know, right?" Mattie raised her hands. "Who knew?"

"I'm so happy for you, Mattie. Garret is quite an interesting guy. I like him a lot and I think you two make a cute couple."

"I never pictured myself with someone like him, Laura Lee. I have to admit that it's exciting but sort of surreal." She inhaled a deep breath and then looked out over the pool. "Am I setting myself up for major heartbreak? I mean, is he going to wake up one day soon and come to his senses?"

"He's already come to his senses by realizing what a catch you are, Mattie. And it's about time someone did."

"But I'm just . . . you know . . . a boring little breakfast cook."

"Oh, sweetie, I can't answer the heartbreak question. Look at me. I mean, I married an accountant. Jack was an ordinary small-town guy going to the same college as me. If anyone had asked me if he'd ever cheat on me or talk down to me the way he did, I would have laughed in their face. So I think you need to look at the person and how he treats you and forget all about the whole fame and money thing."

Mattie angled her head at Laura Lee and gave her a pointed look.

"Oh no . . . don't even say it. Garret isn't your employer. You don't have that obstacle in your way."

"Well, now, I wasn't gonna mention that at all," Mattie said. "But you must have been thinking a lot about your situation or you wouldn't have made that comment."

"Mattie . . ."

"No way." Mattie wagged a finger at her. "You said it, not me, so you can't take it back."

"I was speaking in general terms."

"Don't even try that angle."

"Okay, then we're talking about you, not me. This is your news, your day," she insisted, desperately needing to change the subject.

"Why is it all so scary?"

"Because love is the most powerful emotion of all. To be loved is what we seek most in this life. It's what we were put here for, really." She sliced a hand through the air. "Everything else is all trivial in the end."

"I never really thought of it that way."

"It's true. I mean, even if you're watching a movie full of action, what we care about is the hero and heroine getting together in the end."

"Well, hell's bells." Mattie shook her head slowly. "I feel like I've just jumped off a cliff and I'm free-falling!"

"Exhilarating, right?"

"Um, yeah, but I just hope I find my wings and don't land with a huge splat at the bottom." She smacked her hands together to demonstrate.

Laura Lee laughed. "Oh, sweetie, I don't think that's going to happen. Sure, there will be bumps in the road, but for now don't worry and just enjoy the ride."

"Don't worry, be happy," Mattie sang, making Laura Lee laugh again.

"So, did you tell your mama about you and Garret yet?"

"I'm gonna give it a little time first."

"How about your brothers?"

"Not yet. I'm gonna take Garret to the next bonfire at the marina. You're the first to know."

"Well, I'm honored and I won't say a thing to anyone."

"I'm so lucky to have you as a friend."

"And the same goes here." Laura Lee felt a tug of emotion. Mattie was a friend and also felt like the daughter she always longed for.

Mattie leaned forward. "Oh, and I heard that you danced with Shane. Tell me all about it."

Laura Lee shrugged. "It was a dance, nothing more." She hoped her voice sounded casual.

"Do you want more?"

"Even if I did, it's pointless. Why can't everybody see that?"

"Maybe because it isn't pointless. It's pretty obvious that Shane is into you. I mean, that man talks about you like you're his girlfriend."

"But I'm not. I'm his housekeeper. We spend so much time together and we're just becoming close because of that."

"But are you falling for him, Laura Lee? You can tell me, because your secrets are safe with me as well."

"Of course I'm *attracted* to him, but look, I had my Cinderella night. It's enough," she insisted, but looked away from Mattie so she wouldn't guess the truth. "Once you've been hurt the way I've been trampled on, it's pretty hard to do it all over again."

"No, now, there's where you're dead wrong. I think it's even more reason to give it a shot, because you *deserve* happiness after what you've been through. Think about it that way."

"Okay, I admit that I have thought about it. Look, I think that Shane is a really good man. But he's rich and famous. I would just be a passing folly and risk my job in the process."

"He seems pretty down-to-earth to me."

"Mattie, there is more at stake here than my feelings."

"What if he wasn't rich and famous? What then?"

"I'd go after him in a heartbeat," Laura Lee admitted without really thinking.

"Yes, you said that out loud, so don't even try to take it back."

Laura Lee put a hand over her mouth.

"No, you don't. Talk to me."

"But he is rich and famous, Mattie. The man is way, way out of my league."

"That's nonsense just like the whole I'm-too-old-for-love thing you tried. Look at multimillionaire Mitch Monroe and Nicolina Diamante. That one example busts through the whole age thing, because they are both over fifty. Plus, Mitch is super rich while she was a struggling jewelry maker. And she wouldn't have to work another day in her life, but Mitch supports her jewelry shop because it's her dream. So you have a double whammy where they're concerned. It sure didn't stop them from falling in love, now, did it?"

"An exception to the rule."

"I'm finding out that there are no rules where love is concerned. You heart doesn't care about any of that stuff. You as much as said so yourself. In the end love is everything."

"But my brain does care."

"Okay, well, then I'll keep going with examples to shut your brain up. Not only was Noah Falcon a famous baseball player, but he was a soap opera star too. That didn't keep him from falling in love and marrying high school drama teacher Olivia Lawson. Garret's rock star dad and Maggie McMillan are yet another prime example. Do I need to keep going? How many more exceptions to the rule do you need? And I suppose I'm an example too."

"No, you don't have to go on, but that doesn't mean I should believe in a fantasy that will never happen."

"You don't know that!" Mattie leaned back and looked up at the sky. "You're such a contradiction. If you talk the talk you have to walk the walk, Laura Lee."

"No, what I need to do is to start going home at night and stop having dinner with Shane like . . . like we're a couple. I mean, we take walks. Swim sometimes." She shook her head. "I'm finally in a better place in my life. I need to be more professional and not risk losing my job. I mean, let's get real. I can't be Shane's housekeeper and his girlfriend."

"There are other jobs."

"Not like this one."

Mattie fell silent for a minute. "If you weren't afraid, would you risk it?"

Laura Lee thought about it for a few seconds.

"Be honest."

"Yes," she admitted softly. "I guess I would."

"Then don't be afraid."

"Fear isn't something you can just turn off like that hose over there."

"True. Then be brave. Jump off the cliff like me."

"You are relentless!"

"Yes, and I'm going to do the same thing you did to me." She arched one eyebrow and paused for dramatic effect. "I dare you."

"Dares don't bother me," she scoffed. "Not being able to pay my bills bothers me, though. I don't need to go and make a pass at my boss and then get my sorry self fired. I like being able to go shopping without feeling guilty afterward. I like looking at my bank account and actually seeing money in there."

Mattie sat up straighter. "What if Shane makes a pass at you?" She pointed across the table. "Then it would be on him and you wouldn't be held accountable. Just be all sexy and stuff and see what happens. Put a little wiggle in your walk."

"Would you just listen to yourself?"

"I think it's a good plan."

"I'm not *planning* anything except for doing my dog-gone job. If you don't stop I'm gonna squirt you with that hose again."

"All right. I'll shut up. At least for now."

"Praise the Lord for small favors."

"But—"

"No!" Laura Lee reached over for the hose, stood up,

and pointed it at Mattie. "This thing is still turned on," she warned. "I'm giving you fair warning this time."

Mattie raised her hands in surrender. "Okay!"

"So you give up?"

"I was taught to never give up," Mattie said. "But I will."

Laura Lee nodded but then said, "I don't like that gleam in your eye. Don't you go and try something."

"How come you can play matchmaker but not me? And if you start that life-has-passed-me-by stuff again, I'm gonna push you into the pool."

"You wouldn't dare."

"I know. I'm full of hot air." Mattie stood up and went over and gave Laura Lee a hug.

"Mattie, I know your heart is in the right place and you want to see me happy. I feel the same way about you. But this subject needs to be closed."

"I understand." Mattie nodded slowly. "Well, I've got to go and buy some supplies for the restaurant. I just wanted to share my crazy news."

"It's wonderful news, Mattie. I am so happy for you."

"I knew you would be. Oh, and Garret said that he'd like to come over for a barbecue soon," Mattie added. "I mean, you and Shane already invited us, so . . ."

Laura Lee sighed. "Is there no end to you?"

"Nope. I go on forever."

"I'll ask Shane what night is good and get back to you."

"Promise?"

Laura Lee groaned.

"Laura Lee!"

"Okay, I promise. Are you happy?"

"Yes! Give him a hug for me."

"I will not!"

"I said for me." She tapped her chest.

Laura Lee answered by giving her a quick squirt.

"Hey!"

"You deserved it! Now go or I'll get you from head to toe."

"Okay!" Mattie laughed and then hurried away. But when she was beyond squirting distance, she shouted, "I'm not going to give up on this."

"I told you it's pointless!" Laura Lee shouted back, but had to smile. Mattie seemed so happy that it warmed her heart. She thought about what Mattie said about being sexy, and the little devil on her shoulder whispered in her ear, "Do it. At least give it a try. Wiggle, wiggle, wiggle."

"No!" With a shake of her head she went back to watering the rest of the thirsty plants.

"What's pointless?"

Laura Lee whirled around and this time Shane got a full shot of water on his chest. "Oh no!" Horrified, Laura Lee dropped the hose. It remained turned on and started squirming around like an irate snake. "Sorry!" she shouted, and started chasing the hose without any luck. "I didn't expect you until later."

"The meeting ended early." Laughing, Shane joined her in the mad chase.

When Laura Lee finally pounced and picked up the hose, she accidently squirted him again, this time grazing the top of his head. "Sorry!" she said, but made the mistake of giggling.

"No, you're not." He came at her with purposeful strides, making her back away.

Laura Lee took a step backward. "No, I am," she insisted, but her heart kicked it up a notch. She knew he was playing with her, and damn if she didn't like it.

"I think I need to get you back," Shane said, but she only laughed.

"I'm the one with the weapon."

"And I plan to change that situation."

"Don't come one step closer." She raised the hose and aimed it at him. "I'll shoot."

"Squirt me and I'll toss you in the pool." He angled his wet head toward the water.

"You wouldn't dare."

"You wouldn't dare squirt me or you'll find out."

"Of course I wouldn't," Laura Lee said, and lowered the nozzle to her side. But when he took another step closer that doggone devil on her shoulder gave her a hard nudge and with a little squeal Laura Lee took aim and pulled the trigger.

"No, you didn't!" Shane lunged toward her and tried to snag her around the waist.

"Yes, I did!" With another little squeal Laura Lee dodged him and gave him another quick blast.

"Okay, then you asked for it."

With wide eyes Laura Lee watched Shane take his wallet and cell phone out of the pocket of his khaki shorts. She swallowed hard when he tugged his shirt over his head, distracting Laura Lee with the nice ripple of muscle. That tiny bit of letting her guard down was her mistake. Shane turned and lunged toward her. She dropped the hose and fearing what he was about to do, she beat him to the punch and jumped fully clothed into the pool.

When Shane dove into the water in hot pursuit, Laura Lee swam away, but she was hindered by her laughter. When she felt him grab her foot she kicked him off, losing a flip-flop in the process. She swam for the shallow end, but he swiftly caught up with her and snagged her around the waist.

"Gotcha." When he pulled her to his side she fully expected him to duck her under and braced herself.

Instead he spun her around.

And then he kissed her.

20

Who's the Boss?

SHANE HAD ANTICIPATED KISSING LAURA LEE FOR DAYS, but he still wasn't prepared for the reality of having her in his arms. Her lush, warm mouth made him so hot that he was glad to be in the cool water. Of course in his fantasy the first kiss wasn't going to be in the pool after a long chase. He'd planned on something more romantic like after an intimate dinner or dancing in the moonlight or perhaps his favorite, which was kissing her while taking a steamy soak in the hot tub together.

He'd been dreaming of the erotic moment his lips touched hers, but he hadn't been prepared for the emotional impact. After the slow dance and the evening spent together at Sully's, kissing Laura Lee was number one on his list of priorities. And his list was growing longer with each day spent in her company.

When Laura Lee melted against him Shane deepened the kiss and pulled her closer. She wrapped her arms around his neck, and the kiss went on and on, making him think that kissing him might have been on her to-do list as well. Good, they must be on the same page.

But just when he thought about being bold enough to

cup her cute ass, she pushed at his chest and backed up a step. "What was that?"

"I think they call it a kiss."

"But . . . ?"

"Laura Lee, I was trying to go slow, bide my time until the time was right. I wanted to take you to dinner or do something romantic first, but I just couldn't wait one more minute."

Laura Lee blinked at him, looking confused and so utterly gorgeous that he reached for her once more, but she backed away. "No . . . Shane, you're my boss."

"I'll make you the boss. In fact, I'll do whatever you want me to. Go ahead, give me an order."

"I . . . You . . ." She shook her head and appeared horrified. "No!"

"Why not?"

"Because!" she sputtered.

"Because? You have to do better than that."

She simply shook her head. "This is when you're supposed to say, 'Sorry, I didn't mean to do that.'"

"But I'm not sorry." Shane wanted to take a step closer, but she looked like a scared doe ready to bolt into the woods. He stood very still, not making so much as a ripple in the water. But with her shirt clinging like a second skin, he was having a difficult time not pulling her back against his body.

"I . . . I shouldn't have been so familiar, squirting you and all that. I acted like a silly teenager! And now we're in this pool fully clothed! What is wrong with me? I'm the one who should be sorry." She smacked the water, making it splash, and Shane wanted to laugh but knew better. He also knew that he wanted this sweet woman in his life as something much more than his employee.

"Don't be sorry, Laura Lee. It was fun. Chasing you around made me feel young. I've been so focused on my music, my career, that moments like this have been far and few between. I'd like to start living and not just performing." The thought also went through his head that he didn't want to be fully clothed, but he kept that little detail to himself. "And like I said I've wanted to kiss you for a long time. This was not your doing. Well, unless you count how lovely you are. But you can't help that," he said, hoping she would smile.

She remained still but frowned as if processing that information.

"And judging by your reaction, you feel the same way. Am I right?" he asked with hesitation, but when she sloshed a step backward he wished he hadn't pressed the issue. He watched her warring with the truth and wanted to tell her to stop this nonsense and just come clean. He could see in her eyes how much she wanted him, and waiting any longer for what they both so clearly needed seemed pointless.

"I was . . . swept away in the moment." She made a sweeping gesture that caused more water to fly.

"And now that the moment has passed? Are you still swept away?"

"I am your housekeeper. I sweep your floors." She took another step back. "And now everything is going to be . . . weird."

Shane shook his head. "It doesn't have to be."

"Right. . . ."

She had a point. He did what he didn't want to do and went too damn fast. "No, it won't. This is on me. Okay?"

She paused but then gave him a quick nod. "Okay."

"But would you do something for me please?"

She nodded again. "Of course."

"Forget about the money and the fame and just let me be a man."

"What?"

"Give me tonight, Laura Lee." He held up his index finger. "One night where I'm just an ordinary guy having dinner with a beautiful girl."

"Shane . . ."

"I don't expect anything more. Can you do that for me?"

She looked at him and then said, "I already had my Cinderella moment."

He was surprised by her statement. "Come again?"

"When you danced with me." She smiled this time. It was a soft, sad smile that tugged at his heart unlike anything he'd ever felt before. "But now I have to go back to being your housekeeper."

As if on cue a red rubber flip-flop floated his way and he reached over and grabbed it. "Shall we see if it fits?"

"No."

Shane shook his head. "You're forgetting how the story ends, Laura Lee." His heart thudded and he had to take a step closer. She didn't back up, but her eyes rounded. He put a fingertip beneath her chin and tilted her head up. Her mascara was smudged and tendrils of hair had escaped her ponytail and she was still the most beautiful creature he'd ever seen. "How did the story end?"

She looked at him and swallowed hard. "Happily ever after," she finally replied barely above a whisper.

"Exactly." Shane dipped his head and captured her mouth with a gentle but lingering kiss. He could feel the slight tremble in her lips and wanted to hold her close. But he pulled back and said, "And if you let me in, that's how our story could end as well."

"No." Laura Lee shook her head again. She took another step away from him and said, "We're going to pretend this never happened. I'm going to be professional and do my job."

Shane saw the longing in her eyes, but he also saw stark fear. And fear like that could only come from getting hurt. She wasn't ready to trust him. "I'll pretend, Laura Lee. But that's what it will be ... pretending. When you're ready to let me in, just tell me. I'll be waiting."

She stood there as if anchored to the bottom of the pool and remained silent. He wanted to see her smile and hear her husky laughter. And he wanted to kiss her again.

But instead he walked past her and hoisted himself over the side of the pool. He wanted to look over his shoulder and see if she was watching him, but he forced himself to keep on walking up toward the house. He still had the flip-flop in his hand and thought about taking it back to her, but if he got anywhere near her he might end up pulling her into his arms once again. And that would be yet another major mistake.

The plants she'd been watering were thriving from her care. And when he climbed the back steps to the deck, her touch was there as well. The kitchen smelled fragrant and homey and when he opened the fridge to grab a bottle of water he saw the food she'd prepared for him. While he knew it was her job, Shane still felt the special care she took and knew that the things she did went beyond her job description.

Because he'd been on the road for so many years, Shane never cared much about what his house looked like, more interested in getting much needed rest. He paid very little attention to whatever his interior decorator furnished his house with. But for the first time his house was beginning to look and feel and smell like a real home. Shane knew that this feeling also had to do with the laughter, the conversation at mealtime that had little to do with music and business. While he still received countless requests to do events, Shane turned them all down unless they had something to do with charity. He still wanted to give back, but other than that he was bound and determined to remain retired.

Shane's thoughts returned to Laura Lee and he sighed. She was right. Things were going to be weird. He would just have to tread softly and keep his distance until they found their way back to the easygoing relationship they'd forged. Then he hoped that she would let her guard down for good. Until then, he'd have to keep his distance.

But how could he when there was evidence of her all over the house? Her reading glasses were on the counter next to a romance novel she'd been reading. A note written in her handwriting listed items needed from the grocery store. Shane realized that she already knew his favorite things. He loved her quick laugh, her lively sense of humor. She brightened his days and filled his nights with a fierce longing that he'd not felt before.

And when he went upstairs to peel his wet clothes off, he swore he could smell the lingering scent of her perfume. He wanted her in his arms . . . and in his bed.

But most of all Shane wanted Laura Lee in his life. And so he'd try once more to be patient.

Shane turned on the shower, thinking that because of his success it had been a long time since he was denied what he wanted. He suddenly liked the feeling of a challenge. They were meant to be together. Shane could feel it. Now all he had to do was find a way to make it happen.

21

What About Love?

$\mathcal{W}$HEN GARRET PUSHED OPEN THE HEAVY GLASS DOOR to My Way Recording Studio, he smiled at Teresa Bennett. "Hello, love," he said to the fellow Brit who never failed to make him smile.

"Well, hey, darling. Your father is on the phone, but he's anxious to talk to you," Teresa said, making Garret wonder if the cheeky front desk receptionist knew the reason his father had called him in this late in the day. Garret and Mattie had plans to grill out on the back deck and then head over to the marina for a bonfire. Garret had errands to run, so at first he'd thought about asking to come to the studio tomorrow for the unexpected meeting. But judging by the look on Teresa's face, whatever this was about was going to be interesting at the very least.

Garret's imagination kicked into high gear. Maybe they were going to sign a heavy hitter to the label. With Jeff Greenfield's third top-twenty hit in a row, My Way Records was starting to attract the attention of several artists. Garret's discovery of Rachel Ryan at open-mic night a few months ago at Tootsies had already led to a hit single that was climbing the charts. Although they were small compared to the big labels, they were creating some buzz in and around Nashville.

Garret walked over to the watercooler and filled a cone-shaped cup with cold water. After downing the entire thing, he crushed the cup and walked over to the U-shaped desk. "Okay, Teresa, are you going to give me a hint as to what's going on?"

Teresa gave her hair a flip. "What makes you think I know something?"

"That look on your pretty face is a dead giveaway."

"Ha, you think flattery will get me to spill the beans?"

"Yes."

Teresa tapped a pen to her cheek. "Normally you'd be right. But not this time, kiddo." Teresa had been a backup singer for his father's road band back in his rock-and-roll heyday. Teresa now doubled as the front desk receptionist and a singer on tracks when needed. Once a wild child in her own right, she'd settled down in Cricket Creek and seemed to enjoy working for the small studio.

"Have you been back to London lately?" Garret asked, thinking he could steer the conversation in a different direction and then home in on the reason for the meeting.

"Not in nearly a year. And I've had a hankering for some pie and mash," Teresa admitted with a long, dramatic sigh.

"No pie and mash, but I can tell you that they do have a bloody good shepherd's pie on the menu at Wine and Diner up in town. We should have lunch there someday soon."

"Are you trying to butter me up?"

"Is it working?"

"Nope. How's your mum these days?"

"I spoke with her just the other day. Doing well. Misses me, of course."

"Who wouldn't? Gorgeous as ever, I assume. I hate that I lost touch with Becca after she moved back to London for good. Is she seeing anyone these days?"

"Not that I know of," Garret said.

"I guess that men are afraid to approach a famous fashion model."

"She hasn't modeled for years, but she does keep her hand in the fashion industry."

"Sophia and Grace? All grown up, I suppose."

"Yes, and thinking about coming to Cricket Creek for a visit. Sophia can't get over me moving to a small town and living in a cabin on the river. She thinks I'm pulling her leg even though I sent pictures showing her proof. She says she won't believe it until she visits."

"Did you invite her?"

"Yes, of course. Wait until she sees me in Wranglers and cowboy boots."

"I remember her being a little spitfire when she was a little tot. And Grace?"

Grace is actually thinking of moving to London, but she and Sophia are so close that I'm afraid they'll miss each other too much. But Grace wants to explore her heritage and I don't blame her for that. Unlike me they've spent most of their lives in the States."

When Teresa got a bit of a wistful look on her face, Garret leaned against the desk. "Ever think of moving back?"

"I love the energy of the city, but London is too expensive. And I've grown quite fond of Cricket Creek, crazy as it seems."

"No, I agree with you. There's just something about this town that pulls you in and won't let go."

Teresa arched an eyebrow. "Might have something to do with the cute little blonde I've seen you with, love?"

Garret grinned. "It might."

"Good for you, Garret. That's fantastic news. I'm glad to see that you've settled down. It took me a helluva lot longer to grow up and sometimes I still have trouble behaving."

Garret laughed. "Maybe you'll find yourself some country boy here in town."

"Who could put up with the likes of me? I hardly think so."

"Good point," Garret said, and was rewarded by Teresa tossing a jellybean from a jar she had on her desk. Garret ducked and it hit the window with a ping. "Hey!"

"You deserved it."

"Your teeth are going to rot out eating those all the time."

"Better for me than smoking."

"True enough." Garret was about to try to get a hint from her about the meeting when his father's door opened.

"Garret. Thanks for coming over on short notice."

"It better be good," Garret answered, but felt a bit of excitement when his father nodded.

"It is. Come on in my office. Teresa, hold all calls, okay?"

"I already had that figured out."

"Cheeky thing, isn't she?" Garret asked, and had another jelly bean tossed at him as he walked toward the doorway. He deftly caught it and tossed it in his mouth. "Cherry, my favorite," he said over his shoulder, and had another one hit him in the head.

"Have a seat."

"So, what's up?" Garret sat down in the leather chair and crossed his ankle over his knee.

"Just a little something I want to talk over with you."

"All right, then, carry on." Garret tried to act casual but he could feel energy in the air. Although Garret was pretty much used to his father's transformation from long-haired leather-clad rock star to short-cropped hair and business casual, it was still sometimes a bit surreal. Resentment for his father's absence in his childhood still reared its ugly head on the odd occasion, but his dad's apology and Garret's forgiveness felt like a weight being lifted from his shoulders. Still, if Garret ever had children, he vowed, he would be there for his kids at all cost. "Don't keep me hanging."

"I got a call from Russ Randall a little while ago."

"The producer?"

"Yes."

"That's pretty sweet."

"I know, but he wasn't looking for me. Russ was interested in talking to you."

"Really?"

"I wanted to chat with you before giving him your number so you could process the information first."

"Your beating around the bush is killing me."

Rick chuckled. "Russ didn't want to give me details, but I got as much out of him as he would allow."

"Dad! Get to the point!"

Rick scooted up and leaned forward on his elbows. "Russ wants you to be a judge on the British version of *Sing for Me*. He said that he values your ability as a musician and that he was impressed that you've recently spotted some amazing talent for My Way Records."

"How did he know?"

"Word gets around in this business, you know."

"I know, but word getting around about me has never been positive before," Garret joked.

"Those days are done. This is huge and I'm excited for you."

Garret felt shock running through his veins. This wasn't some reality nonsense but a respected talent show that was a huge success in the ratings both in the U.S. and in England. "Wow." Garret shoved his hands through his hair and looked across the desk at his father. "I have to admit that I'm a bit shocked. But it's really cool."

"It *is* really cool. And even if you choose not to do the show, I want to tell you how proud I am of you, Garret. This is quite an honor."

Speechless, Garret could only nod. "But . . . but what about my work here?"

"That's what I wanted to talk to you about so you'd have your ducks in a row before chatting with Russ. I want you to know that if you want to take the job I'm fine with it. Now, don't get me wrong, you've become invaluable here at the studio, but I don't want that to come between you doing something of this enormousness. Your job as a talent scout and studio musician will always be open."

"I appreciate that." Garret nodded.

"And I had zero to do with this." He made a circle with his thumb and index finger. "Russ called out of the blue. This is your achievement, Garret." He pointed across the table and Garret could see the emotion on his face.

Garret's heart thudded with excitement. "I have to admit that I'm blown away right now."

"You should be."

But then the startling realization set in. "Wait . . . It's set in London, then."

"Not far from your mother, actually. She'd be thrilled, I'm sure."

"Does she know about this?"

Rick shook his head. "I don't see how. Teresa knows because she took the call from Russ and she had the nerve to listen outside my door."

Garret had to chuckle. "Sounds about right."

"I should fire her."

"Like that will ever happen. You two have too much history."

Rick chuckled. "She could blackmail me with the knowledge she has from back in the day. Or write a tell-all book. But she wouldn't. She might have listened in, but she won't whisper a word and we both know it. She was just super excited when she took the call. And besides, I know just as much about her antics."

"I can only imagine." Garret grinned but then nodded slowly. "So, do you think I should do this?"

"Of course. It's an amazing opportunity. And if you're feeling any guilt about time away from the studio, know that the publicity would be invaluable for us too. I know that Maria will feel the same way about your involvement in Sully's South. If you choose to do this we'll work around your schedule somehow. That being said, the only thing you should consider is what is right for you on a personal level. And of course Russ didn't discuss money with me. Your agent will take care of that, I'm sure."

"Yeah . . . ," Garret said, and then closed his eyes and swallowed hard. Mattie. London. He looked at his father.

"What, Garret? Talk to me."

"I've been seeing Mattie Mayfield."

"Ah, and you're wondering how she will take it if you accept the offer?"

Garret nodded and then needed to make his father understand. "This isn't like my relationships in the past. I love her, Dad." It felt so good to say those words out loud. "I really do love her."

Rick smiled. "I can tell by the look on your face that this is serious. I am so happy for you, Garret."

"But we're not to the point where I could ask her to up and leave to come to London with me."

"You're in love with her. What point do you need to get to?"

"Dad, she's a small-town girl and she has her restaurant at the marina to run," he said, pretty much thinking out loud. "We're talking moving out of the country for someone who hasn't been out of Kentucky all that much. How do I begin to bring this up to her?"

"I can't answer that, but if you're asking my advice I'd wait until after you know the details. I do think that the search for talent for the show will start soon. It'll work much like *The Voice* and *American Idol* in that respect, I guess."

"Do you know when actual production will begin?"

"I don't know any details really. I had to pry what I do know out of Russ," he said, and Garret saw the sympathy on his face. "Life throws some curves at you. Tough choices and sometimes the timing is way off."

"You know all about that, don't you?" Garret asked but without the venom he'd once had.

"It's pretty hard to turn down money and fame. But I'm the poster child for how high the cost. I have regrets, Garret, and we've talked about all of them. There's no doubt that I sold out and became a person I didn't know and didn't like. That being said, the journey got me to where I am right here and now. I might have learned the hard way, but I did finally learn what's important in life. I can't make up for the years I lost with you, but there will never again be a time when you aren't in my life. Whether you're in London or here or wherever . . . we will never lose touch or break the bond that we now have."

"That means a lot to me, Dad. And I didn't have to be such a shit over the whole thing. I understand some things better now." Garret leaned back in the leather chair. "You know when Addison broke our engagement she told me to become something in my own right and to not ride on your or Mum's coattails."

"Smart girl. I've always liked her."

"And now that I have the chance for recognition on my own, I could lose Mattie in the process. It's like fate is laughing at me. Or maybe karma for all the people I hurt along the way."

"If karma is the big bitch that everybody claims she is, I wouldn't be sitting here having this conversation with you. Instead I have you in my life, the love of a good woman, and this little studio that I love. But I will tell you this. Money isn't worth it. And don't let your ego get in the way. Take money and pride out of the equation right now."

"What about love?"

"Love trumps money every time. Like I said, I learned the hard way."

"This is crazy. And complicated. I don't know what to do."

"A love that is strong enough can withstand just about anything. That's something only you can decide."

Garret looked up at the ceiling and shook his head. "This is the coolest thing and worst thing all wrapped in one neat little package. Pretty on the outside, but if I open it I feel as if it will explode in my face."

"Talk to Russ and to your agent. And give your mother a call."

"And when do I talk to Mattie?"

"Like I said, after you know more you'll know when the time is right," Rick said, and stood up. He came around to the other side of his desk and gave Garret a hug. "I'm so proud of you and of the man you've become."

Garret grinned. "It was touch-and-go there for a while, though, right?"

Rick shook his head. "You didn't have a normal life. And I wasn't there when you needed me most." For a relationship that was once strained at best, they'd come a long way.

"I learned the hard way too. And I didn't learn once from a mistake but had to make the same ones at least a half dozen times before it stuck."

Rick laughed. "You know what they say about the apple not falling far from the tree."

"I told Mattie that I was a nerd pretending to be a badass. I like being in the background much more than in the limelight. It just took me a long time to figure that out."

"I honestly think you'd be great on the show. You do have a knack for spotting talent and you have a witty, funny delivery. You'll charm the audience."

"Thanks." Garret felt a lump of emotion fill his throat. Validation from his father felt amazing. He felt like a kid hitting a home run in Little League.

Rick reached over and squeezed Garret's shoulder. "If you want to discuss more about this, let me know. You'll have a better handle on the situation once you talk to Russ. At any rate, congratulations. The offer is sweet no matter what you decide."

"Thanks, Dad. Well, I'd better get going. Mattie and I are grilling on my deck and then hanging out at the marina."

"Maggie and I would love to have you two over as well. I can't wait to meet the girl who tamed Garret Ruleman."

"You'll love her."

"I'm sure I will." He gave Garret another brief hug and then took a step back when his cell phone rang. "It's Maggie."

"Take the call, Dad. I'll get back with you on this."

When his father nodded Garret walked out into the reception area. Teresa pounced on him and gave him a hug before doing a little happy dance.

"Are you going to do it?"

"I don't know yet, but you'll be one of the first to know."

Her smile faded just a bit. "Oh . . . your girl."

"Yeah."

"You'll figure it out, Garret. And if you need to bend my ear, I'm here for you, darling."

"I know that, Teresa." He leaned over and gave her a kiss on the cheek. "Well, I'd best be off. I'll talk to you soon."

Garret pushed the door open and walked out into the parking lot. His emotions were a mixed bag, but he was going to take his father's advice and not mention this to Mattie until he knew more about the offer. Garret had to wonder, though, if her love for him was strong enough for her to follow him across the pond to London.

Or was his love for her strong enough for him to give the offer up?

22

Dancing in the Dark

AFTER GETTING THE TEXT MESSAGE FROM GARRET THAT he was running a bit late because of a meeting with his father, Mattie decided to head over to his cabin anyway. He'd given her a key, but this was the first time she'd used it when he wasn't there. Doing so made her feel connected to him on another level. She knew it was simply letting herself in, but the key dangling from her key chain signified so much more to her. Mattie put the vegetables for the tossed salad in the fridge and then scrubbed two big russet potatoes that she'd brought from the restaurant. She'd made a peach cobbler that was still warm from the oven and filled the kitchen with a homey scent of baked goods and cinnamon. Mattie had tweaked the standard cobbler recipe just a bit, adding a bit of brandy to give the dessert a richer, deeper flavor. She'd been reading up on desserts and pastries lately, thinking that she wanted to spruce up the selection on her menu. She considered adding lunch, but if she did it would mean hiring more employees and staying later.

Mattie opened a bottle of red wine and then took a glass from the rack above the sink, thinking about what her daddy would say to her mother when she wanted to make changes to the marina. "If it ain't broke don't fix it," Mattie said, and shook her head. She poured the merlot and then took a sip before letting out a sigh. Adding lunch would also mean less time to spend with Garret, and spending time with him had become a top priority.

Mattie felt a flash of excitement when she thought about going to the bonfire with him tonight. When they arrived hand in hand they would be making their relationship public and official.

She had a boyfriend.

A sweet, charming, sexy boyfriend. And she loved him.

Mattie cradled the knowledge close to her heart. The mere thought of Garret brought a smile to her face. And then knowing that he would be arriving soon, she decided to wait for him in bed. Dinner could wait. The bonfire could wait. But being in his arms could not.

Mattie nibbled on her bottom lip, wondering if she had the nerve to be naked and waiting bold as you please. She looked in the direction of the master bedroom and felt a shiver of anticipation.

Could she be that bold? Her heart thudded at the thought.

Up until now she had let Garret initiate making love, but what would it feel like to slide between the cool sheets and reach for him when he arrived home? She could light candles and have sultry jazz playing in the background. Could she do it?

"Yes. Oh, hell yes."

Deciding she needed more sexy props, she pulled some plump, juicy strawberries from the fridge and located the chocolate dip she'd bought for a sweet start to their night. She washed the fruit and arranged everything on a plate and then headed for the bedroom. Minutes later she pulled the curtains closed, dimmed the lights, and lit several fat candles. She located the cool jazz station and smiled when the sexy stage was set. After a quick stop in the bathroom to freshen up and brush her teeth, she pulled down the comforter and slid between the silky soft sheets.

And then she planned her seduction.

When Garret entered the room she would let the sheet pool at her waist and then reach for a strawberry. But instead of eating it she'd dip it in chocolate and paint a streak down her body and tell him to lick it off. Or maybe she'd strip him first and then paint his body or feed him?

Oh so many choices.

Coming up on all fours, she leaned over and dipped a strawberry in the chocolate, deciding she needed to eat one while she thought of more fun and sexy games. She'd just sunk her teeth into the big berry when she thought she heard the front door open.

"Mattie?"

Oh God . . . Garret was home.

Mattie's nerve suddenly failed her miserably and she decided to scramble from the bed and jump back into her clothes. But in her rush to turn over, her feet got twisted up in the sheet. A moment later Garret walked into the bedroom and found her kicking at the covers with a strawberry stuck in her mouth.

"Oh my God, are you all right?"

Mattie flopped over and stared up at him. She nodded.

"Babe, what are you doing?" He pulled the strawberry from her lips and took a bite.

"Planning a sexy seduction that went way wrong. And please don't tell me I have chocolate all over my chin."

"Okay, I won't tell you."

"Do I?"

"Yes."

"Oh, I suck at seduction."

"What makes you say that?"

"Look at me!"

"I am looking at you." He leaned over and licked the chocolate from her chin. "And I've never seen anything sexier."

"But I bungled it. . . ."

"No, Mattie. This is so you. Cute and funny and sexy as all get out."

"You think so?" When she lowered her gaze he tilted her chin up. Mattie could see the desire there and she smiled. "You can't say I didn't try."

"You don't even have to try. I've thought you were super sexy since the moment I found you pounding your fists on the floor."

"You thought that was sexy?"

"No, I thought that was funny, but I thought your cut-off shorts and little tank top were quite a turn-on. Mattie, you're perfect no matter what you wear. You're elegant in a dress with your hair pulled up and hot as hell in jeans." He gave her a slow smile. "But I love you the best wearing nothing at all . . . well, except for streaks of chocolate," he said, and then dipped his finger in the dish by the bed. "Lie back against the pillows and let me paint your beautiful body."

Mattie nodded and when he swirled the dark chocolate over one nipple she arched her back and giggled. "Oh, it's still cold from the fridge."

"Let me warm you up with my mouth," Garret offered, and she gratefully accepted. His tongue licked and swirled and the heat of his mouth made her moan. When he sucked her nipple she gasped and threaded her fingers through his hair. "I'm supposed to be doing . . . oh . . . this to . . . mmm . . . you."

"Do you want me to stop?"

"I . . . oh . . . ," she began, and when he nibbled lightly she shook her head. "N-nooo!" She pressed her head back into the soft pillow while he painted and licked, going lower and lower. Mattie's heart pounded and warm molten desire, thick as honey, spread throughout her body. He kissed the tender inside of her thigh and she could feel the warmth of his breath on her sex. Her heart thudded in anticipation, but Garret took his sweet time, kissing all around where she wanted him most. . . .

Just when she thought she couldn't stand another moment, he spread her thighs and licked her lightly, teasing her with flicks of his tongue, filling her with the desperate need for release. She closed her eyes, parted her lips, hovering on the brink while she fisted her hands in the sheet. Her entire body tingled and she curled her toes, arched her back ... and then shattered with soaring pleasure.

Mattie blinked, trying to focus while she floated back into her body. She turned her head and watched Garret undress, unable to form words. The ripples of muscle when he tugged his shirt over his head made her breath catch. He rolled on a condom, drawing her attention to the beauty of his body. Finally she said, "I think I've melted into the mattress. I don't think I can move."

"Oh, I think I'll find a way to get you moving again." Garret chuckled and gave her an endearing smile that seemed to squeeze her heart. He sat down on the edge of the bed and traced a fingertip down her cheek. "I love you, Mattie."

Mattie reached up and brought the fingertip to her mouth and kissed it. "I love you too, Garret. You make me very happy."

His smile widened and he bent his head and gave a tender kiss that had her wrapping her arms around his neck. "And you make me deliriously happy too." He eased his body onto the bed and held her close. "I am so very glad that I met you. Mattie, you are the most loving, sweet girl and I can't believe I'm lucky enough to have you in my life."

Mattie nodded and buried her face in the crook of his neck. "It's crazy that you moved to Cricket Creek of all places, don't you think?"

"I can thank my father for that, I suppose." He stroked her hair. "But yes, life is so unexpected sometimes."

Mattie heard a sense of wonder in the inflection of his voice almost as if there was something else he wanted to tell her. But before she could ask him more, he scooted down and kissed her. Mattie's body reacted and she moved against him, loving the feeling of skin against skin. She was surprised how quickly her desire returned and she realized that she could never get enough of Garret. He was nothing like any other man she'd ever met and was everything she wanted. "I love you . . . so very much," she said, and then rolled to the side. "And I'm going to show you."

"Showing is always a step above telling. Show me, Mattie."

Mattie swung her leg over his waist and straddled his body. She splayed her hands on his chest and then leaned over and kissed him on the mouth before she scooted down until she felt the steely hardness of his penis against the folds of her sex. She moved slowly back and forth while watching the play of emotion on his face. She caressed the stubble on his cheeks and then trailed her fingers over his chest. When she felt her body grow warm and wet with need, she rose to her knees and guided his penis up to her body.

He helped, scooting up slightly against the pillows. "Take me inside you, Mattie. Deep. All the way."

"Yes. That's where I want you." She gripped his shoulders, and his hands spanned her waist. Catching her bottom lip between her teeth, she lowered her body onto his erect cock and let him fill her. "Oh!" She sat very still, loving the feeling of him buried deep. And then, through half-lidded eyes, she watched him while she moved oh so gently at first, coming up to her knees and then slowly sinking back down. She did this . . . once, twice until he bucked upward with a hard thrust. Mattie gasped and then rode him faster. When her thighs trembled he gripped her waist and she clung to his shoulders. Her hair tumbled around her face, and her breasts jiggled. She felt wild and free and filled to the brim with the man she loved.

Mattie felt his muscles stiffen and he gripped her waist harder and then cried out her name when he thrust upward and climaxed. Garret pushed his shoulders against the pillows, holding himself buried deeply inside her, and then closed his eyes. His chest moved with each breath and then he opened his eyes. Reaching up, he caressed her breasts, teasing and tweaking until Mattie's head tilted to the side. Her body tingled and seemed to be one giant nerve ending pulled tight. Garret cupped her breasts and moved his thumbs back and forth. "Come up to your knees, Mattie. I want to stroke you."

She did. And while he was still half inside her, filling her, he rubbed his finger over her where she was swollen, sensitive. Pleasure washed over her, intense, almost sharp, and then slid into something warm and sultry. Mattie collapsed against his chest and he held her while she shuddered with little aftershocks.

She stayed on top of him, wrapped around him like kudzu until he gently rolled her to the side. Mattie put her hand on his chest and felt the solid, rapid beat of his heart. Mellow jazz played in the background, and the scent of vanilla candles and chocolate syrup lingered in the air.

She reached up and cupped his cheek and then rubbed her thumb over his bottom lip. When he licked her Mattie felt a jolt of heat and sucked in a breath. "I can barely move and you can get me going again with one little touch of your tongue to the pad of my thumb."

"Really, now." He chuckled low in his throat. When he moved lower Mattie shook her head back and forth against the pillow.

"Garret . . . no . . . I . . ." She tried to speak, to protest, but when he put his mouth where she was so sensitive, almost sore, she moaned. He flicked his tongue over her in an almost not there way and she trembled. "It's too much . . . I . . ." She gasped, but he continued to lick with gentle, tender care. Mattie didn't think she could possibly come again, but she raised her head from the pillow and grasped his head when another orgasm rippled through her body. Her heart raced and her limbs felt numb.

Garret raised his head. "What were you saying?"

Mattie tried to speak, but her voice failed her.

"Oh, Mattie." With a sexy laugh Garret pulled her

against his body and spooned her. "I love you." He cupped her breast and buried his face in her hair. "So very much."

"I love you too."

"Let's take a little nap so we can wake up and do this all over again," Garret said in her ear.

"I think that's an excellent plan."

He answered by kissing her shoulder.

After a few moments Mattie felt his slow and steady breathing, but she didn't want to fall asleep. She just wanted to enjoy lying with him feeling his skin next to hers. With a sigh of pure contentment she watched the candles flicker and the shadows dance on the wall as if swaying to the soft wail of the saxophone.

Having Garret's arms around her felt so good, so right, and he put her hand over his, holding it close to her heart. She smiled, thinking something this good could only get better.

23

(If Loving You Is Wrong) I Don't Want to Be Right

LAURA LEE FOLDED SHANE'S CLOTHES INTO A NEAT PILE and took the laundry basket up to his bedroom. Knowing his routine, she'd managed to avoid him for nearly two weeks. And God, how she missed the man! The words he'd uttered to her after that day in the pool echoed in her mind. *"When you're ready to let me in, let me know. I'll be waiting."*

Laura Lee shook her head and swallowed hard. She brushed at a tear but then cleared her throat and stiffened her spine. "No!" She wouldn't lose her job and have her heart broken, she thought for what seemed like the millionth time. The words were starting to lose the power they once had, because she was so damn miserable! She thought about the lasagna she'd just popped into the oven, the crisp salad in the fridge, and the red wine she'd opened to breathe. But instead of two glasses she'd put one on the counter. She made a small dish of the meal for her to take home, and the thought of eating alone once again had no appeal. Perhaps she'd go to Wine and

Diner and sit at the counter so she could chat with Myra. She shook her head, trying to like the idea, but all she felt was . . . glum.

She could head to Sully's for the Friday night crowd, but memories of dancing with Shane would surely ruin her night. Maybe she should ask for a few days off and get Mattie to go to Nashville, she thought, but Mattie seemed to be attached at the hip to Garret, so she scratched that notion as well. With another sigh Laura Lee thought perhaps she should head to Florida and visit Miranda Mayfield but then thought that last-minute flights would likely be off-the-charts expensive and she'd just bought a cute little used yellow VW Beetle convertible to drive around town instead of the panel van. Putting the top down and having the wind in her hair made her smile, but today nothing seemed to boost her spirits.

Laura Lee put the clothes neatly on the bed and then picked the laundry basket up with a touch of anger. Why in the world did she have to go and fall in love with her boss? Her very famous boss? She glanced at the clock on his nightstand and knew she had to leave soon or Shane would be home and she would have to look at him. Looking at him meant wanting him. "Damn it all to hell and back!"

Still in a snit, Laura Lee hurried down the stairs and checked on the lasagna that hadn't started to bubble around the edges. "For real?" She slapped her hand to her forehead. She had forgotten to turn the damn oven on! Now what? The lasagna took an hour to bake and she couldn't leave the house with the oven on. She glanced at the fridge, thinking she could put the dish in there with instructions on how to fix it, but she knew Shane would be hungry and didn't want him to have to wait that long for dinner.

Laura Lee had no choice. She would have to stick it out until the timer went off. With a little growl of irritation at herself she turned the oven on and stomped around the kitchen. With her hands on her hips she looked around trying to find a chore to do but came up empty. Of course there wasn't one thing left to do, so she guessed she would go out onto the deck and read the book she'd brought with her.

After retrieving the novel, Laura Lee looked at the bottle of wine with longing. While she knew that Shane wouldn't care a lick if she drank a glass of it, she hesitated. Her frayed nerves warred with reason and in the end she poured herself a glass of the merlot and headed outside. She would hear Shane's truck rumble down the driveway and try her best to avoid him. With that in mind she sat down in the lounge chair and took a sip of the wine. The doggone pool also looked inviting. She sure missed swimming, but after the kissing encounter with Shane she couldn't bring herself to indulge in that nice perk either. Great . . . next chapter of the romance novel she was reading led up to a lusty sex scene with the sexy Highlander. Her body reacted and she reached over for another sip of wine only to find that the glass was empty.

"Well, damn." With a grumble she took the glass inside and checked on the lasagna that was starting to show signs of getting done but still had about another half hour to bake. The kitchen smelled divine and Laura Lee had used fresh tender herbs from the garden in the window to season the sauce.

Laura Lee was about to wash her glass, but the wine had made her feel just a bit mellow and she thought that a bit more would help her cope with seeing Shane if he arrived home soon. She poured another glass and then headed back outside. By the end of the chapter Laura Lee was so hot and bothered that she really did need a dip in the pool. She closed her eyes and fanned her face, thinking that reading the steamy book hadn't been such a good idea after all. She needed to start reading mysteries or horror, anything but this sexy stuff. The thought made her put the open book on her chest and she decided that she would just rest her eyes for a couple of minutes. Then she'd take the lasagna out of the oven at the first signs of bubbling around the edges and hightail it home.

The waning sunshine felt good on her face, and the wine did have a soothing effect. She sighed and when her traitorous thoughts turned to Shane she tried to think about the grocery list instead. "Potatoes ... coffee ... milk ... ," she began, but it was like counting sheep and Laura Lee fell fast asleep. . . .

Laura Lee slowly awoke from an erotic dream about a handsome Highlander who looked very much like Shane McCray. As it turned out they really didn't wear anything under the kilt.

She heard voices.

Frowning, she sat up and blinked in confusion. Her first thought was that sadly she hadn't been transformed back in time and wasn't having sex with a Highlander after all. Her second thought was that the sun was starting to set, so she'd been asleep for a while.

Her third thought was ... "Oh no, the lasagna!"

She scrambled from the lounge chair, knocking the book to the floor. But when she came to the sliding glass door, Laura Lee hesitated. Shane stood at the kitchen island with a woman. The lasagna, thankfully, was safely on the counter and she blew out a sigh of relief. But who was the woman? Laura Lee turned and pressed her back to the wall beside the door, not wanting to be seen. Her heart thudded and she closed her eyes, straining her ears to hear the conversation.

At first it was muffled, but then she heard feminine laughter and her heart sank. Feeling a bit guilty, she tilted her head closer to the door, trying to hear the conversation.

"No, Mr. McCray, I can start as soon as you wish. I don't mind if running errands is part of the housekeeping duties."

Laura Lee felt her eyes widen, and her heart thumped so hard she thought that surely they could hear. She put her hand to her chest and listened. At first Laura Lee felt relief that the woman wasn't a romantic interest, but then the realization hit her that she was being replaced! Fired! Her hand went from her chest to her mouth so she could muffle the sob bubbling up in her throat. And then she felt a flash of anger so hot that she wouldn't have been surprised if her red hair burst into flames.

Was Shane that pissed that she didn't fall at his feet when he said he wanted her? She leaned her head around to the door. Breathing hard, she peeked inside and saw that Shane was walking the woman down the hallway to the front door. Fueled with anger and wine and pent-up sexual frustration, Laura Lee felt the fight-or-flight instinct kick in. She looked at the steps and was glad that she'd brought her purse outside with her. Swiping at hot tears, she started for the steps but then swung around and headed for the door. If she was being fired she might as well go down in flames.

Shane walked into the kitchen and stopped in his tracks when he spotted Laura Lee. "You're still here?"

"No, this is a hologram," she said testily.

"But where's your van?"

"The Beetle is mine."

He grinned. "Cute and sassy. It suits you."

She responded with a glare. "You . . . you've fired me?"

Shane nodded slowly and her heart constricted.

"Say it!" She took a step closer and fisted her hands at her sides. "Say it to my face!" She pointed to her face and waited.

"Gladly. I love you."

"Wh-what?" She lowered her hand and swallowed hard.

"I. Love. You." He smiled and closed the gap between them. "Yes, I fired you, but I'm not letting you go." He reached over and tucked a lock of hair behind her ear. "I'm never letting you go."

"I . . ." She looked at him, afraid to believe what was happening.

"Say it back."

Fear gripped her heart and she shook her head.

"Laura Lee, I've missed you more than I thought possible. I don't want you to be my housekeeper. I want . . . I want you to be my wife."

Shocked beyond words, Laura Lee backed up and came up against the counter. She had to grip the edges to keep her hands from shaking. "But . . . but you haven't known me all that long."

"I want to spend the rest of my life getting to know every single thing about you. The one thing I know for sure is that I love you. I'm fifty-eight years old. Why wait one more minute to have you by my side as my wife?"

Still dumbfounded, Laura Lee shook her head.

"I can't imagine not having you in my life." He reached in his pocket and pulled out a little velvet box. "And I want to put this ring on your finger so the whole world knows how much I love you." He opened the box and showed her a stunning pear-shaped diamond solitaire.

She put a hand to her chest. "This . . . this is too soon."

"No." Shane reached over and caressed her cheek. "It's not soon enough. I don't want to spend one more day missing you. I'm retired from music, but I have a new job. Making you happy. I want to take you wherever you want to go. See whatever you want to see. I want to shower you with presents. I want to spoil you silly . . . make you my princess."

Laura Lee finally smiled. "You make it impossible for a girl to say no."

"That's the plan," he said, but then looked up at the ceiling and chuckled. "Actually this wasn't the plan. I had this whole romantic weekend planned, ending with me getting on one knee and proposing. I had no idea you were still here."

"I'm sorry I ruined your plan. I would have been gone, but I forgot to turn the oven on when I put the lasagna in. I've been doing a lot of that kind of silly thing lately."

"Why?"

Laura Lee looked into Shane's eyes and saw love and truth shining there. In that moment all her insecurities flew right out the window and scattered in the wind. "Because you're always on my mind, making me forget what I'm supposed to be doing." She reached over and put her arms around his neck. "I love you. I want to be your wife." She leaned in and kissed him. "So this is how the story ends?" she asked with a trembling smile.

"No . . . this is just the beginning."

Laura Lee felt her nose twitch and she had to swipe at a tear. "Then put that gorgeous ring on my finger."

"Gladly." Shane laughed, but when Laura Lee noticed the slight tremble in his fingers her heart melted. He stared at her hand and then looked at her and smiled before pulling her into his arms. "Now I think we need to eat dinner, drink wine, and . . . make love. What do you say?"

"I say that you have the order backward."

Shane laughed and then took her by the hand. "I'd say you're right."

"Get used to the idea of me always being right."

Shane laughed. "And you get used to being completely spoiled."

"I think you just described every girl's dream."

"Good, and I aim to keep it that way."

Laura Lee followed Shane into the bedroom, thinking that she'd be nervous, but she wasn't. Love was a powerful confidence booster and she knew without a shadow of a doubt that she was going to make Shane McCray one happy man, tonight, tomorrow . . . and for the rest of her life.

24

A Leap of Faith

GARRET LOOKED AT THE ENTRANCE TO BREAKFAST, BAIT, and Books but couldn't bring himself to go in. The time had come when he had to have the conversation with Mattie that he'd been dreading. His heart pounded and his stomach was doing some crazy stuff. He'd waited until the breakfast crowd left, but he couldn't put this off any longer. Just as he was about to open the door, he spotted Mattie running out the back entrance.

"Rusty! Come back here right now, you crazy dog!"

Rusty, however, failed to as much as slow down and continued to make a beeline for the dock. Garret angled his head, thinking that Rusty ran at a fast clip for an older dog. Mattie followed in close pursuit, shouting and waving her arms.

"Rusty, no! Don't do it!"

Feeling a bit alarmed that this was more than stealing ham, Garret decided he needed to follow.

"Please!" Mattie shouted when Rusty ran up onto the dock. "Abigail is gone!"

At closer inspection Garret could see a ski boat idling down the cove, and apparently so could Rusty. Without hesitation the love-struck dog did a flying leap into the water, hitting with a big splash and a lot of determination.

"You can't catch them!" Mattie kept shouting as if Rusty suddenly had a full grasp of the English language. Rusty, however, seemed hell-bent on reaching his destination. Then, to Garret's horror, Mattie jumped in after him.

Garret's cowboy boots clumped against the wooden dock. "Mattie! What in the world are you doing?"

Mattie turned halfway and shouted, "The crazy dog is going to swim out into the river. The current will wash him away."

"He can't possibly swim all the way through the cove to the main channel."

"He'll run up the hill and cut them off at the pass."

"Seriously?"

"Yes!" she said, and started swimming faster.

"Mattie, get back here! It's dangerous out there!" Garret pleaded, but when she kept going he tugged off his boots, dropped his pants, and jumped in after her. Mattie, however, was a strong swimmer, leaving Garret in her wake. She caught up with a furiously dog-paddling Rusty in short order and snagged him by his collar.

Garret worried that Rusty would protest, but he seemed to be tiring and sadly but gladly accepted Mattie's help.

"Crazy dog!"

It occurred to Garret that this desperate plunge must have been something attempted before. He worried, though, that Mattie might struggle to swim back with the Irish setter in tow, so he kept swimming for them.

But by the time Garret was halfway there, Mattie was well on her way back to the dock, so he turned around as well. When Mattie got closer she gave Rusty a shove toward the shoreline before she hefted herself up the steps onto the dock. Garret followed and, winded, flopped down beside her. He glanced over and noticed that Rusty, seemingly not feeling one bit of guilt, did the wet hair shake but then trotted off, apparently knowing he was in big trouble.

Garret came up to his elbows. "So, let me guess, Rusty thought he could catch up to the love of his life."

Breathing a bit hard, Mattie rolled her eyes. "Yes. He knows better but just can't stop himself."

"So, is Abigail a lost cause, then?"

"Well . . ." Mattie turned and gave Garret a slow grin. "Today, Abigail stood up in the back of the boat. She put her little paws up on the seat and watched Rusty leap into the water. I think Rusty's persistence is finally paying off."

"Persistence is always the key." Garret smiled back. "You are such a die-hard romantic, Mattie. One of the many things I love about you."

"Well, now." She leaned over and gave him a lingering kiss. "Pretty romantic that you jumped in after me. Very impressive for a city boy."

"Why, thank you." He smiled, but her mention of the city brought Garret back to the reason he'd gone up to the restaurant to seek her out, and his heart plummeted. "Um, how about coming over to my cabin for a bit? Wash the river water off and have a chat."

"A chat? I can think of better things to do . . . like maybe shower together first?" Mattie wiggled her eyebrows, but Garret couldn't quite muster up a believable smile. She pulled back and gave him an odd look. "Are you going to give me a hint as to what's on your mind?"

Garret leaned over and pushed a strand of her wet hair out of her eyes and then gave her a brief, tender kiss. God, he was having second thoughts yet again.

"I guess not," Mattie said. "But you look pretty serious. Okay, look, I have to close up the restaurant and I'll need dry clothes, so I'll meet you at your place in about an hour if that's okay."

Garret nodded. "Sure." He hated the wary look on her face, but sitting here on the dock in wet clothes wasn't where he wanted to have this conversation.

"Oh, and I forgot to ask if you wanted to go to Shane's for dinner tonight. Laura Lee asked me earlier, but it skipped my mind until now. She seemed to really want us to come and apologized for the late notice."

"We'll see," he said, and forced another smile.

"Whenever my mother said we'll see, it really meant no," Mattie said with a small nervous-sounding laugh. She put a gentle hand on his arm. "Garret, is everything okay?"

"Of course, love." He stood up and offered his hand. "I'll see you in a bit."

Mattie nodded but didn't appear convinced. When she walked off he had the urge to run after her and give her a reassuring hug, but he headed over to the cabin instead.

Garret took a hot shower and then decided he needed a stiff drink. He wondered why in the hell life had to be so damn complicated. After pouring bourbon over ice he peered down at the amber liquid and sighed.

Needing to look out over the river, he headed out to the back deck and leaned against the railing. He gazed out over the small marina and then turned to look at Mattie's little restaurant. She'd explained that her family had worked hard to keep the business through hard times, and Garret knew how much Mayfield Marina meant to her. She had her brothers, her friends, and the quaint town of Cricket Creek. How could she ever up and leave all that behind and go all the way to London for an extended period? Did she care for him enough to do so?

Maybe she did.

And maybe she would be miserable.

Garret scrubbed a hand down his face. Did he even have the right to ask her to do such a thing? They hadn't known each other that long. Perhaps the right thing to do would be to tell her he was going to do the show and that he would return in a few months. And he could fly back and forth now and then. She could come for a visit. But he thought about having a long-distance relationship after having her within a stone's throw away and he knew it would be difficult at best.

God, maybe he was all wrong for her after all and he should leave altogether and let her go back to the life she'd had before he came barging in and turned it upside down. Maybe she'd go back to wanting Colby. Had he inadvertently screwed up her life too? Did he even deserve someone as good as Mattie Mayfield?

Garret set his glass on the railing and gripped the edge. He'd never been this torn up over anything in his life.

"Ah, so there you are," Mattie said.

At the sound of her sweet voice Garret turned around, thinking she looked so pretty in a buttercup yellow sundress that showed off her light tan. She'd pulled her hair up into a French twist and she wore strappy little white sandals. "You look lovely."

"Why, thank you, Garret." She spun in a circle, making the skirt billow out, and then tipped her palms forward. "Do you notice anything different about me?"

"Your hair?"

"Mmm, no. I've worn it like this before." She raised her eyebrows and caught her bottom lip between her teeth, looking so sweet that his heart ached.

Garret took a step closer and then noticed diamond studs glittering in her earlobes. "You got your ears pierced!"

"I did! And it hurt so much I thought I was gonna pass out right there in the mall in front of a little girl sitting next to me who took it like a champ."

"I would have gone with you, love."

"I wanted to surprise you."

"Well, they're pretty."

"I splurged just a little bit. Used tip money I'd stashed away."

"Well deserved." Garret thought it was so commendable that she didn't take anything for granted. "You look just smashing. I want to go out and show you off."

"I thought we might go over to Shane's, so I dressed for dinner. I texted Laura Lee and said we'd let her know if we could make it, and she said no worries."

No worries . . . Garret blew out a sigh. He had a big worry on his mind.

Her smile faded. "Are you going to tell me what's going on?" She walked closer and put a hand over his. "Let's have the chat, Garret."

When he nodded silently she pointed to his drink. "Do I need one of those?"

"Maybe." Garret handed her the glass. "Have a sip."

"Oh boy . . ." Mattie took a swallow and waited. She appeared so vulnerable and he hated that he had to tell her the news.

"I've been offered a job as a judge on *Sing for Me*."

"The TV show?"

"Yes." He nodded and felt a surge of pride at the admission.

"Oh my gosh!" Mattie's eyebrows shot up and she immediately smiled. "That's wonderful!" She looked up at the sky and then laughed. "And here I was thinking you had bad news . . . or you were going to break up with me."

"Break up with you?"

She shrugged. "I dunno."

"Never, Mattie. I adore you."

"Well, I'm relieved. So it's a country music version? Set in Nashville?"

"No." His heart pounded. "In . . . in London."

Her face fell. "Oh." She licked her bottom lip. "How long would you be gone?" She kept her voice light, but he could see the sadness in her eyes.

"Four months or so depending on several factors. I've only been offered one season thus far." He gave her a small shrug.

Mattie glanced over at the river and then back at him. After a few beats of heavy silence, she finally nodded. Her eyes were stormy, but to her credit she managed to smile. "Congratulations, Garret. *Sing for Me* is a huge hit.

I like the American version. It's . . . it's quite an honor. You must be thrilled."

"I want you to come with me."

Her eyes widened. "To London?"

"Yes, I'll rent a flat in Notting Hill, in a beautiful old Victorian house not far from my mother. The studio will be within walking distance from where the show will be filmed. You can come and watch," he said, and when he realized how very much he wanted her to come along, his plea started picking up steam. "We could do some other traveling during the stay as well. Mattie, I'll take you to Paris. Dublin . . . wherever you want to go. Please, say yes."

"But I have the restaurant to run." She glanced over and looked at it before turning her attention back to him. "I mean, I know it must not seem like much to you, but it means a lot to me and to the people who eat there," she said with a slight edge of defensiveness.

"Mattie, love, I know that. I'm not belittling the importance of your shop or what you do."

"I know you don't mean to, but I think perhaps you are."

"I'm not in the least." He shoved his fingers through his hair. "But . . . but could someone else run it for a bit?"

"No. It's my place." She shook her head hard and he saw tears forming in her eyes.

Garret's heart plummeted. "I understand."

"How long have you known about this?"

"A month maybe," he answered quietly.

"Don't you think it would have been fair to tell me then instead of waiting until now?"

"I wasn't sure what I was going to do. Mattie, I've put the producer off for weeks and I have to finally give him an answer." He took a step closer. "But if I'm going to lose you, I'll turn it down."

"And have me live with the fact that you've turned down the chance of a lifetime? The recognition you've wanted and deserve?" Mattie shook her head slowly. "I'd never do that in a million years."

"Then come with me! You'd get to see some of the world."

"My world is here." She lifted her chin and Garret realized he'd offended her again. "This is my home. I can't leave."

"You could. It wouldn't be forever and it would be an adventure for you. We'd get to do so much, and although I'll be busy I'll also have downtime. It is a chance of a lifetime, Mattie, but it can be that chance for you too."

"But what if you want to stay? What if they offer you a permanent position?"

"We don't have to worry about that. We'll cross that bridge if we come to it."

"Really? Don't worry? Garret, I could never live so far away from my family. I know you've traveled and lived in different places, so this is nothing new to you." She waved a hand in an arc. "This is the only home I've ever known."

"Will you consider it at least? Come for a while? If you hate it I'll send you home straightaway."

Mattie closed her eyes and then blew out a sigh. "I was afraid that you'd find it boring in a small town."

"I'm not one bit bored. This offer came out of the blue. This wasn't something that I planned." He took a step closer. "Mattie, I would never do anything to hurt you."

The look she gave him was wary.

"Wow, you don't believe me, do you? Mattie, I'm not that guy from the tabloids."

"I didn't say that."

"You didn't have to."

"This took me by surprise. You're not being fair. You should have come to me with this sooner."

Garret felt sadness wash over him. "You're right and I'm sorry. I suppose I was afraid that you'd react the way you just did and I wanted to hold on to you for as long as I could. But all you have to do is say the word and I won't go."

"I will never do that."

"And you will never go with me."

She nodded. "I'm sorry, Garret. I'm just a small-town girl. I would never fit into that lifestyle."

"Lifestyle?"

"A big city in a foreign country."

"You'd be with me. And I do believe once you're there, you'll truly love it. There is so much to see and do and we'd do it together. It would be an adventure," he said, but when she didn't budge he sighed. "Okay." He took her hands. "But the offer remains open if you want to join me. I love you, Mattie. And I hope someday you'll realize just how much."

"And I love you enough to let you go. Garret, you've enriched my life and given me confidence. But this is only the beginning for you. London . . . and then what? I won't hold you back, but I can't come with you either."

"God, why does this feel like good-bye?" He felt panic at the thought. "I wish this offer had never come my way. Mattie, I'm going to turn it down!"

"No . . . don't say that. You must go. I'll make it easier by leaving." She went up on tiptoe and gave him a kiss and then she turned and walked away.

Garret felt as if his heart were being ripped out of his chest. He didn't think it was even possible to hurt this much. He pictured them walking hand in hand through the streets of London. He knew without a doubt that she'd love the beauty of Notting Hill and the vibrancy of Portobello Road, famous for its shops and fresh markets. He smiled, thinking she'd go crazy in Hummingbird Bakery, but then shook his head. She'd made her position clear and he'd respect her decision.

Garret tossed back the rest of the bourbon and then took his cell phone out of his pocket. It was time to give Russ Randall a call.

25

Crazy Little Thing Called Love

"*M*ATTIE?" LAURA LEE CALLED. "ARE YOU HERE?"

"In the back by the books," Mattie shouted, and a moment later Laura Lee found her.

"You're reading mysteries?"

"I'm sick of romance."

"You are such a liar." Laura Lee sat down on the floor beside her and patted her leg.

"Easy for you to say. You're happily engaged."

"And you've been asked to go to London with a man who adores you. And here you sit for the past two weeks sad and depressed ever since he's been gone. At least call him, Mattie."

"I can't!"

"Pardon me if I don't feel sorry for you. You're feeling sorry for yourself enough for both of us."

"We've gone over this a million times. I can't leave this restaurant! Where would the breakfast crowd go? Who would cook for the fishing tournament coming up? Who would take care of the books? Order the bait? Who would—"

"Me."

"What?" Mattie stopped her rant in midsentence.

"Now that Shane fired me and has a housekeeper doing all my work, I'm bored stiff."

"And you'd want to get up at the ass crack of dawn and cook breakfast?"

"I'd have Shane help me."

"Right ... a famous country singer slinging hash and waiting tables. That's funny."

"It is kinda funny. He'd love it."

"Ha, sure he would." Mattie pretended to read the back jacket of the book, but she felt a little flash of excitement.

"He wants to do it."

Mattie gave up all pretense of reading. "How do you know this?"

"I asked him."

"Laura Lee!"

"Hey, the man is at my beck and call. What can I say?" She glowed with such happiness that Mattie couldn't be angry with her.

"Can he even cook?"

Laura Lee grinned. "He's been having a ball practicing. He can flip pancakes like a pro and crack eggs with one hand. Mattie, you know the whole town will be knocking down the door when they know that Shane will be working here as a short-order cook."

Mattie shook her head. "And what do I pay him? And you? Minimum wage?"

"No, we want to give to the literacy fund that you have here at the shop."

"And you'd do this for several months? What if Shane has commitments?"

"Danny and Mason said they'd help out," Laura Lee insisted. "And Bubba too."

"Why do I think there's more?"

Laura Lee pressed her lips together. "I might have talked to Miranda."

"Mom?"

"Is there any other Miranda I'd tell?"

"Oh, let me guess, she's hoping I'll finally get married and give her the grandchild she's been complaining about not having?"

"Yeah . . . ," Laura Lee admitted with a guilty wince.

"Oh, don't even try to act all sorry. You've been plotting this behind my back!"

"Mattie, I know this isn't just about the restaurant or stocking bait. This is about change. Traveling across the ocean and living away from everything you've ever known. And about this crazy little thing called love."

"Yes." Mattie closed her eyes and sighed. "I'm scared out of my skin. But I miss Garret so much I can't even tell you."

"You don't have to tell me. It's written all over your pretty face. Mattie, I miss that bright smile of yours. You should go."

"Maybe he's over me."

Laura Lee shook her head. "I have it on good authority that he's miserable without you."

"Who?"

"Can a girl get a cup of coffee around here?" shouted a woman with a clipped English accent.

Laura Lee grinned. "Her." She pushed up to her feet. "Follow me."

"Hello?"

"Coming, Teresa," Laura Lee said with a laugh. "Just hold your horses."

"You knew she was coming over?"

"I decided I needed a plan B if I couldn't convince you."

Curious, Mattie followed Laura Lee to the front of the restaurant. A curly-haired woman dressed in a bright red peasant blouse and retro jeans shot Mattie a big smile.

"Mattie, meet Teresa Bennett, receptionist and backup singer for My Way Records."

Teresa extended her hand. "Hello, Mattie. It's nice to meet the girl who captured Garret's heart."

Mattie shook Teresa's hand. "You're friends with Garret?"

"I was in his father's band back in the day. I've known Garret all his life. I'm also friends with his mum. I met Laura Lee a couple of weeks ago when a group of us from My Way Records all went to dinner at Wine and Diner."

"I tried to get you to go, remember?" Laura Lee said to Mattie.

Mattie nodded.

"But you won't do anything but mope around," Laura Lee added.

"That's why I'm here," Teresa said, and then sat down on a round stool. "We need to have a chat."

Mattie went around the counter and poured three cups of coffee and then rested one hip against the counter. "Okay, Teresa, I'm all ears."

"Well, darling, it's quite simple really. Garret is utterly miserable without you." She glanced at Laura Lee. "And I'm told that you're miserable without him too."

Mattie shook her head and looked down at her coffee mug. "It's not that simple."

"Oh, but it is. You need to be together." She shrugged and took a sip of her coffee.

"She's right," Laura Lee said quietly.

"Would you two quit staring at me?"

They both answered with shakes of their heads.

"I've booked you a flight," Teresa finally announced in a matter-of-fact tone. "Laura Lee gave me all your personal information."

"What?" Mattie stood up straight. Her heart thudded.

"You leave tomorrow morning," Teresa said. "So you'd best start packing."

Mattie opened her mouth to protest but then snapped it shut. They were right and it was pointless to argue.

Teresa reached down and pulled a packet out of a tote bag. "This has everything you'll need. Addresses, instructions. Read it over and if you have any questions let me know." She placed the packet on the counter and Mattie looked at it, knowing that her future was in that envelope.

"Does Garret know any of this?"

Teresa smiled. "Not a thing. And I think it's brilliant to keep your arrival a surprise."

Mattie glanced around the restaurant.

"Don't worry, Mattie," Teresa said to her. "I'm on board to wait tables if needed. We've got you covered, love."

Mattie looked at them both and then burst into tears.

Laura Lee and Teresa jumped up and hurried behind the counter. They hugged and cried and then ended up laughing.

Mattie swiped at tears and then crossed her hands over her chest. "I'm overwhelmed."

"I just wish I could be there to see the look on Garret's face," Teresa said.

"I want to see a selfie of your smiling faces," Laura Lee said.

Mattie nodded. "I'll take one. Oh my gosh, I think my heart is going to beat right out of my chest."

Laura Lee made shooing motions with her fingers. "Go and start packing. Teresa and I will be here bright and early to pick you up. You're leaving out of Nashville."

"And Laura Lee is going to spend the night and we're going to paint the town red," Teresa added with a laugh. "It's going to be fantastic."

Mattie laughed. "I'm sure it will be." After one last group hug Mattie hurried out the door and ran all the way back to her cabin.

Tomorrow she was leaving for London!

26

With a Little Help from My Friends

GARRET STROLLED DOWN PORTOBELLO ROAD IN THE heart of Notting Hill, thinking that perhaps the colorful, vibrant surroundings would put him in a better mood. Saturdays were jam-packed with both locals and tourists, since the trading in Portobello Market was in full swing. He started at the southern tip of the market and browsed the antiques stalls, picking up a bric-a-brac here and there but unable to muster up much interest. He headed down the hill to the intersection of Westbourne Grove and Elgin Crescent to the heart of the antiques section, thinking he might want to pick up a little something for his mum. After purchasing a lovely rose pin, he spotted a ceramic Irish setter that looked just like Rusty. Unable not to, Garret bought the small dog and wished for the millionth time that Mattie was with him.

Garret thought about taking a picture of the dog and sending it to Mattie as an excuse to contact her, but he refrained. He wondered, though, what she was doing right this minute. With a sigh he continued on until he came to the fruit and vegetables stands, his favorite part of Portobello Market. Wheelbarrows overflowing with produce, fishmongers, bread stalls, cakes, and cheese were a throwback to years gone by. Owners shouted out their prices, and bargains were to be had near the end of the day. Garret bought a loaf of crusty French bread and a hunk of cheddar cheese, thinking he would munch on the simple meal while watching some auditions of potential contestants on *Sing for Me*. He added a bunch of grapes and a couple of apples to his stash and then couldn't resist a red velvet cupcake swirled with decadent icing.

Feeling a bit of a rumble in his stomach, Garret was anxious to get home and dig into the bread and cheese, so he walked through the Westway Fashion Market without stopping to browse. He turned down Palace Court, where his flat was located in a grand period building. Although not spacious like his cabin in Cricket Creek, the flat came fully furnished with a fitted kitchen and shower room. A winding staircase led to a loft bedroom, and he had a small terrace with a fantastic view. He was within walking distance to the Tube, shops, and restaurants. He thought that Mattie would have found it simple to get around within no time at all. "Not that it matters," he said under his breath.

Juggling his packages, Garret dug into his pants pocket for his keys. Nearly dropping everything, he finally opened the door and headed straight for the galley kitchen. He eyed the bottle of red wine but decided it was a bit too early in the day but it would taste nice later on while he worked. He broke off a hunk of the bread and was about to slice into the cheese when he decided that he wanted to change into something comfortable and maybe drink that glass of wine after all.

While nibbling on the crusty bread he walked into his bedroom and then stopped in his tracks. His heart thudded and he forgot to swallow.

Frowning, Garret walked into the reception room but found nothing out of place. And then he heard another sort of rustling sound. Tipping his head, he looked at the spiral staircase.

Mattie was curled into a cute little position on top of the bed. She hadn't turned down the covers, so she most likely hadn't planned on falling asleep. Her blond hair fanned out over the deep red pillow and he could hear the soft sound of her breathing. He spotted several suitcases to her left and he smiled. From the looks of it she planned on staying for quite a while. For a moment he could only stand there and watch over her, not quite believing his eyes. Because she had obviously had a key, her arrival was a conspiracy that had Teresa Bennett written all over it. His mum had most likely had a hand in this as well.

"Mattie . . . ," he whispered, not wanting to startle her awake. She stirred but didn't open her eyes. Unable not to touch her, Garret walked over to the bed and sat down. At the movement of the mattress Mattie's eyes opened and she looked at him in dazed surprise.

"Garret?" Her voice, husky with sleep, slid over him like a warm caress.

"I think I'm the one who is supposed to be surprised." He smoothed her hair back from her cheek, loving the feel of her skin beneath his fingers.

"I didn't mean to fall asleep, but you were taking forever to get here."

"Sorry, love, I would have run all the way if I'd known you were in my bed."

She gave him a sexy, sleepy smile. "That would have ruined the surprise."

"How did you find me?"

"With a little help from my friends," she said with a grin.

"And why did you decide to come?"

"Because I couldn't live another day without you."

Her quiet admission went straight to his heart. He ran his fingertip over her bottom lip. "And what about the restaurant?"

She chuckled. "There's, like, an entire crew of people taking it over. Shane, Laura Lee, my brothers . . . Teresa. My parents are coming home to pitch in. Can you believe it?"

"Yes. They all love you, Mattie."

"They do, don't they?" Her smile trembled and then she sat up, suddenly fully alert. "I've read a whole stack of books on the plane ride over here. I am a walking encyclopedia about London, especially Notting Hill. You have to take me everywhere."

"I will take you anywhere your little heart desires."

"I like the sound of that."

"And speaking of desire . . ." He leaned in and captured her lips in a sweet lingering kiss. "God, I've missed you so, Mattie. I thought about you constantly," he said. "Oh, and I bought you a present at Portobello Market. Stay right there, I want to go get it for you."

Garret hurried down to the kitchen and took the little ceramic dog out of the paper bag. Taking the steps two at a time, he sat down on the bed and handed the present to her. "Rusty," Garret said with a chuckle.

"Oh my gosh, it looks just like him." Mattie shook her head. "He and I moped around Mayfield Marina like lovesick fools. It was like we had these little gray storm clouds hanging over our heads."

"Ah, no more progress with Abigail?"

"Not other than looking back at him while the boat chugs away, I'm afraid."

"I think there's hope, then." Garret looked above Mattie's head. "I don't see a storm cloud."

"Nope . . . from now on I'm walking on sunshine."

"Brilliant," Garret said, and then pulled her into his arms. "And I'll be walking right there by your side."

"Well, you're going to be walking all over London while I ask a million questions."

"And I'll answer each and every one. It's going to be an adventure, love. I cannot wait." He looked down at her pretty face and said, "I also can't wait to make love to you, Mattie. I want you in my arms."

"You're reading my mind. But we have to do one more thing." She reached over to the nightstand and located her cell phone. "We have to send Teresa and Laura Lee a selfie." She held up the phone. "Ready? Smile!"

They captured the moment of happiness and sent their radiant smiling faces from London, England, back to Cricket Creek, Kentucky.

Garret leaned in and gave Mattie a kiss. "Let the adventure begin."

Epilogue
Sweet Surrender

$\mathcal{M}$ATTIE STOOD ON THE EXPANDED DECK OF HER RESTAU-rant and smiled at Garret. "I ordered the bistro tables. I thought that I wanted blue umbrellas, but then I decided I wanted a variety of colors to represent the vibrant storefronts that inspired me on Portobello Road. What do you think?"

Garret wrapped his arms around her waist from behind and hugged her close. "I adore the idea. I'm amazed at how much you've accomplished in the month that we've been back in Cricket Creek."

"I've talked to Mabel at Grammar's Bakery about providing croissants and pastries. I showed her the pictures of Hummingbird Bakery in London and how they display their cupcakes. We're thinking about adding gourmet cupcakes in the future. Maybe only one day a week to keep it special." She pointed to the grassy area to the side of the restaurant. "I want to have a farmers' market in the fall during harvest, and Gabby at Flower Power said she'd love to sell flowers in the spring. Laura Lee is going to plant an herb garden," she said. "And she agreed to manage the restaurant while we're in London for three months while you film the next season of *Sing for Me*."

Garret kissed her on top of the head. "I hoped she would. I think she really enjoys it too."

"And I think it's hilarious that Shane is insisting that he'll come back as the short-order cook. Not only that, but Shane has been talking to Mason about the possibility of establishing a craft brewery. Is that cool or what?"

"It is, darling. Having this deck built while we were away was brilliant on your part."

"I knew if we were going to make this work I had to learn to do things from London. And of course I was inspired by something new every day. Who knew I was so creative?"

Garret spun her around and gave her a lingering kiss. "I had a pretty good idea. You amaze me, Mattie."

"It's all coming together, isn't it?"

"Yes, it is."

"Well, I have one more surprise."

Garret reached down and took her hand. "What, love?"

"I'm changing the name from Breakfast, Books, and Bait to Walking on Sunshine."

Garret brought her hand to his mouth and kissed it. "Perfect."

Mattie smiled but then said, "You seem a bit distracted. Is everything okay?"

"I do have something on my mind. Can we have a chat over a cup of coffee?"

"Sure. I just made a pot of the new morning blend I've wanted to try. Let's go inside before the painters get here."

"Good idea."

"I'm hoping to reopen in a month." She worried her bottom lip and looked at him.

"Oh, I think you'll make your goal."

Once they were inside, Mattie poured a cup of coffee for him and then turned to get another mug. When he reached for the sugar canister he stopped and said, "Odd, but there's something on my spoon. Care to have a look?"

Mattie put the carafe down and looked at the silver spoon. She saw something glitter and catch the light. Her breath caught and her gaze flew back to his face. "Oh my . . ."

Garret got down on one knee. "Mattie, will you marry me?"

Mattie felt tears spring into her eyes and she could only nod. "Yes," she managed, and he slipped the diamond solitaire ring onto her finger. She held her hand up and looked at it. "Garret, it's stunning. I . . . I love it." She threw her arms around his neck. "I love you!"

"And I love you, Mattie." He spun her around and then kissed her. "You make me so very happy."

She looked down at the ring and smiled. "Let's go tell the whole world!"

Garret laughed. "I thought you'd say that. Let's go!"

They walked outside just in time to see Rusty heading for the dock. The little runabout was heading out for the day and he watched with a forlorn expression while the boat chugged through the cove.

"At least he doesn't jump in anymore," Garret said.

Mattie nodded. "I don't think he'll ever give up hope, though." But just as Rusty started to turn around, Abigail gave a sharp bark, drawing his attention . . .

And then she took a flying leap off the back of the boat and landed with a delicate little splash. Rusty pranced around on the dock and then jumped in the water, meeting Abigail halfway. They swam for shore, shook the water off, and then frolicked around in the grass, looking blissfully happy.

"I guess the lesson is to never give up on love," Garret said.

"It's a running theme in this town. From baseball stadiums to recording studios, there's evidence of it everywhere."

Garret grinned and then pulled her close. "And now there's us. Brilliant."

Don't miss the next charming novel
in LuAnn McLane's Cricket Creek series,

WRITTEN IN THE STARS

Available in October 2015
from Signet Eclipse.

1

The Eye of the Storm

"SIRI, I HAVE NOT ARRIVED!" GRACE GORDON TUCKED A lock of her windblown blond hair behind her ear and sighed. "This is getting super annoying." She held the phone close to her mouth and spoke slowly and clearly. "Walking on Sunshine Bistro at Mayfield Marina, Cricket Creek, Kentucky."

"The destination is on your left. You have arrived."

"No! A big red building is on my left! There isn't a bistro or marina in sight." With her free hand, Grace gripped the steering wheel of her rented convertible and teetered on tears of frustration. "You suck," she said to Siri, but then winced. "Sorry," she said quickly, and then remembered that she was talking to a computer-generated voice.

"No need to be sorry," Siri said.

"Okay, that was a little creepy," Grace mumbled, and tossed the phone over onto the passenger seat. Pressing her lips together, she gripped the steering wheel with both hands while wondering what to do next.

When her phone pinged, Grace reached for it, hoping it was her sister answering the million texts she'd sent her over the past hour. "I should have known," Grace said as she read a message from her mother asking if she'd arrived safely. "No! I'm completely lost," she said while she typed with her thumbs.

Of course, her mother immediately called. Becca Gordon always stepped in when her children needed her. She could usually calm down Grace's mild-mannered sister, Sophia, but Grace was more like her half brother, Garret ... a handful and then some. She missed Garret too!

"Gracie, love, you should have been there by now. Am I right?"

"Mum, what don't you understand about *I'm lost*?" Grace drew out the word *lost* for a few seconds. "As in, I don't know where in the world I'm at except it's somewhere in Kentucky."

Her mother chucked softly. "Oh, Gracie ..."

"It isn't funny!" Grace tipped her face up to the sky just as a bird flew by and pooped on her jeans leg. She let out a squeal of anger.

"Oh come on, darling, it's not that bad."

"Really? A bird just ... just had the nerve to *crap* on me!" She looked around for a napkin from her unhealthy fast-food lunch. Right, the napkin and wrapper had fluttered out of the convertible like butterfly wings, making her feel all kinds of guilt.

Her mother laughed harder.

"Mum! Seriously? What's so funny about my misery?"

"Well, for starters, you revert to an English accent when you get angry or upset. I'm sorry. I just find it rather amusing."

"Seriously? Have you forgotten that you're English and I've lived with you in London for the past two years? That I've traveled back and forth to England all of my life?"

"No, darling, I might be in my fifties, but I'm not forgetful yet. And I've not forgotten that you can get turned around in your own backyard."

"It makes going on a holiday an adventure, and I've

discovered some really cool places, taking the road less traveled," Grace said a bit defensively but had to grin. "And you were often with me."

"Fair enough. You get your lack of sense of direction from me. Sorry."

Grace looked down at her soiled thigh and then cast a wary glance skyward.

"Aren't you using your GPS?"

"Siri is being rather difficult, I'm afraid. This was only supposed to be a two-hour drive from the Nashville airport to Cricket Creek. I'm well beyond that now."

"So I gather that you rented a convertible like you said you would?"

"Yes, and it was nearly instant regret. I thought it would be fun rolling through the countryside with the top down. But driving on the interstate was scary as hell! Everything was super loud. Trucks were terrifying, kicking up rocks and so on. And I littered by accident." She wasn't about to tell her mother it was a cheeseburger wrapper. Even though her mother's modeling days were over, Becca Gordon still only consumed healthy food. "Now I get the whole *Thelma and Louise* ending."

"Put the top up, silly girl."

Grace winced. "Um, I might have zoned out when that whole part was explained to me. Something about a switch and clamps." She looked around, nibbling on her lip. "I was distracted by the cute guy who rented me the car."

"Well, good."

"That I don't remember how to put the top up?"

"No, that you were distracted by a cute guy. You've been all work and no play for far too long, Gracie."

"Ha! I could say the same thing about you. When was the last time you went out on a date?"

Her mother sighed. "Like they say, all the good ones are either taken or gay."

Gracie couldn't really argue with that one.

"Sophia will know how to put the top up."

"Right, I know. She's the smart sister. I'm the creative one. La-de-la-de-da."

"Oh, that's rubbish. All three of you are smart and creative and gorgeous. Sophia had a convertible, remember?"

"Yes, well, at this rate, by the time I find the bistro, it will be dark, and she might have already gone home."

"Have you called Sophia or Garret?"

"Are you kidding? I've blown up their phones. Sophia's goes straight to voice mail, so her phone must be dead. Garret isn't answering, so I'm guessing he might be in the recording studio or taking care of sweet, pregnant Mattie. I can't wait to see her baby bump."

"Yes, poor little thing was put on bed rest. Garret has been so sick with worry. I will be so happy when the baby girl is finally here."

"Me too! I am going to be the best aunt ever. Hey, but speaking of dead phones, my phone is getting there too. I'm going to give Siri another go before my phone peters out."

"Don't you have a car charger?"

"I forgot it."

"Is there someplace you can stop and ask for directions?"

"No, it's all country roads ... trees ... cows." Grace angled her head. "There is a building in front of me and I think there might be lights on. Maybe I should check it out."

"Gracie ..." Becca said in her worried-mother voice. "I don't recommend going into a random building," she said, which really meant *Don't you dare go in there*.

"Don't worry, Mum. I have to be close to the bistro at this point. There's water to the right of this building, so I have to be near the marina too. I'll be fine," she said, but the woods suddenly looked a bit sinister. She squinted, looking for beady little eyes. Sometimes having a vivid imagination wasn't fun.

"Okay, well, text or call me as soon as you can, promise?"

"I will. I promise. I love you."

"I love you too. Give everyone a big hug for me. I'll be there as soon as Garret and Mattie's baby girl is born. I've already cleared my schedule for an entire month."

"Sure thing. Bye, Mum."

"Do be careful. Bye, Gracie."

After ending the call, Grace got a bit teary-eyed. Her mother was the only one who still called her Gracie. Funny, but she often thought that her name didn't fit her personality and that she and quiet little Sophia should switch names.

Grace closed her eyes and inhaled sharply. Oh, she wanted to see her sister! And Garret too. She'd gotten to know Mattie while Garret was in London filming the popular talent show *Sing for Me*. Grace was so happy that her former wild-child brother had settled down with such a wonderful girl. And Garret was going to be a daddy soon. Unbelievable! Sniffing, Grace dabbed at the corner of her eyes. She wasn't much of a crier, but the sheer frustration of being close and yet so far was getting to her. A glance into the rearview mirror made her cringe. "Oh, wow, that can't possibly be accurate." Her gold clip had given up on keeping her long blond hair under control hours ago. She ran her tongue over her teeth and felt something. Wide-eyed, she looked at her teeth in the mirror and saw a black speck. "Dear God, is that a bug on my tooth?" Grace rubbed at it with her finger and then checked it out. Okay, just a tiny gnat but still . . . ew.

Grace desperately wanted water. She groaned and then remembered that she had a couple of bottles in her carry-on bag in the trunk. The water would be warm, but at this point, she didn't care. Besides, stretching her legs would feel amazing. And she needed to find a leaf or something to wipe the bird doo off of her jeans.

Just as Grace opened the car door, she heard a rumble

of thunder. "Don't even . . ." She tilted her face upward and peered at the sky, which had gone from cheerful blue to gunmetal gray. A raindrop splashed on her forehead. Just one. "Please . . . God, no." She held her breath and waited. Nothing.

Sweet, false alarm.

"Okay, time to figure out how to put the top up," Grace said, thinking it couldn't be that difficult. And then, without even another clap of thunder for fair warning, the heavens opened up and rain started pouring. Wind whipped her hair across her face, and she became instantly soaked to the skin. With a shriek of alarm and a glance of regret at the convertible, she ran for the empty building, hoping for an open door and no rats, spiders, or creepy things. Luckily, the door opened and she hurried inside, dripping wet and thoroughly pissed off at Mother Nature. "Is there no end to this crappy day?" she wailed.

"You've still got a few hours left," said a deep voice laced with the South. Startled, Grace looked around and saw metal tanks, lots of them, and it smelled . . . weird. Dear God, what had she walked into? Some kind of drug-making thing? "Got caught in the storm?" a man asked, but failed to appear.

Grace spun around but still didn't see anyone.

"Just a little pop-up thunderstorm. Trust me, it'll soon pass over."

"If you're God, you can stop with the practical jokes."

"Practical jokes?"

"You know, the bug on my tooth, the bird doo on my leg, and now the unexpected rain." She looked around but didn't see the man behind the voice amid the tall tanks and coils. Something hissed and sputtered. To her right was a large vat with something thick and frothy floating on top of it.

"I'm glad you found shelter. It's coming down hard out there."

"Yes, it is." But Grace didn't know whether to be glad

or not. Perhaps she should have listened to her mother. Because Grace had grown up in big cities, she'd been taught to be wary, but her curiosity usually trumped the need for safety. If she were a character in a haunted-house horror movie, she would be the one going into the basement with a flashlight. Her mum would be the one ushering people to safety, and Sophia wouldn't have ventured into the house in the first place. Grace looked around, thinking it was rather odd, finding this whatever-it-was factory out here in the middle of nowhere. Although she was intrigued, her flight-or-fight instinct was starting to kick in, with flight winning. Swallowing hard, she took a step backward, thinking she might need to make a quick exit.

"Well, I'm sure not God, so I have to ask: Who are you and where did you come from in the pouring rain?"

"I think that's my line." Grace always resorted to false bravado when she was scared or intimidated. When something clanked, she edged another step toward the door.

"Well, this brewery is mine, so I think it really *is* my line, if you don't mind me sayin' so."

"Beer?" Grace looked around and felt a measure of relief. "So this is a brewery." She looked around again. "Wow . . . and you're the beer guy."

"Brewmaster, thank you very much. And considered a god to some, so you weren't too far off base," he said with a hint of humor. "By the way, I'm up here."

Grace tilted her head back and saw the source of the voice up on a ladder doing something to a big tank that looked kind of like the world's largest teakettle. He'd poked his head around the side so she could finally see the man with the Southern Comfort voice. "So, there you are."

"Here I am. Not heaven but close enough." He gazed down at her and Grace simply couldn't look away. Longish dark hair framed a handsome face. But he was no pretty boy. Oh no, he had a strong jawline, a Greek nose, and high cheekbones. His rugged good looks were heightened by a sexy five-o'clock shadow. Oh, but it was his mouth that captured her attention. Looking at those full lips made her feel warm and tingly, like she'd just taken a shot of potent whiskey.

Realizing she was staring, Grace lowered her gaze and looked around. "So this is a brewery. I could use a pint about now."

"Welcome to my world."

"Thank you. It appears quite interesting." When Grace looked up again, he gave her the slightest of grins, almost as though he didn't smile too often, and then descended the ladder so quickly that she wondered how he didn't fall. As he walked her way, Grace noticed how his wide shoulders tested the cotton of a standard black T-shirt tucked into faded jeans riding low on his hips.

She just bet he had an amazing butt.

"You look lost."

"Perhaps because I am ..." At five foot nine, Grace was rather tall, but she had to tip her head back to look at his face. Close up, she could see that he had light blue eyes framed by dark lashes. Wow ...

"Are what?"

"Lost. Sort of, anyway." Grace was about to ask him the location of the bistro but a loud crack of thunder had her jumping, sending droplets of water into the air. "Oh! My top is down!"

"Your top isn't down. Trust me, I would have noticed." There it was ... that ghost of a grin again.

"No!" Although it made her realize that her wet pink shirt was clinging to her skin. She plucked at it. "I mean the top of my car ... convertible. I hate to ask, but could you help me put it up?"

"Sure." With a quick nod, he hurried out the door and ran right into the wind and rain like it was nothing. Feeling a bit guilty, Grace watched from the doorway while the top slowly rose upward and then folded downward against the windshield. He swiftly latched it down and then hurried back to the building. "Here, I thought you might want your purse. It was under the dash but getting wet."

"Oh." Grace took the Coach purse and hugged it to her chest. "Thank you so much. I'm sorry you got drenched." But Grace wasn't sorry she got to see the black shirt clinging to him like a second skin. He was muscular but not in a beefy, iron-pumping way—more like his physique was a result of physical labor.

"No big deal." He shoved his fingers through his wet hair.

"The car's a rental, so I didn't know how to put the top up." Grace felt her cheeks grow a tad warm but she lifted her chin. "I should have paid more attention during the demonstration."

"There must be instructions."

"Oh, I guess there's a manual in the glove box." Grace shrugged and then winced. "I just hope the interior dries out."

"Well, it's definitely soaking wet, but it's going to be warm and sunny tomorrow, so you can put the top down later and it will dry out just fine." He extended his hand. "By the way, I'm Mason Mayfield."

"Grace Gordon. Oh wait. Mayfield? You must be Mattie's brother!" She shook his hand, relieved that she was finally on the right track.

"I am. Nice to meet you, Grace."

"Come to think of it, I did see pictures of you in the wedding album that Mattie showed me while she was in London when Garret taped *Sing for Me*." She thought that Mattie's brothers were super hot in tuxes. "I'm Garret's half sister. Sophia's sister."

"Wow." Mason tipped his head to the side. "I wouldn't have guessed that you were Sophia's sister."

"I know. We don't look alike at all." Grace grinned. "Or act alike."

"Or sound alike."

"I spent way more time in London than Sophia. The

accent kind of comes and goes, depending upon my mood, according to my mother, anyway."

"I did meet your mother at Mattie and Garret's wedding. Lovely lady. I'm surprised that you weren't there."

Grace shook her head and groaned. "I got snowed in at the Denver airport and missed my flight. Trust me, I tried to find a way to get there like Steve Martin in the movie *Planes, Trains and Automobiles*, but it was a total fail."

"That's too bad. The wedding was a good time. So, were you in Denver skiing?" The question was innocent enough, but the slight arch of his eyebrow got under her skin a little bit. Now that he knew who she was, Mason most likely thought she was a spoiled diva going on endless holidays and shopping sprees. She wasn't and she didn't.

"Business," Grace answered rather crisply but then felt as she as if she were being a bit rude. After all, he'd just run out into a raging storm on her behalf. "I'm a horrible skier. The fact that my name is Grace is kind of funny, actually. I'm prone to accidents mostly because I'm looking somewhere other than where I'm going."

"Well, be careful in here. There are some things you don't want to fall into." He pointed to the big vat full of frothy stuff.

"I will." Grace hated that because she was the daughter of Becca Gordon, former fashion model once married to rock legend Rick Ruleman, she and Sophia were thought to be rich, spoiled brats. Neither she nor Sophia rode on the coattails of anyone, including their biological father, who worried more about making money than spending time with his daughters. She was about to tell Mason what she did for a living when lightning flashed through the windows, followed by a deafening boom of thunder. Grace yelped and then shivered.

"Oh, hey, are you scared of storms?"

"Not so much, but this seems to be a quite a doozy. I am a bit cold, though. I have dry clothes in my suitcase but . . ."

"Hey, don't worry. I'll be right back with something dry."

"Thanks, but I don't want you to go to any trouble."

Mason shook his head. "I'm not about to watch you shiver." He flicked a glance toward the front window. "And the storm doesn't seem like it's going to let up anytime soon."

"Okay, then, something dry would be splendid."

"I'll be right back."

Grace watched Mason walk away, finally getting to admire his jean-clad butt. *Yep, very nice.* She took a deep breath, finally able to calm down.

Grace looked around, intrigued by all of the machinery. While she did enjoy drinking good craft ale now and then, she'd never given much thought about the actual brewing process. From the looks of things in the huge room, brewing beer was much more complicated than she would have imagined.

Rain pounded on what she vaguely remembered was a tin roof, and although she felt a damp chill, the sound was somehow soothing after her rather stressful drive from the airport. Normally she loved to drive. Having lived most of her adult life in London, she commuted by the Tube, walked the streets, or traveled by taxi. So driving through the countryside had always been one of her favorite pastimes on a lazy Sunday afternoon. Grace grinned, thinking, yes, she often got lost ending up in a village where she explored shops and dined at local restaurants, often with her mother. But Grace hadn't had a lazy or carefree day in a very long time. Of course, all of that had changed as of last week, and now she had more time on her hands than she knew what to do with . . . and it felt rather odd.

Grace noticed that the metal machinery gleamed and the smooth concrete floor appeared spotless. Because it was her nature, she did have to wonder how much money it took to start up a brewery and what Mason's long-term plans were for the business. Lost in thought, Grace turned when she heard his boots clunking across the concrete floor.

Mason walked toward her with long strides. He'd changed into a dry white T-shirt that had the Mayfield Marina logo scripted in green across the front. The jeans were replaced by gray sweatpants and he carried a big plastic bag. He handed it to her. "We sell a few racks of clothes over at the marina. There should be everything you need in there."

"Thanks. Wait. You went all the way to the marina?"

"It's just a short jog down the road. I was already wet." The slight grin returned.

"Really? So where is Walking on Sunshine Bistro, then?"

"Across from the marina, up on the hill a little ways."

"Wow." Grace shook her head slowly. "So I've been this close the entire time?"

"Yeah, you weren't too terribly lost, if that makes you feel any better."

When Mason handed Grace the bag, she felt a little tingle at the touch of his fingers. "No! I feel worse. I've been right here all along."

"You must have missed the right turn. Did you drive by some cabins by a lake?"

"Um, yeah." Grace nodded. "Like three times. Don't tell me: Is that where Mattie and Garret live?"

"No, they live in a cabin overlooking the river. It's actually within walking distance from here too."

Grace groaned.

"Hey, don't feel so bad. GPS and cell phone reception can be sketchy out here, especially when the weather gets crazy."

"Crazy? I thought you said this was a pop-up thunderstorm."

Mason shrugged his wide shoulders. "I was wrong," he said, and as if on cue, lightning flashed, followed by a deep boom of thunder. "A tornado watch was just issued a few minutes ago."

"What?" Grace swallowed hard, wondering if the tin roof would handle a tornado or peel back like the lid of a sardine can. "Should we go for cover or something?"

"I have an alert system on my phone. If we get an alarm or siren, we'll head into a closet or the bathroom. We don't have a basement."

"Oh, boy. And to think, this day started out so normal."

"It's only a tornado watch, not a warning. It'll be fine."

"It's been my experience that when people say *It will be fine* is when all hell breaks loose."

"Is that so?" Mason actually full-on smiled, softening his features. Grace wondered if he knew that his smile was a lethal weapon that could render the female population defenseless. "Well, if all hell breaks loose, I'll keep you safe." The smile faded and she could tell that he meant business.

"Good to know," Grace said in a breezy tone, but she believed him. Although Grace had been taught by her mother to be independent, something about having Mason protect her made her feel warm in spite of the damp clothing.

"I'll keep an eye on the weather."

"Keep *both* eyes on the weather."

Mason chuckled. "Okay, I will. I think you'll find everything you need in the bag. The bathroom is over there on the left." Mason pointed over his shoulder. "As a reward, I'll get you a bottle of ale while we wait out the storm."

"A storm that could spawn a tornado. I guess if I'm going to go flying into the sky, I might as well have a beer in my hand."

"I'll drink to that. So what do you prefer? Something mild? A brown ale? An APA blonde?"

Grace had to hide her grin. She could tell by his expression that he thought she was a wine or martini kind of girl, and while he was right, about a year ago she'd gone to a beer-tasting festival with some girlfriends and been surprised at how many she'd enjoyed. "Actually, Mason, I'm a fan of something dark and more intense."

"You don't say?" He shoved his hands in his pockets and rocked back on his boots. Since when did she find work boots sexy? *Since right now.*

"Do you like chocolate?"

"More than breathing."

"Well, then, I've got you covered. I'll bring you a light medium-body porter that delivers lots of chocolate flavor."

"Sounds amazing."

"I hope you'll think so. It took me a few tries to come up with something I liked," Mason said, and then turned away.

"I'm sure I will. . . ." Grace's voice trailed off softly as she watched his progress. Something warm and delicious washed over her, and she was startled to realize that the foreign feeling was desire. Her mother had been right. She'd been working so hard on Girl Code Cosmetics for the past two years that romance hadn't entered her mind all that much, but it had just resurfaced with a vengeance. Grace was surprised her clothes didn't steam dry right there on her body.

Grace was surprised by her instant reaction to Mason Mayfield. She usually took a while to warm up to a guy, starting with mild attraction that lead to conversation and then maybe a date. As she walked toward the bathroom, she mulled over her attraction to Mason. Perhaps she was used to city-living metrosexual men who, by contrast, made country boy Mason seem so virile.

Just hormones, Grace thought, trying to shrug it off.

Regardless, Mason was one sexy man. She opened the door and flipped on the light, but then made the mistake of looking at her reflection in the mirror. "Holy hell, I look like I've already been through a tornado," she said, thinking that the instant attraction most likely wasn't mutual.

"Oh, stop," Grace said, reminding herself that she was

only in Cricket Creek to help Sophia out at Walking on Sunshine Bistro and to visit with Garret while they all waited with bated breath for his baby girl to arrive. According to her mother, Garret and Mattie hadn't settled on a name yet, even though her mother had tossed endless suggestions at them. After the birth of the baby, Grace would most likely move back to London, where she would start up another company now that she'd sold Girl Code, her wildly successful line of edgy urban cosmetics. Getting involved with anyone local, including sexy Mason, wouldn't work out in the end, and she needed to remember that important fact.

With a groan, Grace peeled her wet clothing off and then dug inside the plastic bag to see what he'd brought for her to change into. She located white sweatpants with *Mayfield Marina* scripted in green lettering down one leg. A light green scooped-neck T-shirt and matching hoodie were in the bag as well. "Nice," she said with a smile.

After slipping into the dry clothing, Grace dug around in her purse for a comb and any cosmetics she could find. A few minutes later, she'd pulled her hair back into submission and added some eyeliner and lipstick. Wrinkling her nose at her reflection, she said, "Well, that's as good as it's going to get."

And then the lights went out.

For a moment, Grace simply stood as still as a statue while thinking in a rather calm manner that she'd never experienced such pitch-black darkness. Surely her eyes would adjust and she'd be able to see enough to make her way out of the bathroom. She blinked and then squinted, but she couldn't see anything. She did the classic holding her hand in front of her face. Nope . . . nothing.

Grace considered herself to be a pretty brave person, but she'd never been a fan of the dark. To this day, she had a night-light in her bathroom. Grace swallowed hard and her heart thudded. Should she yell for Mason? No, surely he'd come looking for her in a few minutes. After all, he knew where she'd gone, Grace thought, and then snapped her fingers, remembering that she had the flashlight app on her smart phone. She fumbled around, bumped into the sink, hit the toilet seat, and came up against the the wall before finally locating her purse. "Yes!" she said when she found her phone, but her triumph was short-lived when she realized that her battery was dead.

With a growl of frustration, Grace decided she needed to exit the bathroom and give a shout for Mason. She dropped her phone back into her purse and located the doorknob, somehow thinking that when the door was open, she'd have at least moonlight shining through the windows or something.

Nope . . . just darkness. "Oh, well . . ." Grace hefted her purse over her shoulder and took a baby step forward, but then remembered the big vat of frothy stuff and decided to stay put and shout for Mason. She inhaled a deep breath, thinking she needed some volume and then spotted a beam of light coming her way. "Oh, there you are! Thank goodness!"

"Sorry. I had to look for a flashlight," Mason said as he reached her side. "I hope you weren't too scared."

"Oh, of course not," she said, barely resisting the urge to grab his arm and cling. And then she heard the wail of sirens. "Oh, no!" She pictured a funnel cloud twirling toward them like in *The Wizard of Oz*. She could hear the howl of the wind and pinging against the windows. "Mason, what should we do?"

"Go into the bathroom for shelter."

Grace nodded and then heard something that sounded like a freight train coming their way. She reached for his arm. "Mason, what is that horrible sound?"

"Let's hope it's not a tornado."

Also available from *USA Today* bestselling author

LuAnn McLane

SWEET HARMONY
A Cricket Creek Novel

Cricket Creek, Kentucky, is no Nashville—it's a sweet, small town outside the big-city limelight. But here, two headstrong country music stars will need to rely on their Southern roots and explosive chemistry to top the charts together.

"No one does Southern love like LuAnn McLane."
—The Romance Dish

Also in the Cricket Creek series
Wildflower Wedding
Moonlight Kiss
Whisper's Edge
Pitch Perfect
Catch of a Lifetime
Playing for Keeps

Available wherever books are sold or at
penguin.com

facebook.com/LoveAlwaysBooks